9/14

Autumn: Purification

Also by David Moody

Hater

Dog Blood

Autumn

Autumn: The City

Autumn: Purification

David Moody

THOMAS DUNNE BOOKS ✖ NEW YORK
ST. MARTIN'S GRIFFIN

THOMAS DUNNE BOOKS.
An imprint of St. Martin's Press.

AUTUMN: PURIFICATION. Copyright © 2011 by David Moody. All rights reserved. Printed in the United States of America. For information, address St. Martin's Press, 175 Fifth Avenue, New York, N.Y. 10010.

www.thomasdunnebooks.com
www.stmartins.com

Library of Congress Cataloging-in-Publication Data

Moody, David, 1970–
    Autumn : purification / David Moody.
        p. cm.
    ISBN 978-0-312-56999-0
    1. Zombies—Fiction. 2. Survival–Fiction. 3. Regression
(Civilization)—Fiction. 4. Communicable diseases—Fiction. I. Title.
    PR6113.O5447A953 2011
    823'.92—dc22

                                                    2011020834

10 9 8 7 6 5 4 3

Prologue

Forty-seven days ago, more than ninety-nine percent of the population had been killed within an impossibly short period of time. Right across the world, without any warning or explanation, the pattern was repeated as billions of lives were inexplicably ended—snuffed out and switched off with neither dignity nor malice, unimaginable numbers of innocent people discarded and abandoned and left to rot where they'd fallen. Just a handful of terrified survivors remained, none of them able to understand or even to begin to come to terms with what had happened to their friends, family, lovers, children . . .

Within forty-eight hours, almost a third of the dead rose again. The germ (or disease or whatever it was that was responsible) had spared a key area of these creatures' brains. Somehow unaffected, a spark of primordial instinct had survived the infection, leaving the bodies physically dead but still compelled to move; lifeless but incessantly animated. And as the flesh which covered these stumbling aberrations had rotted and decayed, so the unaffected region of the brain had grown in strength and had continued to drive them forward. First their most basic senses had slowly returned, then a degree of control. The corpses didn't know what, who, or where they were. They didn't know why they existed nor what they wanted. They had no need to eat or drink, to rest or sleep, or even to blink or breathe . . . they just *were*. This combination of increasing self-awareness and decreasing self-control gradually manifested itself as anger and hostility. Sentenced to spend every minute of every day shuffling pointlessly through the empty world, even the slightest unexpected sound or movement was enough to attract their limited but deadly attention.

With Britain (and presumably the rest of the world) now otherwise almost completely silent, the mobile dead moved randomly from their supposedly final resting places, staggering in all directions on rotting, unsteady feet away from the towns, cities, and other centers of population where they'd died, spreading aimlessly across the land like a drop of ink slowly flowing outwards over blotting paper.

Except here.

Here, in apparently nondescript fields miles from anywhere of any perceived importance, for no immediately visible reason, thousands upon thousands of inquisitive, rancid bodies had arrived, cramming themselves into the space of just a few square miles. An endless mass of empty, skeletal husks which had once each had individual identities and lives and reasons to exist, but were now nothing more than emotionless collections of tattered rags, gray-green greasy flesh, withered muscle, and brittle bone.

At the outermost edge of one of the vast fields, the disheveled carcass of what had once been an affluent investment banker lifted its head and looked up, barely able to focus its clouded eyes. Surrounded on all sides by scores of similarly bedraggled cadavers, the remains of the once powerful, dignified, and well-respected man shuffled awkwardly forward, slipping and sliding through churned mud, and clawed clumsily at those bodies which stood in its way.

Survivors.

This place was different from everywhere else. It didn't know what, but it knew there was *something* near here and it had an instinctive, insatiable desire to get even closer to whatever it was. It didn't know why—it barely even knew what it was doing—but it couldn't stop.

Buried deep underground, far below the rotting crowds, almost three hundred survivors existed in the unnatural semi-darkness of a subterranean military base. It was impossible for them to exist there without revealing their location. The world was a silent, lifeless, empty place now, and the sounds made by the people underground, no matter how slight, echoed through the silence. The heat they produced burned like a fire. In the otherwise cold and vacuous land, the corpses were attracted to them like moths towards the last light on Earth.

What had begun as a few random corpses stumbling upon the underground military base by chance had now grown into a crowd of vast, almost incalculable proportions. The movement of the loathsome creatures inevitably attracted more and more of them from the surrounding area: a slow-motion chain reaction. Now, several days since any of the soldiers had been aboveground, almost one hundred thousand bodies had gathered around the bunker, every last one of them fighting to get nearer to its impassable entrance.

The dead investment banker's way forward was blocked by more bodies. It lifted its emaciated arms again and then, with unexpected force, lashed out at the figure immediately in front. Soft, putrefying flesh was ripped from bone as the decaying office worker tore the unsuspecting creature ahead of it apart. The sudden outburst of violence spread rapidly through the nearest cadavers on all sides, rippling out farther into the enormous crowd in every direction before petering out again as quickly as it had begun. All across this massive, decomposing gathering the same thing was happening time and again, each of the bodies interested only in getting closer to whatever it was that was different about this godforsaken place.

Apart from the wind blowing through the swaying branches of trees and the fighting and continual shuffling movement of the dead, the world around the buried base appeared frozen. Even birds had learned not to fly too close because of the reaction their fleeting appearances invariably caused. In spite of the fact that the corpses were individually weak and clumsy, what remained of the rest of the world instinctively feared them and did all they could to keep their distance. In such huge numbers as this, the dead were unstoppable.

Deep underground in the military base, the living fared little better. Despite being relatively strong and still able to act rationally, they were afraid to move. It was obvious to all the lost and terrified souls buried in the concrete maze below the fields and hills that the sheer number of bodies on the surface would eventually be too much for them. Their options were desperately limited and frighteningly bleak. They could either sit and wait (although no one knew what they'd be waiting for or how long it would take) or they could go aboveground and fight. But what would that achieve? What use was open space and fresh air to the military? The disease still hung heavy in the contaminated air, and every one of the soldiers and their officers knew that a single breath would, in all probability, be enough to kill them. Those survivors immune to the disease who also sheltered underground knew that they would fare no better from such a confrontation. Any attempt to clear the bodies from above the base might help in the short term, but the noise and movement such an act would inevitably cause would doubtless result in countless thousands more cadavers being drawn nearer to the shelter, and there were potentially millions more out there.

Below the surface the survivors and the military were forced to remain apart. Designed to cope with the aftereffects of chemical, nuclear, or biological attack, the base was remarkably well-equipped and technologically advanced. The air being pumped through the complex was pure and free from infection. The survivors who had taken shelter there, however, were not. Decontamination had been halfheartedly attempted at first, but the woefully underprepared military scientists had known from the start that it would be a futile exercise. The germ could be washed away from equipment and from the soldiers' protective suits, but the survivors had been breathing contaminated air for more than a month and they were riddled with infection. While the deadly contagion had no obvious effect on them, even the slightest exposure might be sufficient to contaminate the base and kill everyone in it.

The military occupied almost all of the complex—everything beyond the entrance to the decontamination chambers—leaving the thirty-seven survivors with the main hangar and a few adjacent storage, utility, and maintenance rooms. Space, heat, and light were severely limited. After fighting through the hell aboveground to get here, however, the limitations of the military facility were readily accepted and hugely appreciated. The alternatives which awaited them back out on the surface were unthinkable.

1

Emma Mitchell looked at her watch. Two o'clock. Was that two in the afternoon or morning? She thought morning, but she wasn't sure. In the permanent darkness of the base it was impossible to tell the difference between day and night anymore. There were always people sleeping, and always people awake. There were always people gathered in groups and huddles talking in secret whispers about nothing of any importance, and there were always people crying, moaning, and arguing. There were always soldiers moving through the decontamination chambers or coming out into the hangar to check, double-check, and triple-check their stockpiled equipment.

Two in the morning or two in the afternoon, Emma couldn't sleep. She lay in bed next to Michael Collins and stared into his face. They'd made love a while back, and she felt ridiculously guilty. It had been the fourth time they'd had sex in the three weeks they'd been underground, and each time he'd fallen asleep as soon as they were finished and she'd been left alone feeling like this. When she'd asked him, he'd said that being with her made him feel complete, that their intimacy made him feel like he used to before the rest of the world had died. Although Emma felt that way too, sex reminded her of everything she'd lost and made her wonder what would happen if she lost Michael. She didn't know whether she slept with him because she loved him, or if it was because they just happened to be there for each other. One thing of which she was certain was that there was no room in her world for romance and other long-forgotten feelings anymore. He had no trouble, but she couldn't imagine ever being relaxed or aroused enough to have another orgasm. There was no longer any seduction or foreplay. All she wanted was to feel Michael inside her. He was the only positive thing remaining in her world. Everything was cold apart from his touch.

In the final days before finding this bunker, Emma had grown to hate the cramped motor home that she and Michael shared. Now she never wanted to leave it. It was a small, private space where the two of them could shut themselves away from everyone else and she appreciated it. The others had no choice but to spend all day, every day together, and Emma didn't know how they coped. She needed this space to be able to cut herself off from what was happening elsewhere. Yesterday she'd overheard two soldiers talking about the air getting thinner on the lower levels of the base, that the sheer weight of the bodies aboveground was beginning to cause problems and block vents and exhaust shafts. She'd spoken to Cooper about it and he hadn't seemed surprised. The thought of what it must be like aboveground now made her want to lock the motor home doors and never open them again.

Emma heard a noise outside. She sat up and wiped the nearest window clear of condensation, the heat from her and Michael's bodies contrasting with the cold air in the vast hangar. Supplies were being delivered. Two suited soldiers emerged from the decontamination chambers to begrudgingly deliver rations to the civilian survivors. Emma was surprised they were given anything at all. She often tried to imagine what life must be like for the soldiers. Were they just going through the motions, waiting to die? How long would the contagion outside last? Was the air clear now, or would it stay contaminated for another month, year, or decade? How would they know? Would any of the soldiers ever be brave or stupid enough to risk going aboveground and breathing in? Donna Yorke had suggested that was why the military had been so acommodating toward them. She said she could see a time when they might want to use the immune survivors to either try and find a cure or, once the bodies had rotted down to nothing, just to scour the surface for food, water, and supplies.

Emma put on Michael's thick winter coat and stood up and moved to another window. It was hard to make out what was happening outside—the hangar lights were almost always turned down to their lowest setting to conserve power, only getting any brighter when the military was heading outside, and that hadn't happened for more than two weeks. Two days after the civilians had first arrived, the army had opened the doors and made a futile attempt to clear the mess they'd made getting in. They'd been beaten back by the number of bodies outside. The first few hundred had been obliterated with flamethrowers but there were thousands more behind. Distracted thinking about the carnage that day, she watched Cooper checking over one of the vehicles he and the others had arrived here in. It was obvious from his manner, attitude, and priorities that he was military—or was he now ex-military? Regimented and confident, she'd often seen him exercising or demonstrating to small groups of people how to use the military equipment which surrounded them. She knew it was important to keep themselves and their vehicles in good order. She was under no illusions. Today, tomorrow, or in six months' time, they'd have to leave the bunker eventually.

"Something wrong?"

Emma turned around and saw that Michael was sitting up in bed. His dark eyes looked tired and confused.

"Nothing. Couldn't sleep, that's all."

He yawned and beckoned her over. She climbed back into bed and he grabbed hold of her tightly as if they'd been apart for years.

"How you doing?" he asked quietly, his face close to hers.

"I'm okay."

"Anything happening out there?"

"Not really, just a delivery of supplies, that's all. Does anything ever happen around here?"

"Give it time," he mumbled sadly, kissing the side of her face. "Give it time."

2

"Morning, you two," Bernard Heath said in his loud, educated voice as Michael and Emma walked together into the largest of the few rooms that the survivors were permitted access to.

"Morning, Bernard," Emma replied. "Bloody cold, isn't it?"

"Isn't it always? Get yourselves something to eat, they left us quite a lot last night."

Holding onto Michael's hand, Emma followed him as he weaved through the crowded room. About six meters square, it was used by the survivors as a dormitory, a meeting place, a kitchen and a mess hall. In fact, it was used for just about everything. As bleak, grim and imposing as its gray, featureless walls were, the fact that the room was always filled with people made it just about the best place for any of them to spend their time. At least here they weren't always looking over their shoulders or sitting in silence, not daring to speak. At least here they could, for the time being at least, try to relax, recuperate, and heal.

A basic shift pattern had been drawn up shortly after they'd first arrived at the bunker. Although there had been the few expected protests and missed shifts, most people were prepared to pull their weight and contribute by cooking or cleaning or doing whatever other menial tasks needed to be done. Rather than evade work as some of them might have done before, almost all of the survivors now willingly worked as hard as they could. How much of the work was done for the good of the group was questionable: most simply craved the responsibility because it helped reduce the monotony and boredom of the long, dark days. As many of them had already found to their cost, sitting and staring at the walls of the bunker with nothing to do invariably resulted in thinking constantly about all they had lost.

Emma and Michael collected something to eat from Sheri Newton—a quiet and diminutive middle-aged woman who always seemed to be serving food—and sat down. The faces of the people around them were reassuringly familiar. Donna Yorke was at a table nearby talking to Clare Smith, Jack Baxter, and Phil Croft. As the couple began to eat, Croft looked up and spotted them. He nodded at Michael.

"Morning," Michael said as he chewed on his first mouthful of dry, tasteless rations. "How are you doing today, Phil?"

"Good," Croft replied, wheezing. He took a long drag on a cigarette and coughed.

"You should think about giving those things up," Michael said sarcastically. "They'll be the death of you, mate!"

Croft grimaced as he coughed and then managed a fleeting smile. It was a sign of the grim hopelessness of their situation that death was just about the only thing they could find to laugh about. The group's only doctor, Croft had been seriously injured in a violent crash as they'd approached the military bunker. The dank conditions underground were not ideal and did nothing to aid his recovery. Although the only remaining visible signs of his injuries were a scar across his chest and an unsteady limp, as a trained medic, Croft knew that his body had sustained a huge amount of internal damage and that he would never be fully fit again. With his private discomfort and pain continuing, and with the military on one side and thousands of decomposing corpses on the other, the potentially harmful side effects of smoking were the very least of his concerns.

Cooper marched angrily into the room, his sudden, stormy entrance instantly silencing every conversation and causing everyone to look round. He fetched himself a drink, yanked a chair from under the table, and sat down next to Jack Baxter.

"What's the matter with you?" Jack asked.

"This place is full of fucking idiots," the ex-soldier answered. Since returning to the base he had steadily distanced himself from his military colleagues. Perhaps symbolically, he now wore only the lower half of his uniform, and he only kept the boots and trousers on because they were the most practical clothes he possessed. In fact, they were just about the only clothes he had.

"Now who's he talking about?" Croft interrupted. "Who you on about now, Cooper?"

Cooper took a swig of coffee. "Bloody jokers in charge of this place."

"What have they done?"

"Nothing, and that's the problem."

"What do you mean?" Donna asked, concerned. She knew

Cooper well enough to know that there had to be a reason behind his sudden foul mood. He was usually much calmer and more controlled than this.

"They won't tell me anything anymore," he explained. "They've been ordered not to. I just can't understand their logic. What are they going to gain from keeping us in the dark? We've seen more of what's happened out there than they have."

"Sounds typical of what I've seen of the military so far," Jack said. "So is that all that's bothering you?"

Cooper shook his head.

"No, it's more than that. I've just been talking to an old mate of mine, Jim Franks. Jim and I go back a long way and I know I can trust him. Anyway, he's been telling me that they think they're going to start hitting real problems soon."

"Supplies?" Baxter wondered.

"No, they've got enough stuff here."

"What kind of problems, then?" Emma asked, starting to feel uneasy.

"Big fucking problems," Cooper continued. "Nothing they weren't expecting, but big fucking problems nonetheless."

"Such as . . . ?"

"You've got to remember that I was talking to Jim through the intercom on the front of the decontamination chamber and he was trying to keep quiet in case anyone caught him speaking to me, so I didn't get a lot of detail. It's the bodies. They've been taking readings around the base and the damn things still keep on coming. Jim told me that the air filtration system's still working at the moment but it's really starting to struggle and the problems we've heard about with ventilation are getting worse.

Seems that more than half the exhaust vents are blocked or almost blocked, just like we said they would be."

"So what are they going to do about it?" Croft said, asking the question that everyone was thinking.

"There's no way of clearing the vents from down here," he replied, "so they're going to have to go aboveground again."

"But what good's that going to do?" Emma said, terrified at the prospect of the bunker doors being opened again. "Do they think they can just clear the bodies away? As soon as they move any of them hundreds more will take their place."

"I know that and you know that," Cooper said dejectedly, "but they don't understand the scale of the problem. This is why I don't understand them not talking to us. The reality is that the people making the decisions down here don't have a fucking clue how bad things are up on the surface. Until you've seen it for yourself, until you've been out there in the middle of it, you just can't imagine what it's like out there, can you?"

"So how are they planning to keep the vents clear?" asked Donna. "Like Emma says, as soon as they've cleared them more bodies will be lining up to block them again."

"Jesus, I don't know. My guess is they'll try and cover them or build something over the top. You've got to remember that this place was designed not to be noticed. You'd have to look hard just to find the bloody vents 'cause they're not obvious, but that doesn't matter anymore. I think they're planning to fight their way through to them and then just do whatever they have to to block them off. They'll try and cover the top of them or maybe leave people out there to guard them. A trench or a wall might do it . . ."

"Pity the poor bastards who get sent out there to build bloody walls," Jack said. "Christ, it's hard enough just being up there, never mind having to build a bloody wall. I tell you, you wouldn't get me back outside for anything."

"You reckon? Keep things in perspective, Jack," Cooper said, looking directly at him. "We've got a massive advantage over this lot at the moment because we can survive out in the open. So who says they're not going to try and use us to do whatever it is that they're planning? Argue all you like, but if you've got a gun held at the back of your head, you'll do whatever they bloody well want you to do."

"You really think it's going to come to that?"

"Perhaps not yet, but . . ."

"But what?"

"But they might do eventually. Put yourself in their shoes. You'd probably do the same."

The conversation stalled as each of the survivors stopped to take stock of Cooper's words. He knew how the military minds worked better than any of them. He'd never been anything other than straight and direct. There was no point trying to soften the blow.

"How long?" Donna asked.

"How long until what?"

"How long before they open the doors and go out there?"

"No idea. I don't expect they know either. We'll just have to sit and wait."

"It has to happen sooner or later, doesn't it?" Michael said, his voice filled with resignation. "It's inevitable. They used to call it

Chaos Theory, didn't they? If something *can* go wrong, eventually it will."

"You're a happy bugger, Mike! Keep looking on the bright side, eh?" grinned Jack.

"He's right, though," Cooper agreed.

"We've all seen it happen," Michael continued. "We started off in a village hall. There were about twenty of us there. We thought we'd be okay but we had to get away. One of us went back and the place had been completely overrun. We found ourselves a house in the middle of the bloody countryside miles away from anywhere, but that wasn't safe enough either. Built a bloody fence around it but it didn't last."

"Same with us and the university," Donna said. "It seemed ideal to start with but it didn't last. Things change and we can't afford to just sit still and wait and hope and—"

"And you're right, the same thing's bound to happen here eventually," Cooper interrupted. "Something's going to give— more vents will become blocked, the disease will manage to get in somehow, or something else will happen. It'll take luck more than anything else to keep anybody safe down here."

"So what do we do about it?"

"There's not a lot we can do right now," he answered. "We just need to be ready for it when it happens, and be prepared to get out of here fast if anything goes wrong."

3

Three days was all it took. It was midmorning when it began.

Michael was standing in front of the motor home, talking to Cooper about the sorry state of his battered vehicle. Although it had been cleaned and overhauled to the best of their abilities with their limited resources, the machine still looked desperately dilapidated. Their conversation was interrupted abruptly when the hangar lights were switched on full, filling the cavernous space with unexpected illumination. Having been forced to live in almost complete darkness for weeks on end, both men covered their sensitive eyes and, for a fraction of a second, found themselves thinking more about the sudden pain and discomfort than the possible reasons why the lights had been turned on now.

Michael was the first to react.

"Shit," he cursed as he looked around, still shielding his eyes. "This must be it."

Cooper saw that the doors into the main decontamination chamber were opening. From deep inside the base a steady stream of dark-suited figures began to emerge. Close to one hundred troops quickly filed out into the hangar. Although their formation and manner lacked something of the discipline and precision Cooper had come to expect from his former colleagues, they were still clearly well-organized and ready to fight.

"Christ, they mean business," he said.

"What do we do?"

"Get everyone ready to get out of here."

They sprinted across the huge room together, cutting through the soldiers' ragged formation. The sudden light and noise had already alerted the other survivors. Anxious faces started to appear before Michael and Cooper were even halfway across the hangar.

"What's happening?" Steve Armitage asked.

"What's it look like?" Cooper replied. "They're about to open the fucking doors!"

Steve hadn't even had a chance to respond before a crowd of panicking survivors had shoved him out of the way and spilled out into the hangar.

"Get ready to leave," Cooper shouted, loud enough for everyone to hear. He hoped they weren't going anywhere, but he felt duty bound to prepare the group for the worst possible scenario. "Get your stuff together and get everyone into the vehicles."

Without question or delay the frightened crowd began to hurriedly make its way across the cavernous chamber toward the police van, prison truck, and motor home. Bernard Heath looked around for Phil Croft. He grabbed the medic's arm and steadied him. Croft could walk, but his injuries prevented him from getting anywhere with any real speed.

"Get the kids," Michael yelled to Donna across the small,

square room where the youngest members of the group tended to gather. She was one step ahead of him, ushering the four children toward the door of the little storeroom they used to play in. She was trying not to let them pick up on her sudden fear. Emma, frightened and moving against the flow of most of the others, grabbed hold of Michael's arm.

"What's going on?" she demanded. "What are they doing?"

"Get into the motor home," he told her. "I'll be over in a couple of minutes."

"But . . ." she protested. Michael pushed her away, desperate to get her to safety quickly.

"Don't ask questions," he shouted after her, "just get yourself over there."

"Is that everyone?" Cooper asked as he returned to the hangar after checking that the last rooms were clear.

"Think so," Jack replied as he looked back across the immense cavern, watching the rest of the survivors trying to cram themselves and their belongings into the back of the group's three vehicles.

"You two get yourselves over there and try and get that lot sorted out," Cooper ordered. Although no one had ever nominated him as their leader, the authority and command in his voice were unquestionable. Michael and Jack turned and ran toward the others.

As Cooper watched the soldiers, the roar of engines suddenly filled the air, echoing around the immense space, and an armored personnel carrier took up position at the foot of the ramp which led up to the main entrance doors. Two smaller jeeps were driven out of the shadows and parked immediately behind the first vehicle. He cautiously moved forward, his military mind keen to try and work out his ex-colleagues' tactics.

"Cooper!" shouted Michael as the final few survivors jostled for space in the group's battered transports. "Come on!"

Cooper ignored him and instead moved closer to the troops. He estimated there were somewhere between eighty and a hundred soldiers in the hangar and there was no doubt that this was a major operation. He knew that the officers—who, as far as he could tell, were still buried safely within the deeper confines of the base—would never risk sending such a large number of men aboveground unless they had absolutely no choice but to do so.

He took a chance. He had nothing to lose.

"Hey," he said, standing in shadow and reaching out and grabbing the arm of the nearest suited figure at the back of the ranks. The soldier nervously spun around to face him. The protective mask and breathing apparatus obscured so much of the trooper's face that Cooper could see only his eyes. "What's happening?"

"Vents are blocked," the young soldier answered, his voice muffled but clearly anxious.

"So what's the plan?"

The soldier glanced around, not sure whether or not he should even be speaking to Cooper. He figured that the preparation of the troops and equipment closer to the front of the hangar was a sufficient distraction for him to risk a few more words.

"They reckon we can get by for now with at least two of the vents clear, so we're going out there to sort 'em and to make sure they stay working."

"So are you staying out there?" Cooper whispered. The soldier shook his head.

"You've got to be fucking kidding," he replied quickly. "No, that's what the jeeps are for. The vents are low on the ground. Plan is to leave a jeep straddling each vent to block them off and stop those bloody things out there from clogging them up again."

The soldiers began to move forward. The trooper shrugged off Cooper's hand and retook his position in the formation. Still curious, Cooper moved back toward the others but instead of getting into one of the vehicles with them, he clambered up onto the front of a huge, unused military transport to try and get a better view of what was about to happen. Out of breath and red-faced, Jack appeared at his side.

"What's happening now?" he asked, panting with nerves and effort as he hauled himself up beside the soldier.

"They're going to try and clear a couple of vents," Cooper explained. "They're planning to leave those jeeps parked on top to try and keep the bodies away."

"Got to get to the damn vents first," Jack said. "Do they even realize what it's like out there?"

"They will in a couple of minutes. Anyway, they don't have any choice if they want to keep breathing. If there was another way I'm sure they'd have tried it by now. No matter what you might think, they're not stupid—"

He stopped talking abruptly as the doors began to open. At first nothing seemed to happen. Then a dull scraping noise became audible over the rumbling sound of the military machines poised to drive out into the open. A second later and the first chink of light appeared. A slender shaft of harsh gray-white brightness between the two gradually separating halves of the door, increasing as the entrance opened farther.

"Christ," Jack said under his breath, trying not to panic. "Jesus Christ."

As soon as the gap was wide enough, bodies began to spill through into the hangar. Forced forward like a viscous liquid by the weight of rotting flesh pushing hard against them from behind, the first corpses stumbled down the ramp toward the soldiers with unexpected speed, many tripping and falling, unable to properly coordinate their awkward movements. The soldiers responded instinctively, pushing them back and firing at them until they had managed to temporarily stem the flow of dead meat. From somewhere deep within the ranks a muffled order was given and a row of four soldiers armed with flamethrowers stepped forward out of the darkness. They pushed their way farther into the diseased crowd and unleashed their devastating weapons on the nearest creatures, sending controlled arcs of dripping, incandescent flame shooting out of the bunker door and up into the cold morning air. Virtually tinder dry, the bodies caught by the fire were incinerated almost immediately.

Another order was given and the personnel carrier began to creep slowly forward, climbing steadily toward daylight and then emerging out into the open, pushing deeper into the burning crowd, grinding charred flesh and bone into the mud beneath its heavy and powerful wheels. To the front and on either side the flamethrower-carrying soldiers took up protective positions and advanced cautiously, matching the laborious pace of the massive vehicle and destroying as many corpses as their flames would reach. Beyond the mass of burning bodies, countless more abhorrent figures continually pushed themselves closer and closer to the center of the disturbance attracted by the fire, noise, and sudden movements, oblivious to the danger. At the bunker entrance the two jeeps finally emerged out into the mayhem, each of them defended by another flamethrower-carrying soldier and other troops armed with more conventional but clearly less effective weapons.

As the military convoy slothfully eased away from the front of the base, the remaining troops formed a heavy protective line of defense across the still open entrance. The air was filled with billowing clouds of thick, black smoke, and the choking, suffocating smell of burnt corpses. Unable to see what was happening from where he was perched, Cooper jumped down from his high viewpoint and moved up the ramp to get closer to the troops.

"Cooper," Jack yelled at him, "come back. Don't be stupid."

Cooper ignored him and continued to edge farther forward. Now he was standing a short way behind the line of heavily armed soldiers, he could see that the personnel carrier and its entourage had managed to carve a deep, gently curving channel through the center of the immense crowd of corpses. The vehicles moved painfully slow through the bloody mayhem, still surrounded by a protective guard of soldiers who continually fired into the writhing, squirming, surging masses all around them. Hundreds of rotting figures were being obliterated by flame and gunfire and yet, undeterred, hundreds more continued to stagger across the mass of burning remains to take the place of those which had fallen.

Some three hundred meters away from the entrance to the base now, the driver of the personnel carrier turned to the officer next to him.

"Where's the vent?" he demanded. "Where's the fucking vent?"

Those troops who hadn't yet been aboveground had been unable to anticipate the disorientating visual effect of so many bodies being packed tightly together on the ground. Shaking with nerves, one overawed officer tried to trace the path they had already taken on a map. He looked up briefly to check his bearings but the land around them was featureless and little was visible except for the frantic, uncoordinated movements of the swarms of dead, searing arcs of flame, and dense, billowing clouds of noxious smoke.

"Should be somewhere over there," he yelled, pointing over to his right as he checked his instruments, then tried to find a more accurate visual reference. The driver steered the carrier as directed, shielding his eyes from a blast of sudden brightness as more bodies were drenched with fire and destroyed. He watched in disbelief as the creatures around them burned and yet continued to move. Inexplicably ignorant to the flames which quickly consumed them, the rotting cadavers staggered relentlessly forward until their last decaying muscles, nerves, and sinews had been burnt away to nothing.

"Got it," the driver said with relief as he caught a momentary glimpse of the exhaust vent amongst the seething sea of decaying figures. Originally standing just a few inches above ground-level and camouflaged by mud, moss, and weeds, the location of the vent was made obvious today by the mass of once-human remains which had accumulated around it. The first cadavers had been attracted by the faint noise and the heat coming up from the depths of the base, but after that many more bodies had become entangled with the low metal structure and they in turn had been trapped in place by countless more figures pushing against them, until the metal vent was partially obscured by writhing mounds of cold gray flesh.

"Drive straight over the top of it," ordered the officer, his composure returning. The driver did as instructed, turning the vehicle toward the vent and accelerating through the bodies. The soldier moving just ahead of them continued to soak the apparently endless crowd with fire, burning away the nearest of the hordes of lumbering cadavers, which were scrambling ever closer to the convoy.

Other than the metal vent, this patch of land was relatively flat and featureless. The driver of the personnel carrier powered over the top of the metal covering as ordered, smashing burning bodies away to either side and managing to scrape away a thick layer of once-human remains.

Someone gestured high in the air and a group of soldiers descended upon the vent. Some took position and started to sweep the bodies with machine-gun fire, keeping them at bay, while two soldiers began digging out the vent, shovelling away blood, guts, and gristle, and picking out bones and snagged shreds of clothing. They worked with furious speed, not looking up, but increasingly aware of bodies edging ever closer, grateful for the frequent bursts of flame and gunfire which held the advancing dead back.

Now that the way was clear, the driver of the first jeep, following close behind, gestured for the driver of the second to position his vehicle so it was straddling the vent, as they'd planned back in the bunker. The second driver pulled forward carefully, until the metal opening was positioned directly beneath the center of the mud- and blood-splattered vehicle. He leaned precariously out of his door to make sure he was in the right place, and saw that there were just a couple of inches' clearance between the top of the vent and the bottom of the jeep. Perfect.

He shouted to his colleagues, then jumped out and, with the soldiers already on the ground, they raced after the troop-carrier and the other jeep, which were now heading toward the next nearest vent to repeat the maneuver.

From behind the defensive line of soldiers standing in the entrance to the bunker, Cooper still struggled to see what was happening. Clouds of repulsive-smelling smoke blew back into the base and stung his eyes, filling his nose and throat with a charred, nauseating aftertaste.

"What's happening now?" Jack asked. The longer the soldiers had spent outside, the more Jack's curiosity had overtaken his nervousness. He'd gradually crept forward until he was standing just behind Cooper's shoulder.

"Can't see what they're doing. I've lost sight of them."

"Do they even have the slightest idea what they're—" Jack started to ask before a sudden blast of flame silenced him. He could feel the heat on his face, prickling his skin. When the smoke and heat-haze cleared, he saw the remains of a small pocket of bodies which had exploited a gap in the ranks and surged forward. The fact they were burning now didn't matter. They'd got dangerously close.

"This doesn't look good," Cooper said quietly. "These things are relentless."

The heat from another arc of flame, this time even closer than the last, sent the two men scuttling farther back into the base.

"Bloody hell," Jack cursed, recoiling from the intense heat.

"Look at the chances they're having to take here, Jack," Cooper said as the soldiers struggled to keep the dead at bay. "And for what? This is just to keep breathing, for Christ's sake!"

Jack didn't have a chance to respond. The soldiers protecting the entrance suddenly lowered their weapons and dropped back en masse. For a moment the two survivors feared the arrival of an unstoppable deluge of dead bodies but it didn't happen. Instead the personnel carrier burst back into the bunker followed almost immediately by the full complement of tired, shell-shocked, and battle-dirtied troops.

The shooting and fire-bombing continued until the doors closed.

Jack stared at the world outside for as long as he was able. The return of the powerful armored vehicle and the troops had disturbed the air and, momentarily, had caused much of the dirty smoke to disperse. Just for an instant, his view of the outside world was clear and uninterrupted. He could see mounds of dead flesh: the charred and mangled remains of hundreds of bodies lying twisted and blackened on the muddy ground. Beyond them he could see thousands more cadavers, all fighting to get closer to the base. Like a dense, gray fog those bodies which had so far escaped destruction scrambled over the remains of those which had fallen, desperately trying to reach the soldiers and survivors buried underground.

Jack missed seeing the sky and feeling the wind on his face, but the ever-present claustrophobia and the smell of dry, recycled air was a small price to pay to be kept safe from the hell outside.

4

"And that's all they're prepared to tell you?" Croft asked.

Cooper shrugged his shoulders nonchalantly. "That's about it. To be honest, I don't think there's much more to tell. They've cleared two of the vents and cremated a ton of corpses. That was all they went out there to do."

"But are they going to need to clear more vents? Will they go out there again?"

"I don't know."

"And how long do they think those vents are going to stay clear? How long's it going to be before they're clogged up with bodies again?"

"I don't know," Cooper said again, clearly irritated by the doctor's relentless and pointless questioning. "Look, Phil, it doesn't matter how many times you ask me, or how many different ways you ask, I don't know anything more than what I've already told you, okay? The blokes I know have been told not to talk to me."

It was several hours since the soldiers had returned from

outside and the doors to the base had been resealed. Croft, Cooper, Jack, and Donna were sitting in the relative comfort of the motor home with Michael and Emma. The brief glimpse of outside light earlier had made the bunker's prison-like gray walls feel more confining than ever. They could still see the bunker through the windows of the motor home, but the extra layer of separation gave the illusion of being a little further detached than usual from their nightmarish reality.

"What bothers me," Jack said quietly, cradling a beaker of water in his hands as if it was finest malt whiskey, "is that they're still coming. After all this time it doesn't look like anything's changed. I looked out there today and I could see as many bodies as I saw on the day we first arrived here, maybe even more. It's been three weeks now, for God's sake. Why don't they just piss off and find somewhere else?"

"Because there *is* nowhere else," Donna reminded him. "You know this, Jack. Even if there are hundreds more survivors scattered round the country, they'll all have hidden themselves away like us by now. They might not be underground, but they'll be out of sight, and I'll tell you something, I bet they've all got their own bloody huge crowds hanging round them just like we have."

"It wouldn't make any difference whether we were underground or up a bloody mountain," Michael added. "Doesn't matter how quiet or careful we are, they'll keep going until they find us."

"I know," Jack said dejectedly.

"Did you see what kind of condition they were in today?" Donna asked.

"Didn't get much chance, sorry," Jack sarcastically replied. "I would have got a bit closer but the soldiers and the flame-throwers and the thousands of burning bodies kind of put me off. Next time I'll try and—"

"What I mean is," Donna snapped, annoyed by his attitude, "were they still as mobile as they were before? When we came down here they were starting to get really aggressive. I just won-dered if they've changed or got any worse?"

"I couldn't tell. Honestly, Donna, it was hard to see any-thing much from where I was standing."

"It's difficult to say what kind of condition they're in," Cooper added. "Like Jack said, we couldn't see much more than fire and smoke out there. But what really concerns me is the fact that the guys who were left defending the entrance were kept busy all the time the doors were open."

"So?"

"So even though there was a bloody huge engine driving through the middle of them and a squad of soldiers firing at them nonstop, plenty of them were still trying to get in here. We've been saying all along that these things just react to dis-tractions. That might still be true, but to my mind a troop car-rier surrounded by blokes with flamethrowers should be a damn sight more distracting than a line of soldiers standing in an open door. I think the bodies that came towards the base must have chosen to try and get in here."

"You *are* joking, aren't you?" Jack balked.

"I don't joke, Jack, you should know that by now. Those things outside, their flesh and bone may be getting weaker, but we've said all along that they're getting smarter too, haven't we?"

"Are you serious?" asked Croft.

"I'm just guessing here," he replied. "It might have just been coincidence or a fluke that they found themselves close to the entrance. The bodies could have been heading towards the men out in the field and then been distracted by those that were left behind to protect the base."

"How could they be getting smarter when they're rotting away?" Jack wondered, looking at Dr. Croft for an answer to his obviously unanswerable question.

"How the hell am I supposed to know?" the doctor snapped angrily. "Bloody hell, I'm sick of this. Stop assuming I know what's going on. I keep telling you, I don't know any more than you do." Annoyed and hurting, Croft swung himself around in his seat and kicked the motor home door open with his feet. "Mind if I smoke?"

Michael shook his head.

"How many you down to now, Phil?" Jack asked.

"One and a half boxes," he replied as he relit an already half-smoked cigarette and slowly inhaled. "I tell you, I'm going to go out of my bloody mind if I can't get more cigarettes."

"How long do you reckon that lot will last you?" asked Emma.

"I've been limiting myself to smoking half of one each day. So I've probably got a couple of weeks left as long as you lot stop asking me stupid bloody questions and winding me up."

"What then?"

"Not much choice really, is there?" Croft said dejectedly. "I can either give up or go out and get some more!"

"You should try looking closer to home," Jack suggested.

"I bet they've got fags and drink and everything in their stores down here."

Cooper shook his head.

"You'd be surprised, Jack. This whole operation was thrown together in minutes. They've probably got less kit and supplies stashed away than you'd think."

Across from Cooper, Michael sat on the edge of the uncomfortable sofa which doubled as the bed he shared with Emma. Emma shuffled nearer to him and he wrapped his arms around her as she rested her weight against him. The others looked away, each of them feeling suddenly awkward and almost embarrassed. Emma and Michael's relative intimacy made them feel uncomfortable. They'd all lost everyone who'd ever mattered to them, and even the idea of such tenderness felt alien now—an uneasy reminder that the world they'd given up was gone forever.

"I always wanted a van like this," Jack said suddenly, looking around and making a conscious effort to start a more trivial conversation. "Me and Denise were planning on getting ourselves something like this when I retired. We were thinking about selling up and living on the road for a while."

"I wouldn't recommend it," Michael said. "It's not all it's cracked up to be. We were living on the road for a couple of weeks before we found this place, weren't we, Em? Didn't enjoy it!"

Jack smiled.

"Seriously, though, I've been thinking about it a lot," he rambled, looking out through the motor home window and imagining he could see something other than gray concrete walls. "Just think what it'll be like when the bodies have gone. Picture it, we'll have the whole country to ourselves. We'll be able to go where we like, when we like."

"So where would you go?" Croft asked him.

"I think," he began, stretching in his seat and staring up thoughtfully at the low metal ceiling above his head, "I'd like to try and travel right round the coast. I'm going to wait until next summer, then I'll start south and work my way west. I won't plan a route, I'll just keep going and one day I'll end up back where I started and see how much it's changed."

"But you could have your pick of the biggest houses or whatever you wanted," Emma said. "You could sit on your backside and relax. You'd still want to travel and live rough?"

"I'm getting used to living rough now. It'd be strange to be comfortable again. I like the idea of being on the move, taking whatever I need from wherever I can find it."

"Think you'll ever do it?" Donna asked.

Baxter looked deep into his beaker of water and thought hard for a moment. "I hope so."

"You make it sound easy."

"There's no reason why it shouldn't be. But there's no way of knowing other than doing it, is there?"

"It's going to get harder every day," Donna said, sounding tired and dejected. "As time passes there's going to be less and less for us to take out there. The last bits of food will rot. Buildings will start to crumble. Everything we used to know will gradually disappear."

"Christ," Jack groaned, "here's looking on the bright side, eh?"

"I'm just trying to be realistic, that's all."

35

"Anyway," Croft interrupted, "we've got to get out of here before you can start sightseeing, Jack."

"I know. Frustrating, isn't it? It's us who can survive out there, but it's the bloody army who'll decide whether we can go outside or not."

"Think they'll try and keep us locked down here, Cooper?" Croft asked.

"Unless us being here puts them at risk, I don't think they'll be in a hurry to get rid of us," Cooper answered. "I still think we might be useful to them. I think they might be making plans."

5

"What's the matter?"

Emma had woken up alone in bed. After a brief moment of blind panic she'd found Michael at the other end of the motor home, sitting behind the wheel and staring out through the windscreen into the gloom of the hangar. The hands on the dashboard clock said it was almost four. When he heard her he glanced around momentarily and then looked out again.

"Nothing's the matter," he replied. "I was just thinking, that's all."

"What about?"

"You know, the usual."

"What's the usual?"

"All this bullshit," he answered, gesturing outside the motor home. Emma sat down next to him. He sounded uncharacteristically abrupt and distant.

"Is it me? Have I upset you or . . . ?"

"Why do you always assume it's got anything to do with you, Em? What could you have possibly done to upset me?"

"I don't know. Maybe if you'd talk to me and tell me what's wrong I could help . . ."

Michael turned around to face Emma and pulled her closer. She was shivering with cold.

"It's nothing you've done. Believe me, you're just about the only thing I'm not worrying about right now."

"It's just that when I woke up and found you weren't there I started to think . . . you know what it's like . . ."

"I know."

She paused for a moment. "So what exactly *were* you thinking about?"

He nodded in the direction of the heavy entrance doors, which separated the fortunate few inside from the vast crowds of rotting flesh outside the base.

"The bodies."

"What about them?"

"You remember how many were outside when we first got here?"

"Thousands, why?"

"Jack said he thought there were just as many of them out there today, maybe even more."

"I know, I heard him. So?"

"So even though we've been buried down here for weeks, they're still managing to find us out."

"We knew this was going to happen . . ."

"I know that, but if they've been able to find us when we've been keeping quiet and out of sight, what the hell's going to happen now? What's going to happen now that those bloody idiots have started going out there with their guns and their flamethrowers and God knows what else? I think that every last corpse that's anywhere near here is going to end up outside those doors, trying to get in. And then more will come, then more. And the more there are out there, the more pressure this base is going to be put under just to keep functioning. Sooner or later they'll have to go aboveground again and then, when they do, it'll just make matters worse. It's a vicious cycle, and the dumb bastards in charge here can't even see it. They'll keep at it until this fucking place falls apart."

"Do you really think that'll happen?"

"I think it's inevitable," Michael answered quietly, his voice low and unemotional. "I've said it before. It might happen tomorrow, the day after tomorrow, or the day after that. It might happen in the next hour or it might not happen for weeks. The one thing I'm sure of is that it will happen eventually."

6

"You on your own, Cooper?"

Cooper shuffled closer to the intercom fixed on the wall next to the heavy door which separated the decontamination chambers and the rest of the buried base from the hangar. Well away from most of the rest of the group of survivors, he had been sitting talking to Bernard Heath when they'd become aware of sounds of movement coming from inside the decontamination area. Through a six-inch-square observation panel he'd recognized Jim Franks, just about the last of his ex-colleagues who still dared to risk speaking to him.

"I've got Bernard Heath with me," Cooper replied, his voice deliberately low, "but it's okay. Bernard's all right."

A pause.

"Okay, mate, if you trust him, I trust him," the subdued, disembodied voice said. Franks and Cooper had known and respected each other for years. The rest of Cooper's former colleagues had either been ordered or had chosen to stop communicating with him. Many now felt uneasy around him and distrusted him because he was "out there with them" instead of "in here with us." Others thought that being a bona fide, natural-born survivor somehow made him a different person from the Cooper they had known and served alongside previously. Those few troops who still remained committed and loyal to the military simply feared incurring the wrath of their superiors if they dared speak to him. Others had become completely isolated and withdrawn and just didn't speak to anyone anymore.

"How are things going in there?" Cooper asked, huddling closer to the intercom.

"Not so good," Franks replied.

"Why, what's happening?"

Another brief silence, then he answered.

"The men are scared 'cause no one knows what's happening or why it's happening. And we know we're on our own here now, so the fucking jokers who are running this place are starting to think they're in charge of what's left of the country and that they can do what they please. The men are pretty shook up after what happened outside. It's getting pretty fucking intense in here."

"Did you go out?"

"Not this time," Franks replied, "but it'll be my turn sooner or later. You know better than I do what we're up against here."

"It's not good," said Bernard.

"Seems to me it's fucking awful, never mind 'not good.' Jesus Christ, we've got people walking round down here talking about fields full of thousands of dead bodies and—"

"So what's happening?" Cooper interrupted, repeating his original question, keen to get an answer.

"Christ, Cooper, you know what it's like when you're getting ready for a fight. You've got some blokes who can't wait for it all to kick off so they can get going, then you've got others who spend most of their time crying into their fucking pillows like babies. All that most of us want to do is just get out of this hole, but we keep being told that what's out there is worse than what's down here and . . . and I don't know where this is all going but something's going to give sooner or later."

Cooper was worried that Franks had mentioned a fight. As far as he was concerned a fight in their present position would inevitably mean the military risking absolutely everything for absolutely nothing.

"I wish I could give you some good news," Cooper said, "but I'd be lying if I did because there's been no good news since this whole bloody thing started. Believe me, though, mate, you're in the best place you can be. Make sure you stay down there as long as you can. I've told you before, every move you make up here will bring hundreds of bodies swarming round you like flies. You might be stuck down there, but at least you're alive and you're not having to watch every step that you take. My advice is to keep your head down and get through this as best you can because—"

"You've got no fucking idea," Franks snapped, raising his voice to a dangerously loud volume. "For Christ's sake, Cooper, don't be so fucking naive. You know the kind of people that are in here. There's only so much of this they're going to take. There's only so much *I* can take."

"You don't have any choice. Go aboveground again and—"

"Try telling that to this lot."

"Seriously, Franks, I know how it seems, but you've got to—"

"Remember Carlson?" Franks interrupted.

"Keith Carlson?"

"Kevin," Franks corrected. "Remember him?"

"The chef, right?"

"That's right."

"What about him?"

"They found him in his bunk yesterday morning. Stupid fucker had slit his wrists."

"Christ," Bernard said quietly.

"He's not the first and he won't be the last," Cooper said quickly, blunt and unsympathetic.

"I know that," Franks continued, "but the problem isn't what he did, it's how to get rid of him. They can't decide what to do with the body. People are so fucking paranoid down here that they're talking about trying to burn him or cut him up into little fucking pieces, for God's sake. I've just seen blokes fighting over the corpse."

"Fighting, why?"

"Because they want to make sure he's dead. Jeavons and Coleman are standing guard over the body watching it, ready to hack it to fucking pieces if it starts to move."

"It's not going to move," Heath said, his voice sounding unintentionally condescending. "That would probably only happen if the body had been exposed to the outside air. I don't think—"

"I know that and you know that," Franks said angrily, "but you try convincing a couple of hundred soldiers who are scared out of their fucking minds and who feel like they've been backed into a corner. These people are trained to fight, not to sit around doing nothing. They're talking about dumping the body outside when we go aboveground again."

"Makes sense," Cooper said, "but that could be weeks away yet."

"I don't think so."

"Something planned?"

"It's starting to look that way."

"What?"

"Not sure, no one's saying much. Just rumors, that's all."

"Such as . . . ?"

The conversation faltered momentarily. Through the observation panel Cooper watched as Franks looked over his shoulder and checked he was safe to keep talking.

"I started to hear a few rumblings yesterday, and I've heard more today from people that I trust so it looks like there's some truth in what they're saying. Problem is we're not getting enough air down here and it's probably going to get worse. They cleared a couple of exhaust vents but they need to do more. There's no way of unblocking them from this side 'cause they'll risk infecting the whole fucking base, so at best it looks like we'll be heading up again soon to get a few more of them cleared."

"If that's at best," Bernard asked quietly, not sure he wanted to hear the answer, "then what's your worst-case scenario?"

Cooper glanced across at him, sharing his concern. Another pause and then Franks spoke again.

"Some of the boys who went out last time," he explained, "told the chiefs that they managed to get rid of hundreds of those things up there."

"They did," agreed Cooper. "Problem is there's tens of thousands more of them left."

"Rumor has it," Franks continued, "that they're looking at trying to organize one massive push. Rumor has it we're all going aboveground to torch the whole fucking lot of them."

7

The lights came on. Donna immediately jumped up from her seat as the doors to the decontamination chambers began to open.

"Oh, Christ," she said anxiously, glancing across at Emma, Clare, and Bernard, who were standing nearby and who were also staring at the slowly opening door.

Alerted by the sudden brightness in the hangar, most of the other survivors had already begun to furiously scramble across the vast cavern toward their vehicles. As the first heavily suited soldiers began to emerge from their sealed shelter, the frightened crowd of men, women, and children once again sprinted toward the police van, prison truck and motor home.

A steady stream of troops again took up position on the ramp just short of the entrance doors. Standing to the side of the main column of soldiers, an officer furiously marshaled proceedings. Just as they had done previously, a number of engines were started and another armored personnel carrier drove out of the shadows.

This time the powerful vehicle was accompanied by four jeeps and was surrounded by a phalanx of eight, flamethrower-carrying men. The men moved quickly toward the front of the short convoy, ready to escort the vehicles out into the open and burn a path for them through the seething crowds of the dead.

It was Saturday afternoon, three o'clock.

"What do you reckon?" Donna asked Bernard. The two of them had stopped halfway across the hangar and were watching the troops intently. "Think they're just going to try and do the same as they did before?"

"Looks that way," he replied, his voice quiet and trembling slightly. "I just want them to get it over with. If they're really going to do this, I just want them to do it now and stop all this stupid and pointless—"

His words were cut short as the ominous mechanical rumbling began, which signaled the opening of the main doors. He swallowed nervously and licked his dry lips, unable to look away from the entrance to the bunker, too scared to keep watching but even more afraid not to. The outside world slowly began to appear. Because of the slope of the entrance ramp he saw the clouds first—a dirty, gray-black, rain-filled sky that hung over the desolate scene and which made the day seem almost as dark as night. And then it began. An unexpected split second of silence and calm was ended by a sudden deluge of bodies which began to pour into the base before being pushed back and obliterated by the soldiers with flamethrowers. From that distance Bernard couldn't make out the individual corpses. He saw just a featureless mass of movement, constantly writhing and lurching, spilling forward into the advancing flames. For a gut-wrenching, seemingly endless moment, the weight and force of the advancing bodies seemed to put the farthest forward of soldiers on the back foot, almost forcing them back into the base again before they were able to dig in and start pushing forward. Their vastly superior power and strength soon allowed them to eat into the crowd with relative ease. Brutal and one-sided, as the battle quickly unfolded the familiar smell of burning again began to fill the cavernous hangar, carried along by suffocating clouds of dirty smoke.

"We need to get ready to move," Michael said. Donna reacted instantly but Bernard failed to respond, transfixed by the hellish sights he could now see outside. The personnel carrier began to drive forward, followed first by the jeeps, then by other heavily armored vehicles. The entire convoy was surrounded by a ring of soldiers who launched spitting jets of flame into the crowds.

"Cooper reckons they're really going to go for it this time," Jack Baxter said, suddenly appearing behind Bernard. "He says they might even be trying to get rid of the whole lot of them. What good do they think it's going to do? Get rid of this lot and more and more will come to take their place. They'll never do it."

"You can't reason with them," Cooper said, watching the soldiers marching out. For half a second he wondered whether he should have been fighting with them. "Put yourselves in their shoes," he continued. "We don't know much about what's happened, but we know a hell of a lot more than they do. We might not have the hardware they've got, but we're better placed to deal with all of this than they are. All they know is they can't breathe the air outside because it will probably kill them, and those bloody things out there are preventing them from getting the clean air they need. They're seeing the bodies as the enemy, and the only option they think they've got left is to blow the whole fucking lot of them to kingdom come."

"But don't they understand?" Jack pointlessly asked before Cooper interrupted.

"No, Jack, they don't, not fully. They haven't seen half of what we've seen."

"But the bodies won't stop, will they? They'll keep coming until there's nothing left."

Outside the bunker, the farthest advanced troops had made steady progress. The area immediately surrounding the base—which already resembled a churned and bloody World War I battlefield—was swarming with movement. The bodies approached from all angles and were beaten back by soldiers who had been kept waiting underground too long and who were desperate to fight. They laid into the approaching cadavers with anger and hate, this sudden outburst of brutality finally helping them to release their pent-up frustrations and previously stifled emotions. Those who had not been aboveground before, although shocked and terrified by what they saw all around them, were surprised by the relative ease with which the corpses could be destroyed. But from their vantage points low on the ground, the vast numbers of the dead and their relentless determination were as yet unclear.

Heavy artillery was quickly deployed. Mortars and shells

were fired into the endless crowds beyond the immediate perimeter of the base. In the near distance explosions shook the ground constantly, each blast tearing huge numbers of bodies apart. Closer to the entrance, the personnel carrier had almost reached another exhaust shaft. Walking alongside one of the vents, and shielded from the battle by the protective ring of fire which surrounded the convoy, the senior officer in the field, a hard bastard and veteran of many conflicts called Jennens, watched events unfolding around him with a degree of cautious satisfaction. His men and women were making steady progress, despite the appalling conditions. A sudden sharp shower of hissing rain had drenched everything. Grimy pools of water puddled across the churned, furrowed land, the ferocious heat from the flamethrowers turning them to steam. Captain Jennens's boots crunched cindered flesh and charred bone into the mud.

Another vent was easily secured. Jennens peered into the distant gloom beyond the scattered remains of the hundreds of bodies which had already been destroyed. He'd seen some appalling sights in his time, but never anything like this. The size and ferocity of the apparently endless crowd were remarkable and terrifying. As soon as one patch of the dead was scythed down, more surged forward to take the place of the fallen. He watched with an uneasy fascination as still more of the dark, skeletal creatures scrambled, tripped and crawled through the mayhem toward his soldiers and certain destruction. Did the damn things not realize they'd be annihilated? In the midst of the confusion Cowell, one of Jennens's most trusted men, appeared at his side.

"We can do this, sir," he said, shouting to make himself

heard through his face mask and over the squally wind and rain and the constant noise of battle. The ground rumbled momentarily as a small mortar landed short of its target and exploded nearby, sending a gruesome shower of blackened body parts flying through the air. "If we're going to do this at all, then we should do it now."

Jennens thought for a moment. Cowell was right. The opposition, although huge in numbers, was clearly weak and seemed incapable of offering any tangible, coordinated resistance. Although wiping them out wouldn't give the soldiers any more freedom, this was, unquestionably, a perfect opportunity to take back some of what they'd lost. The defensive position they'd initially intended to take had already become offensive and attacking. If they could destroy enough of the bodies and beat the remainder of them back far enough and keep them at a distance, they would be able to fortify the entrance to the bunker and properly clear and secure the exhaust vents. There was still no way the military personnel could survive outside the base, but Captain Jennens immediately recognized the psychological importance of ridding themselves of their perceived enemy.

"Shall I give the order, sir?" Cowell asked, keen to take this overdue, decisive action. Jennens looked around the battlefield again. In the short time he'd been standing there, his troops had made even more progress through the diseased crowds. The enemy was pathetic and defenseless against the comparative might of the military. All the dead had were numbers. Jennens knew they had nothing to lose.

"Do it," he commanded.

* * *

"Can't see," Jack whined, edging closer to the soldiers charged with protecting the hangar entrance. "I can't see a bloody thing."

"Stay back, Jack," Michael warned him.

A sudden noise from behind the small group of survivors startled them momentarily. Cooper spun around to see that the decontamination chamber doors were opening again.

"Shit," he cursed as a second ragged column of nervous soldiers appeared from the depths of the base. There seemed to be almost twice as many of them this time.

"What's all this about?" asked Bernard, feeling increasingly anxious.

"My guess," he answered as more than a hundred soldiers filed past them, "is they've decided to try and clear them away completely. I think this is the showdown we were promised."

As they emerged from the shadows into the light of the hangar, the soldiers increased their speed, breaking into a gentle jog for a few paces before accelerating and sprinting out into the semidarkness with weapons held high, ready for battle.

"This is not good," Jack said, feeling his stomach churning with nerves. "This is not good at all."

As the fighting outside increased in ferocity and volume, Cooper ushered the others toward their transports. Michael climbed into the motor home and found that it was already crowded with frightened people, each of them clutching the few personal belongings they'd managed to salvage in the sudden confusion. In the front, Donna had taken up the position he usually occupied behind the wheel. Emma was sitting next to her.

"Are you two okay?" he asked, leaning into the front cabin.

Donna gripped the steering wheel tightly in readiness. "You want your seat back?"

"It's okay," Michael answered. "There are enough people in here already, I'll find somewhere else. Look, Donna, if anything happens, just put your fucking foot down and get out of here, okay?"

"Be careful, Mike," Emma said, but he'd already gone.

Both the motor home and prison truck were full—most people choosing the comfort of one or the security of the other— but there was still space in the police van. Cooper called him over.

"Just got a couple of folks in the back of this," he said, gesturing over his shoulder at the van. "Do me a favor, just make sure that either you or I are behind the wheel if we need to make a move, okay?"

"Okay."

Breathless and red-faced, Bernard Heath appeared from around the back of the van.

"I've done a quick head count," he wheezed. "I think everyone's accounted for."

Cooper nodded and then stood and watched as the soldiers continued to pile out through the bunker door.

Outside the base, a wide swath of land had already been cleared. The majority of the soldiers had now been formed into long attacking lines, sweeping slowly out across the land from the bunker entrance, tasked with destroying as many of the bodies as they could. The jeeps had been positioned over all but one of the vents and the main objective of the excursion had been achieved. What was happening now was largely unplanned but so far it was still relatively well coordinated. From positions just behind the advancing troops, heavy artillery was being fired over their heads, relentlessly pounding the land and the shadowy hordes, destroying scores of bodies with every shell. All around, momentary bursts of brilliant yellow, orange, and white light pierced the deteriorating monochrome gloom, illuminating the grotesque bodies for a fraction of a second at a time like camera flashes. The troops moved steadily away from the base entrance, their progress quick and largely unimpeded.

The forward attacking line of ground troops fanned out as they moved away from the bunker, preventing the crowds getting any closer. A bloody and relatively constant gulf of several meters' width remained between the advancing soldiers and the dead. Ignorant to the danger they faced, those creatures which had so far escaped the wrath of the military continued to try and move ever closer, dragging themselves over the putrefying remains of the thousands of corpses that had fallen before them.

"Aim for the head," a sergeant yelled, trying not to think how much he sounded like a character from the horror movies he used to watch as his troops unleashed another furious volley of bullets and flame at the seething mass of cadavers. Undeterred, and without a single flicker of emotion, the dead continued to surge forward.

A short distance farther down the military line, Sean Ellis, a soldier with a short but impeccable service history stood up to his ankles in blood, mud, and rancid flesh and picked out individual corpses from the constantly shifting crowd up ahead. With the skill and concentration of a highly trained marksman he managed to shut off from the rest of the mayhem unfolding all around him and aimed at individual bodies in turn, shooting them in the head and obliterating what remained of their brains. They dropped twitching to the ground and were immediately trodden down by more grotesque figures advancing from behind. Conditions were becoming steadily worse with smoke, flame, and rain combining to make it impossible to see clearly through the deteriorating light of this stormy autumn afternoon. To his, left and right Ellis's colleagues continued to fight, each of them destroying as many bodies as they were able, but the crazed creatures continued to advance. For every one that Ellis destroyed, ten more immediately seemed to take its place. And beyond, he realized, there were thousands and thousands more. Out of view an endless number of them crawled through the darkness toward the fighting.

"Christ," the soldier on his immediate right cursed. "How many of these fucking things are out there?"

They continued to shoot and the bodies continued to advance, spilling ever forward like a thick, dark sludge. Ellis didn't have time to think or speak, concentrating instead on firing bullet after bullet into the rotting crowd. An arc of white-hot flame burned through the air just ahead of him, illuminating the full horror of the scene for a few heart-stopping seconds. The disintegrating faces of hundreds of corpses were suddenly visible and Ellis was transfixed, staring at them in horror and revulsion, praying for the light to fade and the dark to return. The nearest corpses were less than ten meters ahead.

The ragged line of soldiers, still advancing, reached a ditch where a meandering stream had once run diagonally across the battlefield but which had, over the course of the last few weeks, become clogged and filled with a compacted layer of putrefying human remains. The trooper on Ellis's right, struggling to keep focused on the fighting and not lose his nerve, slipped down the slight incline, ending up on his hands and knees in the middle of the stagnant trench. A powerful wave of gut-wrenching nausea swept over him as he looked down into a mire of decayed faces, limbs, and other body parts, all immediately recognizable as such. He pushed himself back up and tripped and stumbled farther toward the approaching bodies on the other side of the ditch. Bile began to rise in his throat and he started to salivate. He knew he was going to vomit, but he also knew he had to stop himself at all costs. He turned back around to look for help and another searing jet of fire lit up the stormy sky above him. A fraction of a second later a shell dropped short of its intended target and landed just meters away, exploding instantly and showering the troops with mud, shrapnel, and dribbles of flesh. Knocked to the ground again, the soldier panicked and scrambled back away from the front line. He was aware of a sudden stabbing, burning pain in his back, but he ignored it and kept moving. Once steady on his feet again he reached over his shoulder and rubbed at the part of his neck and right shoulder which hurt the most. He could feel a small, jagged shard of metal which had ripped through his suit and pierced his skin. He brought his hand back around and saw that it was glistening with blood, and he knew his suit had been compromised. Panicking, he lifted his weapon and turned back to face the dead. Just for a moment longer—no more than a few seconds—the adrenaline numbed the pain and kept him fighting.

Aware that a gap had opened up in the attacking line to his side, Ellis looked around. The wounded soldier next to him continued to fire into the swarming bodies until the infection took hold. As he emptied another round into the crowd the inside of his throat began to swell, then it started to bleed. Knowing he was dying but not knowing why, the soldier slowly turned on the spot, desperate for help. Frozen in position by a spontaneous nervous reaction, his finger remained on the trigger of his rifle, releasing a continuous burst of bullets. Ellis was the first of eight soldiers to drop, shot through the abdomen and neck.

The sounds of battle were muffled down on the ground. Though he was weighed down by his breathing apparatus and other equipment, Ellis managed to roll over onto his back in the mud. He looked up into the dark gray sky above his head and waited. The heavy rain clattered down on his face mask, drowning out all other noise. He was aware of sudden, frantic movement all around him and then complete and utter darkness. He felt the crowd of emaciated bodies crawling over him as they marched toward the base.

"Listen," Cooper said as he stood by the transports next to Michael and Bernard.

"What?" Bernard nervously demanded.

"Something's happening."

The men stood in silence, listening to the noises reverberating all around them, amplified by the vastness of the hangar.

"What?" Bernard asked again.

"Can't you hear it?"

"Hear what?" Michael demanded, feeling increasingly un-easy.

"Just listen . . ."

Michael did as Cooper said, and now it gradually became clear. There had been a subtle change to the sounds of battle drifting into the bunker from outside. Where before there had just been the constant pounding of gunfire and mortar explosions, now he could hear screams and shouts over the relentless tumult. Everything suddenly sounded desperately frantic and uncoordinated, as if all order and control was steadily disappearing. He looked up the ramp toward the entrance door and saw that while some of the troops who had been left behind to guard the bunker were edging forward, others were beginning to shuffle back.

"They've got no idea how many bodies are out there, have they?" Michael said anxiously. "You tried to tell them, didn't you? Christ, there must be thousands of corpses for every soldier."

"It'll be all right, won't it, Cooper?" Bernard asked, though he already knew the answer to his question.

Cooper ran the length of the hangar and up the entrance ramp until he was almost level with the soldiers left to guard the base. He looked out into the darkness where the frequent flashes of brilliant light and flame and random explosions provided more than enough illumination for him to see what was happening outside. He was an experienced soldier, and he'd been involved in enough operations to know when an army's tactics were working and when they were not. He could see at least two areas ahead of him where the bodies were now between the soldiers and the base. The creatures had somehow managed to work their way through the lines of troops. Relentless and emotionless, the dead hordes continued to move forward past unexpectedly isolated pockets of men and women who were surrounded and swallowed up by the decaying masses. It was a horrific, nightmarish scene which transfixed Cooper until the headlamps of the personnel carrier in the near distance distracted him. It was powering back toward the bunker, its lights jerking up and down as the driver forced the massive vehicle over the uneven ground at speed. Both frantic soldiers and dead bodies occasionally crisscrossed in its path and were obliterated as it raced back to the safety of the base.

The corpses were close. Too bloody close.

"What can you see?" Michael shouted from the bottom of the ramp. Cooper didn't answer, he just continued to survey the mayhem outside. Incredibly, the balance of power on the battlefield seemed to be shifting. The longer he watched, the more chaotic and disorganized the soldiers were becoming. Three freshly opened gaps in the military's defenses became four, then five, then more. The troop carrier thundered back and all around individual troopers began deviating from their orders, falling out of formation and running for cover, firing wildly at anything which moved. And then, high in the air over all of the madness, a single orange flare appeared in the sky. It hung above the carnage, lighting up the cloud base and bathing everything below in a strong and eerily beautiful light. Cooper forced himself to get back down to the others. He knew the flare was the signal to retreat.

"They're coming back," Cooper yelled as he sprinted. He'd barely finished speaking when the personnel carrier crashed back into the base, careering out of the darkness and skidding down the incline, out of control. Michael and Bernard dived for cover in opposite directions as the heavy machine plowed along the length of the hangar and then collided with the front of their police van, sending it spinning around through a quarter turn and shunting it hard against the wall. Michael ran to help those who had been waiting inside the vehicle, unaware what was happening and unable to protect themselves from the sudden violent impact. He could hear them screaming in confusion and pain as he yanked the doors open. One of them—an elderly man whose name he could never remember—was dead, his bloodied face smashed against one of the windows.

"What the hell do we do now?" he yelled to Cooper as he pulled the remaining survivors out. Cooper ran toward the personnel carrier. Most of the soldiers who had been inside had already fled toward the decontamination chamber and were hammering on the door to be let back inside.

"Get them in here."

As Michael ushered the shell-shocked civilians toward the military vehicle, the first of the foot soldiers began to return to the base. They stumbled down the ramp, still firing indiscriminately into the darkness behind them. Seconds later they were followed by the first wave of dead bodies. A sudden loud noise and a flash of frantic movement distracted Cooper. He looked up and saw that one of the jeeps had crashed into the side of the entrance door. The soldier who'd been behind the wheel was now limping down the ramp but he'd barely made it halfway down the slope before he was overcome by advancing bodies, their speed increased by the incline.

"We've got to get out of here now," Cooper said to Michael. "If they can't get that door closed then in a couple of minutes this place will be full of those fucking things. We can't afford to wait."

"Go!" Michael screamed at Donna and Steve Armitage, who was behind the wheel of the prison truck. The noise in the cavernous room was deafening and intense and at first neither of them reacted. Michael gestured frantically and angrily toward the bunker doors until Steve finally acknowledged him and began to pull forward, steering the clumsy prison truck around stockpiles of military equipment. Donna, who'd never driven the motor home before, followed nervously.

As the two vehicles moved up toward the entrance, many more soldiers and bodies swarmed back down into the base. Individually the corpses were slow and largely uncoordinated, but their collective movement down the steep incline gave the impression of speed and control. Gunfire continued to ring out. As more soldiers forced their way back inside and the fighting intensified, so the hangar quick filled with more deadly gunfire and the occasional flashes of barely controlled flame.

Emma searched desperately from the front of the motor home, hoping to catch sight of Michael as they drove deeper into the confusion. Next to her, Donna struggled to control the unresponsive vehicle. She followed the prison truck, concentrating on staying close to its taillights and matching every move

Steve made. She glanced into her door mirror. Deeper in the base behind them she could see frantic movement all around the back of the personnel carrier. In the midst of it all she saw Bernard Heath struggling to climb inside. She watched helplessly as he was brought down by gunfire, a stray round almost cutting him in half. A torrent of bullets thudded into his right leg, his crotch, his abdomen and his shoulder. By the time he hit the ground he was dead.

"Oh God," she said, her eyes stinging with tears. "Bernard's gone down."

"What?" Emma demanded, spinning around and trying to get a clear view through the back of the motor home. She caught a glimpse of his body on the ground before another surge of corpses blocked her view. Where the hell was Michael?

Out of sight of the motor home, Michael pulled the door at the back of the personnel carrier shut.

"Move!" he yelled. He lurched forward and then fell back into a seat as the soldier driving the transport turned it around and pulled away.

"Put your fucking foot down," Cooper ordered. The driver didn't argue, quickly overtaking both the motor home and the prison truck and powering up the access ramp. Countless staggering shapes—both living and dead—were dragged beneath its huge wheels.

"Which way?" the nervous trooper stammered through his cumbersome face mask. Bright electric light was replaced by comparative darkness as they drove out into the open. Intense battles were still raging on all sides as soldiers fought to get back into the bunker. The gunfights provided some illumination but not nearly enough for Cooper to be able to make sense of what was happening around them. He knew that the main track away from the bunker was blocked by the truck the survivors had crashed when they'd first arrived there weeks earlier, so now he needed to find another route away. The vehicle he was in would be able to cope with any terrain, no matter how rough or uneven, but the prison truck and motor home following behind would both struggle with anything more than the gentlest of gradients. Resigned to the fact that conditions would probably be bad whichever direction they chose, he made a snap decision.

"Follow the line of the valley," he ordered, gesturing left and choosing what he thought would be the most level route, shouting to make himself heard over the noise of the engine and the relentless *thud, thud, thud* of the endless stream of bodies which launched themselves pointlessly at the metal sides of the personnel carrier. "Just keep going straight. We're bound to pick up a road or a track at some point."

Driving through the bloody mayhem and devastation which continued to unfold all around them, the three vehicles disappeared into the darkness.

The hangar was filled with bodies. Individual soldiers still managed to offer a degree of resistance but their ammunition and their will to fight were almost completely gone. Terrified and exhausted, several disorientated troops had ripped off their cumbersome face masks in desperation and were almost immediately infected and killed. Others were brought down by cross fire. Many more were ripped apart by vast, surging crowds of crazed corpses, huge numbers launching themselves at each of the troopers.

The senior officer left belowground ordered the decontamination chambers to be locked and sealed. One hundred and seventeen troops were buried underground. Almost double that number remained trapped in the hangar and out on the surface, some still fighting, the majority dead or dying.

8

Michael crawled the length of the personnel carrier to get to Cooper, being thrown constantly from side to side as the vehicle clattered across the uneven ground.

"So what the hell do we do now?" he demanded, knowing full well that his question was a pointless one.

Cooper had already dragged himself into the front of the vehicle and was sitting alongside two protective-suited soldiers. There were a further two troopers sitting in the back with Michael, and three other survivors. Obviously the soldiers had been out fighting on the battlefield for some time, and the survivors gave them as wide a berth as was possible in the close confines of the military vehicle. Their cumbersome survival suits were covered with a layer of mud, blood, and stinking gore.

Cooper didn't even bother trying to answer Michael. Frustrated, Michael asked another question.

"Do we just keep going all fucking night?" he cursed, holding on to the back of Cooper's seat as the armored vehicle suddenly lurched down an unexpected incline. He looked out through the blood-splattered windscreen and saw that the driver's view was frighteningly limited. "There's less than half a tank of fuel in the motor home," he continued nervously. "We can't keep going indefinitely."

When Cooper still didn't acknowledge him he slumped back angrily in the nearest seat, then turned to look out of the back of the vehicle. Behind them the devastating and ultimately pointless battle continued to rage with frequent explosions and brilliant flashes filling the dead world with light for a fraction of a second at a time. The personnel carrier dipped awkwardly to one side as the ground over which they drove became increasingly rough and uneven. Following close behind was the prison truck and, farther back still, Michael was able to see the lights of the motor home as it struggled to keep up. He wished he was with Emma. How had this been allowed to happen? How had everything fallen apart so quickly? A couple of hours ago the bunker door had still been sealed and they'd been relatively safe and protected; now people had died and for what? They were exposed and vulnerable once more, running without direction again. He couldn't stop thinking about Bernard. He pictured him now, lying dead on the hangar floor, surrounded by scores of bodies and soldiers still trying to fight. Christ, he hoped Bernard had died quickly. He hoped he wasn't suffering. Imagine lying helplessly in the middle of that nightmare, unable to move and slowly bleeding to death, just waiting for it all to be over . . .

"We're bound to hit a road at some point," Cooper finally said, snatching Michael from his dark and increasingly depressing thoughts, bringing him back to reality. "Then we'll stop and try and work out where we are."

"Don't be stupid, how can we stop? If we stop then we're going to—"

"If we're sensible we can afford to stop for a little while," Cooper interrupted, his voice slightly louder—just enough to silence Michael's outburst. "We'll stop and regroup and decide what to do next. If we're quick there won't be time for any more than just a few bodies to find us."

Michael nodded and grunted to show he'd understood, but he'd stopped listening. All he was interested in was Emma, and nothing else mattered. He watched the constant movement all around them as bodies turned and traipsed through the night after the ragtag convoy.

In the prison truck, Steve Armitage skillfully steered along the wide furrowed tracks that the military vehicle in front of him was leaving in the mire. At his side was Phil Croft, terrified and shaking with nerves but still alert, watching the world outside like a hawk. In the back of the truck more survivors sat huddled in the darkness together, not knowing where they were now or where they were going, each one of them racked with an uncomfortably familiar sense of disorientation and hopelessness.

More than fifty meters behind the truck, Donna groaned with effort as she struggled to keep control of the motor home. It was an old, overused, and unresponsive vehicle which gave a rough ride on level road at the best of times, never mind in these treacherous conditions. Inside the vehicle no one spoke. A far more ordinary machine than the other two vehicles it followed, its wide windows afforded those survivors crammed in the back a clear view of the dead world around them, a view which many of them would have preferred not to have seen. Now more than a mile from the bunker, there were still vast crowds of bodies swarming across the land all around them. Donna did what she could but the ride was increasingly unsteady. The motor home hadn't been built to cope with thick, churned mud and sudden dips and climbs. The steering was slow and heavy and the vehicle's rear end constantly threatened to slide out of control. In the back no one dared speak for fear of distracting their nervous driver.

Emma glanced up at the outline of a house nestled amongst the trees on the brow of a low hill. Even from a distance she could see movement and knew it had been overrun. It reminded her of Penn Farm, and she felt as terrified and helpless now as she had when she and Michael had lost the farmhouse. Her dark thoughts were interrupted when they suddenly stopped moving.

"What's wrong?"

Donna gestured up ahead. Emma looked out and saw that Cooper was outside the personnel carrier. He was untying a frayed rope or chain that had been keeping a wide metal gate closed. The headlamps of each of the vehicles illuminated huge numbers of unsteady bodies, which began to collide with the transports as they crisscrossed the scene randomly. Fortunately for Cooper, the light and engine noise was far more of a distraction than he was. They watched as he swung the gate open, kicked away the nearest corpse, and then ran back to his vehicle.

"Should be easier from here," Donna said quietly, her voice sounding tired and resigned. "I don't think we'll—"

A foul-looking, withered cadaver slammed into the front of the motor home. Donna jumped back with surprise and then leaned forward and peered down as it began to batter the bodywork with clumsy, barely coordinated hands. It was an appalling sight. In the time that the survivors had been underground, the condition of the bodies had continued to steadily deteriorate. This monstrosity, judging by the length of what remained of its lank, shoulder-length hair and its shredded clothing, had been female. The lower part of its face was virtually indistinguishable. The hole where its mouth should have been was double normal size and its jawbone hung down, ripped away from one side of its head. Its skin was green-black and covered in ruptures and holes where the flesh had been eaten away. The corpse's empty eyes stared unblinking into the headlights of the motor home.

"They're moving," Emma said, looking anywhere but at the body. Donna lifted her head and then gently accelerated, hoping that the initial movement might be enough to push the body away to the side. When it still didn't move she jabbed her foot down hard instead and the repellent figure was carried forward several meters before being dragged down and crushed under the motor home wheels.

Matching the route of the prison truck and personnel carrier, Donna carefully steered the motor home through the gate and pulled out onto a narrow gravel track.

9

The convoy pushed on through the evening and into the night, following the twisting road through the darkness, not knowing where they were heading.

There were nine people in the personnel carrier, and for the most part none of them spoke. Cooper kept himself occupied by constantly watching the road ahead, scanning for bodies and searching for somewhere they could stop for a while and regroup. They had hardly anything with them—very little food or water, only a few weapons—and it was obvious that getting hold of some supplies was a priority. He'd known it was going to be like this if they'd needed to evacuate the base at speed. He'd intended to stockpile supplies in readiness, but the military had provided them with minimal rations and had maintained such strict control over their equipment that it had been impossible for him to build up any reserves. They'd hardly had enough to survive on as it was, let alone any to save.

In the back of the vehicle Michael stared at one of the soldiers who was leaning against the door, sobbing.

"What's your name?" he asked. The suited figure turned and looked at him.

"Kelly Harcourt," she replied. Michael was surprised, although he knew he shouldn't have been. He'd assumed that under all the battlefield dirt and the shapeless protective suit, the trooper was male. Although it was dark and most of her face was hidden by her breathing apparatus, he could just make out her eyes and the bridge of her nose. She looked too young to be in uniform.

"First time you've been aboveground?"

She nodded. "They told us what it was like," she said quietly, "but I never expected this."

"Believe me," he said, "whatever they told you, it's worse. You haven't seen anything yet."

The conversation ended as quickly as it had begun. Michael regretted sounding so negative, but what else was he supposed to say? Lying to the soldier to try and make her feel better was pointless. Maybe he should have just shut up and said nothing? It seemed the harder he tried, the less he achieved. He and Emma had worked damn hard to survive since the first day, and for what? He thought about the places he'd been since then—the community center in Northwich, Penn Farm, the bunker—none had been as safe as they'd first seemed. He silently admitted to himself that he was as helpless, vulnerable, and scared now as he'd been almost two months ago when the nightmare had begun.

Was this how it was always going to be?

Progress along the debris-strewn roads was slow. The landscape through which they traveled was relentlessly dark and bleak with the bodies being the only things apart from them which still moved. By chance they occasionally walked out in front of the personnel carrier, but for the most part they were slow to react to the noise and light produced by the short convoy and stumbled aimlessly into the empty road after the vehicles had gone.

They'd been driving for more than an hour when they reached the outskirts of a small town where they changed direction, choosing not to risk driving straight through. They drove toward a collection of large, nondescript buildings sited just off the main road. The soldier driving the personnel carrier slowed down as they entered an overgrown retail park. When they looked deeper into the shadows they were able to make out a pub, a cinema, a couple of office blocks, and several dilapidated factories, as well as shells of buildings in various stages of construction or demolition. It looked like the area had been in the middle of a large-scale regeneration project when the project managers, the architects, the backers, the bankers, the construction workers, and everyone else involved in the project had died. Michael looked around the site hopefully. There didn't appear to be more than a handful of bodies around, although he knew they'd start coming before long.

He leaned forward and grabbed Cooper's shoulder. "Let's try here. Might as well."

Cooper nodded and the driver cautiously led the convoy deeper into the estate, following a winding block-paved road which connected a number of car parks the size of football pitches, largely empty save for a scattering of vehicles—some crashed, others long abandoned by their dead owners. He slowed down outside the pub. Cooper made a suggestion.

"Head for that place."

He gestured beyond the pub, past the cinema and over toward a warehouse-sized store with metal shutters over the windows. The driver kept moving forward, swerving instinctively but unnecessarily around three clumsy, lurching bodies which tripped out of the shadows. The store was in the farthest corner of the estate at the top of a slight rise, bordered on its left side and along the back by a high chain-link fence. Beyond the fence were trees. As they approached, Cooper noticed a cordoned-off loading bay at the side of the building.

"Over there," he said. "Go through the gate."

The driver did as instructed, accelerating up the hill and then carefully guiding the personnel carrier into the enclosed area. Still following close behind, the prison truck and the motor home did the same. The personnel carrier came to a sudden, juddering halt. Desperate to escape its confines, Michael climbed out quickly and jogged across the loading area to the gate. Cooper appeared at his side and, between them, they pulled it shut and secured it. A lone body had managed to squeeze through before the gap was closed. Cooper grabbed its neck and smashed its head repeatedly against the side of the prison truck until it stopped moving.

"Let's get everyone inside," Michael said. "If we get under cover quickly enough we shouldn't attract many of them. We might even be able to spend the night here if we—"

73

Another body rushed him from the side, grabbing hold of him with surprising strength. He stopped himself reacting when he realized it was Emma. She wrapped her arms around him, knocking him off balance.

"I didn't know if you'd got out," she said, barely able to contain her relief. "I looked but I couldn't see you . . ."

"This is all very touching, but we don't have time for it," Donna said disapprovingly as a lone body lethargically dragged itself up toward the gate. "Get out of sight, for Christ's sake."

The survivors and soldiers nervously emptied out of their respective vehicles and waited at a side entrance into the dark and silent building. Gavin Stonehouse, the highest ranking of the four remaining soldiers, led the way through a door which had been propped open for the last seven and a half weeks by the atrophied right leg of a dead member of staff. He held his rifle out in front of him, ready to fire but not sure what good it would do. The group followed behind in a close but uncoordinated bunch and were completely silent until Jack Baxter spoke.

"We should make a bit of noise," he said, "just in case there's any of them in here. We should try and get them out of the shadows."

"It's all shadows in here, Jack," Michael said, looking around and trying to make sense of their dark and dismal surroundings. "I think we should give it a minute. Get everybody inside first."

They had entered a huge and probably extensively stocked household store, and they were presently walking through the middle of a large electrical department. To their right was a bank of blank television screens; to their left a similarly lifeless display of stereo equipment.

Stonehouse stopped moving.

"So what now?"

"Get some bloody light in here for a start, I can't see a damn thing," a nervous voice from the darkness replied. Michael recognized it as belonging to Peter Guest, a quiet whisper of a man who generally kept to himself and to whom he had spoken only a handful of times.

"There's bound to be something in here we can use," Donna said hopefully as she looked around through the gloom. She could hear something moving close by, but she wasn't sure whether it was living or dead. The longer she listened, the more she thought she could make out.

Standing just to Stonehouse's right, Phil Croft lifted his cigarette lighter and flicked it into life, the dancing orange flame burning an immediate, bright hole in the darkness. A body which had by chance stumbled perilously close, suddenly increased its speed and turned and scrambled through the shop debris toward the light. It lurched for Stonehouse, knocking him off-balance into a huge TV screen which rocked precariously on its stand. Stonehouse calmly picked himself back up, shoved the corpse away on its already unsteady feet, and then lifted his rifle and shot it through the head. It dropped heavily to the ground, its face a caved-in mass of putrefied flesh and splintered bone. The gunshot echoed endlessly around the store.

"Nice one," Donna said. "Christ, make some more noise, why don't you? We'd better get some damn light sorted out now because every dead body in this fucking place will be on its way over to us."

"Did it cross your mind that there might be a reason why none of us bother carrying guns?" Jack added. "A single shot might take one of them out, but there are thousands of the bloody things out there, and the noise you make getting rid of one will bring a hundred more sniffing around you."

Donna began to search the nearby shelves for something to illuminate the dark building. Others followed her lead. Kelly Harcourt, the soldier Michael had spoken to earlier, disappeared back outside and then returned with a handful of torches from the personnel carrier.

"Why the hell didn't you bring those in with you in the first place?" Donna yelled at her, snatching one of the torches.

"Give her a break, Donna," Jack said as he took a torch and shone it around. Several circles of bright light tracked around the vast shop floor in different directions, occasionally illuminating corpses slowly lumbering towards them.

"Stay here and wait for them to come to us," Cooper ordered.

The first body hauled itself into view. Moving awkwardly and dragging one useless foot behind, all the torches were immediately focused on the creature. Its face—as much of its face that remained intact—was badly discolored and had an unnatural, waxy sheen. Decay had eaten away much of its nose, right eye, and cheek, and its few remaining yellowed teeth, grinding constantly, were visible through the largest hole in its flesh. It still wore the tattered remnants of a store attendant's uniform: a blue shirt—with a collar that now appeared several sizes too big because of the body's emaciation—and a red tie. Donna found it bizarre that the body was still wearing a tie. It even had a name badge still pinned to its shirt pocket, though the name had been obscured by mold and dribbles of blood and other bodily discharges. Cooper disposed of it by swinging a fire extinguisher and virtually knocking its head from its shoulders. It collapsed to the ground as three more bodies stumbled into the light.

Half an hour was enough time for the survivors to rid themselves of the remaining corpses and dispose of them in a heap outdoors. Many of the group then busied themselves around the building, collecting anything that might prove useful, happy just to be occupied for a while. The bodies outside hadn't materialized in the vast numbers the group had come to expect. They took advantage of their nonappearance to raid all the edible food and drink they could from the kitchen of the pub nearby and the concessions stand in the foyer of the cinema opposite—mostly confectionary and cans of drink, but it was better than nothing. By the time those who had gone outside were safely back inside the store, there were some twenty bodies gathered around the front of the building and half as many again clattering against the fence surrounding the loading bay, still nothing like the massive numbers they were used to around the bunker.

"They're not a problem when they're like this and there's only a few of them," Cooper explained, trying to educate Stonehouse. "Problem is, if you're not careful, one of them will attract another, then another, and so on and so on until you've suddenly got hundreds to deal with. And there are thousands upon thousands of the fuckers out there, so keep the guns as a last resort. Softly, okay?"

Stonehouse sat opposite Cooper, slumped dejectedly in a chair in an officelike area of the store where he guessed customers would previously have sat with staff and applied for credit. Jack sat with them. Donna, Emma, and Michael were also nearby, as were several others. A short distance away, the three other soldiers sat in silence on a pile of large cushions and garishly colored beanbags which looked like they had originally been designed for use in children's bedrooms.

"So what happens now?" Stonehouse asked. Jack looked at him and tried to imagine how he must have been feeling, trapped in his uncomfortable protective suit, knowing that if he took it off he'd almost certainly suffer a quick and painful death. Jack imagined he might have been able to handle it himself for a few hours, maybe even a couple of days at a push, but the four soldiers now traveling with them would have to exist like this indefinitely. He didn't know how they'd be able to eat, drink, or do anything else. Surely it would only be a matter of time before they were forced to take off their suits. Whether they realized it or not (and he was pretty sure they did), they were just waiting to die. Just prolonging the inevitable.

"We should stop here for as long as it's safe," Cooper replied, finally answering the soldier's question, "then see what we've got and work out what we need—"

"Then what?"

"We move on, I guess."

"Where to?"

"How the hell am I supposed to know?"

"Problem is," Jack said, "nowhere's safe anymore. Christ, you lot with your bloody guns and your tanks and everything else couldn't look after yourselves, could you? What hope do you think *we've* got?"

Cooper looked up and shook his head to silence him.

"Come on, we've talked about this a hundred bloody times already, Jack," he said before turning back to face Stonehouse again. "The bodies are rotting. They're more controlled than they were before, but the fact is they're still decaying. They'll reach a point before too long when they're just not able to function."

"And how long's that going to be?"

"A few more months, I guess."

"Months? Fucking hell, are we supposed to sit here like this for a few months?"

"You might have to. Could you last that long?"

"I doubt it. Anyway, getting rid of the bodies won't get rid of the germ. The air's still going to be full of shit we can't breathe."

"So what are you going to do?"

"Doesn't look like we've got any option but to try and get back to the base," Stonehouse replied. "Whatever happens we're dead if we stop out here. Might as well try and get back if we can."

"You've got nothing to lose," Jack said quietly.

"Seems to me everything's lost already."

10

Clare Smith's watch said it was a quarter to three. The cavernous store was echoey and cold. She lay restless on the floor next to Donna on a dusty mattress they'd dragged over from the furniture department hours earlier. She was physically exhausted but unable to sleep. She raised herself up onto her elbows and looked around. Perhaps as many as half of the others were awake too.

Clare needed to relax but she couldn't get comfortable. Her guts were twisting with sudden waves of cramps. It was probably just nerves, she told herself, either that or the overdose of sugary food she'd had earlier. Whatever the reason, even the thought of eating now made her want to vomit. She'd had diarrhea an hour ago. Christ, that had been humiliating. She'd sat on a dried-out toilet pan in the farthest corner of the building and had cried with the discomfort and degradation. She was sure that everyone had heard her. Even now after living rough for almost six weeks and going without even the most basic of human necessities, sometimes it was still too much for her. She was a teenage girl and despite what had happened to the rest of the world, her body had continued to develop as it would normally have been expected to. She'd started her first period just a few days ago. Donna had helped her and had reassured her as much as she could but it hadn't been easy. Donna was struggling too. Everyone was struggling.

Clare lay back down again and looked up at the high ceiling, studying the metal girders supporting the roof and the lights. She wished they could switch them on. They'd been living in almost constant darkness for weeks now.

Her eyes were heavy but she still couldn't sleep. She knew that as soon as day broke they'd be up and out again and she didn't know when they'd next be able to stop. She didn't know if she'd have enough strength to be able to make it if she didn't get some rest. It was hard enough to just keep going when they didn't know where they were or what they were going to do or . . .

She could hear something.

She sat up and listened. In the distance she could definitely hear a faint, mechanical sound. More soldiers escaped from the bunker, perhaps? The world was otherwise so completely silent that this new and unexpected noise seemed eerily directionless. Was she imagining it? Was it just her tired mind playing cruel tricks, or maybe there was something else hiding inside this unfamiliar building?

It was getting louder.

She realized she wasn't the only one who'd heard it. Another couple of people were sitting up now. She leaned across and shook Donna.

"What?" Donna grumbled lethargically before suddenly remembering where she was and jumping up fast, worried that something was wrong. "What's the matter?"

"Listen."

The noise was definitely moving closer now. It sounded like an engine, but not anything they recognized. It continued to steadily increase in volume and then gradually became clear; a constant chopping, thumping sound over the engine groan. Donna knew what she thought it was, but she refused to believe it. Louder and louder now until the building felt like it was shaking with the deafening sound. Michael got up and ran to the front of the warehouse, pressing his face against the glass, trying to look through the holes in the security grill. High above the store, from out of nowhere it seemed, a brilliant shaft of bright white light suddenly shone down. It swooped along the length of the industrial estate several times and then stopped, illuminating the loading bay at the side of the store. It took a few seconds for the reality of the situation to sink in: there was a helicopter hovering directly overhead.

"Is this one of yours?" Jack asked Stonehouse.

"Nothing to do with us," he answered.

Cooper grabbed one soldier's rifle and disappeared out through the side door they'd originally used to enter the building. Stonehouse and Jack followed him out into the loading bay and ducked down next to him beside the prison truck, all of them shielding their eyes from the bright light and whipping wind. The pilot of the helicopter skillfully lowered the machine and set it down in the space between the three vehicles. Cooper anxiously watched every meter of its slow descent.

The helicopter's engine and its lights were extinguished. The swirling rotor blades began to slow and the noise faded away, the all too familiar sound of bodies clattering against the wire-mesh fence immediately filling the void.

"Who the hell is this?" Jack asked. Before anyone could answer, the doors on either side of the helicopter cabin opened. Two people jumped down, both of them instinctively crouching down to miss the still spinning blades. A well-built man and a smaller, more rotund woman stood together in front of the aircraft and looked around for signs of life.

"Hello," the man called out. "Anyone here?"

His calls provoked a sudden, intense reaction from the crowd of corpses on the other side of the fence, but nothing else. After a few seconds spent silently weighing the options, Cooper stood up and stepped out of the shadows. He still held the soldier's rifle tightly in his hands, making sure it was clearly visible, but he kept the barrel very obviously pointed down toward the ground.

"Over here," he shouted. The man and woman turned and walked toward him. To his relief they looked relatively normal: scruffily dressed, unarmed civilians. "Where the hell did you pair come from?"

"Just outside Bigginford," the man replied. "I'm Richard Lawrence. This is Karen Chase."

"Everything all right, Cooper?" Michael asked, suddenly appearing outside, flanked by a soldier and two others. A further crowd of people stood in the doorway just behind them, watching intently. Cooper ignored them all and moved closer to the new arrivals.

"How the hell did you find us? We've only been here for a few hours."

"Not hard from up there," Richard answered, nodding back toward the helicopter. He brushed his long, windswept gray hair out of his face so that he could clearly see Cooper. "We saw the crowds earlier so we knew something was happening around here," he continued, referring to the battle at the bunker. "So we've been on the lookout for anyone trying to get away. And you lot stick out like a sore thumb."

"Why?"

"I've been flying helicopters for years," he explained. "You get used to how things should look from up there. It's easy to spot things that are out of the ordinary, especially when everything else is so fucked up. You don't often get vehicles like the ones you've got here parked around the back of places like this. Not exactly delivery trucks, are they?"

He had a point, Cooper silently admitted.

"How many people have you got here?" Karen asked, looking at the crowd by the door.

"Don't know exactly," Cooper replied. "Between thirty and forty."

"We should talk inside," Michael suggested, already walking back toward the door, acutely aware of the effect the helicopter's arrival had had on the steadily increasing mass of bodies nearby. The strangers followed him inside, and by the time they reached the main area where the rest of the group had been camped, just about everyone was up and awake and aware of what had happened. Nervous and subdued conversations were immediately silenced as the two unfamiliar figures entered the store. Suddenly the center of attention, Richard and Karen found themselves standing in the middle of the group feeling awkward and exposed, nodding acknowledgments to the few faces they were able to make out in the half light.

"This is Richard Lawrence and Karen Chase," Cooper announced to the others. "They've come from Bigginford."

"That's miles away," Jack said quietly.

"They've got a bloody helicopter, you idiot," Croft sighed, frustrated by his stupid comment.

The room was suddenly silent in hushed expectation. No one spoke, and yet each person had countless questions to ask. Donna cleared her throat.

"So do you spend all your time flying around in the middle of the night looking for survivors?" The tone of her voice was unexpectedly abrasive, clearly lacking in trust.

"Not usually," Karen replied, matching her mistrust.

"So how did you know where to find us?"

"We've known for some time that there was something going on around here."

"But we didn't know what," Richard continued, playing with his short white-tinged beard as he spoke. "All we could see from up there was a few thousand bodies. We knew something had to be attracting them, but we didn't know what it was."

"So where were you?" Karen asked.

"Underground," Jack said.

"I flew over this area a couple of days ago and it was pretty bloody obvious that something was going on. There was a hell of a lot of smoke around but I couldn't see what was happening. We came back again and saw the fighting. We thought that some of you might have got away so we spent the last couple of hours flying around trying to find you."

For a moment no one spoke, everyone considering the explanation they'd just heard. It sounded feasible. They didn't have any reason not to believe what they'd been told.

"So how did you end up with a helicopter?" Emma asked.

"I used to fly for a living," Richard told her. "I used to work for local radio, those 'eye in the sky' traffic broadcasts they used to do. I was up there when this all kicked off. We were in the middle of a broadcast and it got the reporter. Beautiful girl, she was. Died in the seat next to me . . ."

"So are there many of you?"

"Not as many as you, by the look of things,' Karen replied. "There are just over twenty of us, but we're split at the moment."

"Split?"

"We've been based at Monkton airfield since this all started, but we're getting ready to move on."

"So where are you going?"

"You probably know what it's like from your own experiences," Richard said, taking up the story. "You make a damn sound out in the open these days and you'll find yourselves surrounded by those bloody things out there before you know what's happening. What with the helicopter and the plane—"

"You've got a plane too?" Jack interrupted, amazed.

"Only a small one. Anyway, with the noise we've been making we've been surrounded by thousands of them since we first got to the airfield."

"So where are you planning to go?" Michael asked, repeating the question. "Surely it's going to be just as bad wherever you end up?"

"We've found an island," Karen said.

"An island?" Emma gasped, her mind immediately filled with images of sun-drenched beaches and endless, yellow-gold sand.

"It's just off the northeast coast," she explained. "It's cold, gray, and miserable and there's hardly anything there, but it's a hell of a lot safer than anywhere on the mainland."

"How big is it?" Michael asked quickly. "What kind of facilities have you got there? Are there many buildings or do you—"

"It's early days yet," Karen said, holding up her hand to stop his barrage of questions. "We spent a lot of time looking for the right location and we finally think we've found it. It's a little place called Cormansey. It's about a mile and a half long and a mile wide. There were about five hundred people living there originally. There's one small village where most of them lived, and a few houses and cottages dotted all around the place. There's an airstrip on the far side of the island and—"

"What about bodies?" Michael wondered, desperately trying to keep his sudden excitement under control. Richard explained.

"We're planning on culling what's left of the local population. We're trying to fly a few people over each day to gradually get the place sorted out. We've only known about it for a few days. I flew three people over yesterday morning and three more today. That's how I came to be flying over this place."

"So what's the plan?"

"We've sent some of our strongest people over there to start clearing the land. They're going to work their way down the length of the island, getting rid of the dead. Like Karen says, we think there were only a few hundred people there originally and from what we've seen it looks like a lot of them are still lying facedown on the ground. As far as we can tell there aren't any indigenous survivors so that just leaves us with several hundred corpses to get rid of and a bloody big cleanup operation."

Jack stared at the pilot in awe. Like everyone else around him, he was slowly beginning to come to terms with the implications of what he was hearing. Imagine being somewhere where they were free to move and there were no bodies anywhere. Imagine being somewhere where they could make as much noise as they damn well pleased without fear of the repercussions. It sounded too good to be true. Perhaps it was.

"Once we've got enough people over there we'll start moving into the village," Richard continued. "We're planning to clear it building by building until we've got rid of every last trace of the dead."

"What about power and water?" Croft asked, his mind racing.

"Come on, Phil," Donna said pessimistically, "don't get ahead of yourself. How do we know any of this is true?"

"They turned up here in a bloody helicopter, Donna," Cooper said, annoyed by her attitude. "Why should they lie? It might not all be as easy as it sounds, though."

"We never said it was going to be easy," Richard said. "It's still early days and we've got a lot to do, but there's no reason why we can't make this work. And who knows, in the future we might be able to get fuel and power supplies working again."

The future, Michael thought to himself. Bloody hell, these two survivors who had suddenly appeared from the sky were in a strong enough position that they could actually allow themselves the luxury of stopping to think about the future. Okay, so they clearly still had a huge amount of work ahead of them and the danger they faced was far from over, but at least they could sense an end to it. They could see the direction that the rest of their lives might possibly take. He, in comparison, didn't know which way he was going to run or what he was going to have to face in the morning.

The conversation continued as more previously silent survivors suddenly found their voices and asked more and more questions of the new arrivals. As those questions were patiently answered, the clear, rational details of the plan being presented became increasingly apparent. Individually, people started to understand the potential importance of what they were hearing.

In a brief pause, a single unexpected question came.

"Do you know what happened?" a woman asked, her voice quiet, unsure whether she should have asked that. Every other conversation stopped.

"Do you?" Richard asked the group rhetorically. The room had become deathly silent. "What about you?" he asked again, this time looking directly at Stonehouse and the other three suited soldiers grouped around him. "You must have known something."

"We weren't told anything," Cooper replied for him.

"You're military too?"

"I was."

Richard looked into space, and thought carefully before he spoke again. "Look, I can tell you what I've been told, but I can't tell you if it's right or wrong."

"How can he possibly know anything?" Donna demanded angrily. "There's no one left who could have told him."

"You don't know that for sure . . ." Croft said, trying to placate her.

"There's just no way," Donna said, looking at the helicopter pilot and pointing her finger at him accusingly. "You can't know . . . you just can't."

"Like I said," Richard continued, unfazed, "I can tell you what I've seen and heard and you can choose whether or not to believe me or forget it. It makes no difference to me what you think. My gut feeling is that what I've heard is right, but that doesn't necessarily mean it is."

"Just stop all this bullshit and tell us!" Peter Guest shouted. His angry outburst was completely out of character for such a normally withdrawn man. As Michael waited to hear more, he asked himself whether he really wanted to listen to what Richard was about to say. What possible difference would it make? How would knowing what had happened change anything now? It might make him angrier. It might make the situation worse. It might even affect his relationship with Emma, although he couldn't see how. Regardless of what might or might not happen, he knew that he had no choice but to listen to Lawrence. He wanted to know why his world had been turned upside down so quickly and so cruelly, why everyone he'd known had been killed in a single day, and why his life had become nothing but a relentless, exhausting struggle.

Richard cleared his throat, sensing the group's collective unease. He looked around the dark room, staring in turn at each of the faces he could see.

"You really want to know what did this?" he asked. Silence. "Then I'll tell you what I've been told."

11

Richard Lawrence sat down on the edge of a counter and started to talk.

"I was hiding about a week after it started. Me and another bloke called Carver had shut ourselves away in the ruins of a castle. Sounds impressive, but it wasn't. It was just a gatehouse, a couple of towers, and a few sections of crumbling wall dotted around a field, but it had a moat that was still half full of water and we reckoned that would be enough to keep pretty much everything out. We blocked the drawbridge and used the helicopter to get in and out, landing it in what was left of the main courtyard and living, sleeping, and eating in a little wooden gift shop. It was more like a shed than anything else.

"We were still flying the old helicopter I'd used for work but we were getting low on fuel. We either needed to find somewhere to fill it up or we had to get ourselves another aircraft. On the tenth day we ended up flying low over a couple of army bases and government buildings trying to spot any decent equipment we could take. We didn't see anyone at the first base, and there were just a handful of soldiers in suits and breathing masks at the second. There were plenty of bodies around, though. I guessed that some of the military knew what had happened, but it looked like hardly any of them had managed to get to shelter in time.

"You'd have thought we'd have picked up a load of survivors while we were out there because of the noise we made, but we hardly found anyone. I still don't know whether that was because there just wasn't anyone left or because they were too afraid to let us know where they were when they heard us. Anyway, this one afternoon we were flying over the motorway going south towards Tyneham when Carver spots a car moving in the distance. We follow it, and when the driver clocks us he pulls over and stops in a service station car park. We get out of the helicopter and the driver starts calling us over. He's a real awkward, gangly looking lad in his late teens. His name's Martin Smith and he's really nervous and anxious and emotional. I reckoned we were probably the first people he'd seen since it happened. He keeps bursting into tears. There are bodies starting to appear all around us but he's not even looking at them and it's like he's thinking about something else. Carver keeps the bodies at bay while I try and calm him down. 'She knows what happened,' he says as I walk up to him. 'She might be able to help. She might be able to do something.'

"By this point I'm thinking that the kid's lost his mind, and that's perfectly understandable given the circumstances because we've all come close to losing it recently, haven't we? He's pointing into his car. I look inside and lying across the backseat is a woman in a protective suit with a face mask and everything. It's not a military suit, it's different. It looks cleaner—less practical and more scientific than anything the army would have. I open the car door and lean inside. The woman doesn't move. When I touch her shoulder she opens her eyes for a second and then lets them flicker shut again and I can see that she's in a really bad way. Her face is thin and white and it's obvious that she hasn't eaten or had anything to drink since it all kicked off. She smells as bad as the bodies and the back of her suit's all soiled and dirty. I try to talk to her but I don't get any response. I can't even get her to open her eyes again. Carver shouts over to me because now there are more bodies around than he feels comfortable with and so, being as careful as I can, I pick her up and take her into the service station. Carver and Smith follow me inside. We take our chances and leave the helicopter, knowing that we'll fight our way back out to it if we have to.

"I lie the woman down on a plastic bench in this little burger bar. The place stinks of rotting food and rotting bodies. Carver has a quick look around for supplies but there's nothing worth having. I sit down with the kid next to where I left the woman, making sure we're out of sight of the windows. I ask him who she is and he tells me her name is Sylvia Plant. I ask him how he came to be with her and he starts to calm down a little and tells me his story. He tells me that she was a friend of his parents and that she worked in the monitoring center at this place called Camber, which is about thirty miles away from where we were sitting. He says she used to work with his dad a few years back, but that he hadn't seen her for a long time since his dad retired. I know the place he's talking about. It's one of those faceless buildings where lots of people used to work but no one ever talked about what they did. I start thinking he's going to tell me this woman is responsible for everything that's happened but he doesn't. He tells me that she found him about three or four days earlier. She'd been driving around since it started, looking for survivors. He tells me that she was sick then because she hadn't eaten and she'd been getting progressively worse ever since. I start to press him and I start getting hard with him because I want to know what's going on.

"Smith says he asked the woman if she knew what was going on and she told him that she did. She told him that she'd been cleaning a lab when it happened, and that was why she was wearing the suit. Everyone else around her had been caught and killed. She'd said she'd walked around the building for hours looking for help. She hadn't found anyone, but she'd been able to piece together what had happened from things she'd seen. She'd used security passes belonging to dead colleagues to get into the parts of the building where she'd never been able to go before. She said that this was all caused by something she'd first heard rumors about years ago. There had been stories doing the rounds for almost as long as she'd worked at Camber.

"Remember the Star Wars project? Back in the eighties before the end of the Cold War there was a lot of noise made about this plan to build a shield to protect countries from nuclear attack. I don't know if it ever got off the ground but according to this woman, when terrorists really started hitting their targets with force, the same countries started working on ways to protect themselves from the threat of attack by other nonconventional means. She said that they wanted to create an artificial germ which would latch onto chemicals or poisons in the air and neutralize them—that was the plan. She found out that development had been going on for some time. She also found out that a version of this 'supergerm' had been created and that it was thought to be stable. It was intelligent and self-replicating and, because of increased terrorist threats, it had already been released. Apparently that happened a couple of years ago now. Smith says the woman told him we've all been breathing the germ in every day since then.

"Anyway, the woman told Smith that finally there was a chemical attack and that rang true because I remembered hearing something on the news just before this all started. There was a gas attack on an airport terminal in Canada. Smith says that the woman saw reports of huge numbers of deaths in the surrounding areas, way out of line for the amount of poison that was supposed to have been released. Seems that the germ tried to do its job and neutralize the attack, but it mutated as it did it and, whatever happened, it set off a chain reaction that spread. It was the mutated germ that did all of this. It changed to try and protect us and became something that killed just about everyone. Bloody ironic, isn't it?

"Smith tells me that the woman pieced all this together from various bits of information she found. She saw records showing that communications had been lost with most of Canada, and then with the United States. The information stopped coming altogether pretty soon after that.

"You can call it bullshit if you like and dismiss everything I've just told you, but it's the only explanation I've heard so far. We can all probably come up with a hundred other reasons why all of this might have happened, but this is the only version I've heard that has any evidence to support it. Smith wasn't lying to me, he had no reason to, and the woman had no reason to lie to him either. And if she really was from the monitoring center at Camber, then she would potentially have had access to all kinds of confidential information. I believe what I heard. Everything happened so quickly because the germ was already there. As the mutation spread, everyone died around us. There's no way we'll ever know why the corpses got up and started to move. It was designed to prevent death, and maybe it did its job after all. Maybe it destroyed the bodies but spared the brain. Whatever actually happened, it doesn't matter now.

"We sat there with Smith and the woman for another few hours until it was dark. We pushed our way through the bodies back to the helicopter and flew back to base. The woman was dead by late the following afternoon. Smith is still with us."

"Rubbish," Phil Croft said, disturbing the heavy silence which had descended upon the already quiet room. "Utter bollocks."

"Might be," Richard said. "Doesn't really matter, does it?"

"And is that it?" Donna said. "Is that all you've got to tell us?"

"What else do you want me to say? I've told you everything I know. What you do with it is up to you."

The exhausted pilot stood up, stretched, and walked back toward the helicopter to fetch himself some food.

12

"Do you believe him?" Emma asked, looking straight into Michael's eyes.

"I believe he's telling us the truth about what happened with this guy Smith," he answered, "but whether I believe the rest of the story or not is a different matter."

"There's no reason he'd make it up."

"True."

"I think I remember hearing about something happening in Canada. I think it was probably the last thing I saw on the television."

"Me too, but that doesn't mean—"

"And I'm sure I've heard about that place at Camber too, and there had to be a good reason for the woman to be wearing a protective suit."

"Also true," Michael said, struggling to sound interested.

"Bit of a coincidence that they managed to find Smith,

though, and that Smith found the woman or the woman found him."

"Suppose so, but it's as much a coincidence that we were all sat in here together tonight, isn't it? It's only because of coincidence that Richard Lawrence found us and even that you and I came across each other."

Emma yawned and stretched her arms up into the cold early morning air.

"Ironic, isn't it?" she said. "If it is all true, I mean. Something originally put there to try and protect us ends up doing all the damage."

"Sounds about right for this fucked-up planet. Anyway, there's no point going on about it. We can't prove or disprove it and even if we could it doesn't make any difference. What's happened has happened, and that's all there is to it. There's nothing any of us can do about it now."

"I know."

"It reminds me of something my dad used to say," Michael said, smiling wryly and allowing himself to reminisce for the briefest of moments. "When things weren't going his way at work he'd get really wound up and sometimes we'd go for a pint together and try to put the world to rights. Dad worked for a steel manufacturing company until they went bust. Every day he'd come home and tell us that they'd lost orders to other local firms or to companies overseas. Mum used to get worked up about the work going out of the country but Dad didn't. He said it didn't matter where the work was going, the fact was that his firm had lost it. He used to say to her that if you got knocked down by a car, did it matter what color it was? That's how I feel today. Like I said, what's happened has happened, and finding out why or what did it just isn't important. I can't get excited about any of this bullshit. We are where we are."

He stopped talking, and in the sudden quiet he thought about his dad again. He hadn't thought about his parents for days now, maybe even weeks. Michael had subconsciously built a wall around the past to stop painful memories from getting in the way.

Emma stood up and walked to the front of the building. She looked out of the front of the store, shielding her eyes from the brilliant orange sunrise which was shining through the grill and beginning to fill the building with bright, warm daylight. The long, tripping shadows of occasional stumbling corpses stretched across the gray car park toward them.

"What are you thinking?" she asked, concerned by his sudden silence.

"Nothing," he lied. "What about you?"

"I've got all kinds of stuff going through my head," she admitted. "I don't want to get carried away here, but . . ."

"But what?"

"But I can't help thinking that we might have found a way out of all of this, Mike. This time yesterday we were buried underground just sitting and waiting. Today we're—"

"This time yesterday we were relatively safe," he interrupted, correcting her. "Today we're exposed and vulnerable and on the run and we've got nothing."

"Christ, you can be such a negative, miserable bastard at times," she said angrily. "Can't you be positive for once?"

"I *am* positive," Michael protested, "but I'm a realist too. Until I've seen this island and I've stood on the beach and shouted at the top of my voice and no bodies have come crawling out after me, then I'm going to stay skeptical. We need to be careful here and not rush into anything that's going to cost us."

"So what are you saying? That we should just say our good-byes and wave these people off into the sunset?"

"No, that's not what I'm saying at all, but you know what I think. If something can go wrong—"

"It will go wrong. I know. Change the bloody record, will you? It doesn't mean we have to sit around and wait for crap to happen, for God's sake. It doesn't mean things *can't* work out right for us, does it?"

Michael chewed his lip and thought about what she'd said. Perhaps she was right and he was being too negative. Truth was, he'd already lost too much to risk being positive. He couldn't stand the thought of them building themselves up, only to be knocked down again.

"Sorry," he mumbled apologetically. "You're right, I'll shut up."

"I don't want you to shut up," she said, moving back toward him, "I just want you to give this a chance. Have an open mind. Come on, Mike, think about what might happen if this works out. If this island is everything they say it is, then before long you and I could have a house together. We could have our own bedroom with a proper bed. We could have a kitchen, a garden, a living room . . . We could have privacy and space."

"We thought we'd got all of that at Penn Farm."

"I know, but this is different, I can feel it. If it hadn't been for the bodies then we'd probably still be at Penn Farm, maybe even somewhere better. Bloody hell, if it hadn't been for the bodies then we could be anywhere we damn well please. And now we're talking about going someplace where there aren't any bodies."

"No, we're not," Michael said, quickly slipping back into his negative mind-set. "Not yet, anyway. At the moment we're talking about going to an island and clearing a couple of hundred bodies from it. There's a big difference."

Emma shook her head. It wasn't worth talking to him when he was in this kind of mood. She turned and walked away, fed up with arguing pointlessly. Michael watched her go. He hadn't wanted to upset her but he couldn't bear to see her getting carried away with half an idea that might eventually end up costing them everything.

For a while he sat alone and watched the bodies outside.

13

Trying to get to the airfield and join the other survivors there was the only sensible option available to the group. Any other logical alternatives were nonexistent. They had nowhere else to go.

In their days and weeks of incarceration underground, the structure of the group had barely changed: some people had naturally held back, trying to blend into the background, watching everyone else doing the work around them and never actively contributing themselves. Other, more confident people had, by default, begun to take control and organize. In the cold light of day this morning, however, there had been a subtle shift in several people's attitudes. The introduction to the equation both of the soldiers—who, until yesterday, had maintained an enforced and cautious distance from the group—and the arrival of the helicopter had dramatically altered the makeup of the frightened little community. Individuals who had previously been content to hide away in the shadows were now keen to push themselves to the fore, desperate not to get overlooked and left behind.

"I'll do it," Peter Guest said anxiously, stepping around Jack and grabbing a map from Richard Lawrence's hands. "I'll navigate. Show me where we are."

Richard took the map back from him and folded it down to a more manageable size. He pointed to the general area where they were presently hiding. He had spent the last half hour writing down basic directions to Monkton airfield for them to follow and had just asked for a volunteer to navigate. Showing more enthusiasm than he had done at any time during the previous month, Guest anxiously began reading through the directions and cross-referencing them with the map, plotting the route to Bigginford and the airfield beyond.

"You travel with Cooper in the personnel carrier," Michael suggested. "Steve can follow behind in the truck and I'll follow him."

"Not in that motor home of yours, you won't," Steve Armitage said from across the room. He'd been outside checking over the three vehicles and had just returned, breathless and cold. He wiped his greasy hands on a dirty rag which he threw into a dark corner. "It's knackered, mate. Axle's broken. I'm not surprised after the journey we had here last night."

"Shit," Michael said under his breath.

"What are we going to do now, then?" Emma asked, feeling strangely saddened by the loss of the vehicle which, until recently, she'd grown to hate.

"We'll have to go out and find something else," said Donna, who until then had been sitting nearby and listening silently.

"We won't all fit in otherwise. There's bound to be something around here we can use."

"There aren't too many bodies out there," Steve said. "I reckon we'll be all right to go and look around as long as we're sensible and quick."

"Can't we try and manage with just two trucks?" Emma wondered. Michael was about to answer when Stonehouse spoke.

"You're going to have to get yourselves two vehicles," he announced. Standing at the back of the small group of people, the soldier walked to the front. An imposing figure in his heavy protective gear, carrying his rifle and flanked by one of his men, his sudden movement was unexpected.

"Why's that?" Cooper asked, genuinely confused.

"Because we're going back to the base," he replied. "It's our only option."

"Don't be stupid," Croft said. "The place was overrun yesterday. You can't go back there."

"We can and we will. We can't stay out here."

"But we need your vehicle and—"

"We need to get back underground. We're completely fucked if we stay up here."

"Doesn't look like you've got much choice," Michael said. "You're dead whatever you do. Might as well come with us and—"

"And what exactly? Sit and watch you lot run? Sit in these bloody suits and wait to die?"

"At least you'd be giving *us* a chance," Croft yelled at him, his face suddenly flushed red with anger. "Do things your way and everyone loses."

"Tough shit."

"Bastard," he said as he moved toward the soldier, limping and wincing as he landed heavily on his feet, aggravating his still painful injuries. Stonehouse shoved him out of the way, and the doctor, already off-balance, crumbled to the ground at his booted feet. Stonehouse lifted the butt of his rifle and held it inches away from Croft's face.

"Leave it, Doc," Cooper said. He turned to face Stonehouse. "Just fuck off and go."

"What the hell are you doing?" Croft yelled from the floor, looking up at Cooper in disbelief. "Have you gone completely mad? We need that vehicle!"

Cooper looked down at him and glared. He grabbed his arm and pulled him to his feet.

"No," he replied abruptly. Stonehouse watched, surprised by his ex-colleague's reaction. He had anticipated some kind of resistance from Cooper at least.

"Christ, Cooper," the incensed doctor cursed as he brushed himself down, "there are only four of them. We'll end up driving to Bigginford in a convoy of twenty bloody cars if we're not careful."

"No, we won't," Cooper calmly replied. All eyes were suddenly on him as he began to walk toward the exit, away from the confrontation. Then, without warning, he suddenly stopped, turned around, and ran back in the opposite direction, diving through the air and smashing into Stonehouse and the soldier standing next to him. In the confusion the two troopers were knocked flying to the ground. Stonehouse was quickly up on all fours, but Cooper grabbed hold of his face mask under his chin and yanked it up and off his face. The second soldier, immediately aware of what was happening, began to scramble away but Cooper was too fast for him. He jumped onto his back and pulled and tugged at his suit, his mask, and his breathing apparatus until it came free and he could see the soldier's bare flesh underneath. He was aware of the other two soldiers running away, fleeing deeper into the vast store, and he readied himself should the troopers on the ground get back up and attack.

Stonehouse was the first to drag himself onto his feet. He grabbed his rifle and ran angrily toward Cooper. But before he got anywhere near, the infection caught him. Choking, and with a look of pained surprise on his face, he fell back on top of the other soldier, who was still on the ground, already suffocating. Fighting for breath, Stonehouse shook and convulsed, still grasping his rifle tightly. Eyes bulging, he stared at Cooper until he lost consciousness.

"You killed them," Donna gasped, appalled. "You bastard, you killed them."

"They were dead already," Cooper responded with disdain, "and they were about to kill us."

14

Michael, Jack, and Cooper ran together through the silent car parks of the industrial estate, desperately searching for another suitable vehicle to get them to the airfield. There were more bodies around than there had been last night, but they knew they had no choice but to do this.

"Van," Michael said as he pushed his way past another lurching corpse, "over there."

He pointed to the far right corner of the football pitch–sized car park they had just entered. On its own next to an office building was a red mail van. Lying in the road in front of it was the gnarled body of a postal delivery worker. The woman's motionless corpse was twisted and looked like a piece of washed-up driftwood, eaten away by decay. The strap of an empty mail bag was still wrapped around her neck.

Cooper ran around and yanked the driver's door open, while Michael frantically fished around in the wizened corpse's pockets for the keys. He threw them to Cooper, then got up and fought off two bodies which had stumbled uncomfortably close. He had Stonehouse's rifle slung across his back. Unexpectedly nervous, he swung it around and primed it. Cooper had taught him to shoot while they'd been underground but, until now, he'd never actually needed to fire a weapon. They usually had to deal with many, many more corpses than this, and guns were only good for getting rid of them one at a time. Holding his breath he brutally shoved the barrel of the rifle into a dark hole on one side of the nearest body's broken nose, aimed up into its skull, and pulled the trigger. A deafening crack rang around the car park, echoing off the walls of every building in the immediate vicinity. Michael was knocked back by the unexpected force of the weapon. He tripped over his own feet and fell as a shower of crimson gore and splintered bone erupted from the back of the creature's head, splattering the wall behind it.

"Push the damn thing!" Cooper shouted from the front of the van. He couldn't get it started. Michael picked himself up off the ground and shot the second corpse in the side of the head before swinging the rifle onto his back again and running around to the rear of the vehicle where Jack was already pushing. He shoulder charged the van, the sudden impact starting it rolling forward slightly. Cooper jumped out of his seat and began to shove against the driver's door, leaning in through the open window to steer.

"Christ, Cooper, have you still got the bloody handbrake on?" Jack half-joked, red-faced and wheezing as he strained against the back of the van. He threw his full weight forward again, screwing his eyes shut with effort. When he opened them again he saw that more gangling, decomposing bodies were creeping dangerously close.

With all three of the men pushing, the van finally began to gain momentum. It started to roll across the car park with relative ease and Cooper jumped back behind the wheel. He slammed his foot down on the clutch and tried again to start the engine. After a few seconds of ugly mechanical groaning and straining, it finally spluttered into life. He accelerated away, revving the engine hard and leaving Michael and Jack running after him through belching clouds of dirty exhaust fumes. He turned the van around and went back to collect them, making only the briefest of diversions to wipe out another couple of meandering cadavers which had dragged themselves into the car park.

Inside the store, Emma had managed to find the two remaining soldiers who had disappeared when Cooper had attacked the others. They were hiding together in a large stockroom.

"Just leave us alone," one of the soldiers sobbed as he heard Emma approaching. His strained voice was full of desperation and fear. "That bloke Cooper's a fucking psychopath. He's always been the same. He'll fucking kill us!"

The frightened trooper cowered away in the shadows. A couple of meters away from him, Kelly Harcourt pressed herself back against a storage rack hoping she would melt away into the shadows, her heart thumping in her chest.

"He's no psychopath," Emma said as she took a few cautious steps farther into the room, trying to pinpoint their exact location. "He's a survivor, that's all." She peered across the room, sure she'd just seen a flicker of movement out of the corner of her eye. "You'd probably have done the same if you were in his position."

She didn't find it easy defending Cooper's actions, no matter how relieved she was that he had reacted so quickly. She'd also forgotten that, until recently, these two soldiers had served alongside him. They probably knew more about him than she did. *Was* he a psychopath?

"He'll do it again," the male soldier whimpered. "All he's got to do is open our suits and we've fucking had it. That's all that any of you have to do."

"But no one's going to do that to you, are they?" Emma sighed. "Why the hell would we?"

"You'll do it if you have to," Kelly shouted, the sudden volume and direction of her voice immediately giving her location away. "You'd kill us just as quickly as you get rid of those bloody things outside."

"You're wrong. Cooper didn't have any choice. Stonehouse forced him to do it."

Just ahead and to her right Kelly slumped against the racking and slid down to the ground. Emma could see one of her feet sticking out into the aisle. She walked toward her, then crouched down at the side of the terrified soldier. Kelly lifted her head and looked up at Emma.

"I just don't know what to do," she admitted. She had tears running down her face, but no way of wiping them away. "I can't handle this."

"It's all right," Emma said quietly, putting a gentle hand on her shoulder. "We're all struggling." She paused, not sure if Kelly was listening or whether it was even worth continuing. "Listen, I'll be straight with you: you two have got the worst deal of all here. You're stuck between a rock and a hard place. You're trapped in those bloody suits and it must be hell, but you don't have much of a choice, do you? You can try and find some transport and get back to your base, you can stay here, or you can come with us. Like I said, as long as you don't put anyone at risk, then—".

"Then what?" she demanded. "Then Cooper won't kill us?"

Emma sighed with frustration. She got up and walked back toward the door, keen to return to the others.

"Look, we're too busy trying to keep ourselves alive here. No one's interested in killing you."

15

Under the unfocused gaze of a crowd of fence-rattling corpses, the group piled into their vehicles. As many of them as possible crammed into the back of the personnel carrier—the strongest vehicle in the convoy. Cooper took the wheel with Peter Guest at his side, ready to navigate. Steve Armitage took up his now usual seat behind the wheel of the prison truck. Steve had begun to fiercely guard his position. Apart from the fact that few other people could have driven the truck as well as him, the responsibility, power, and control which he attached to the role made him feel worthwhile and alive. Strange, he thought, that what had previously always felt like such an ordinary and menial job should now give him such purpose.

Fewer survivors traveled in the back of the prison truck than on earlier journeys, the spare space being taken up with useful supplies and equipment which the group had stripped from the store. Just a handful of people needed to ride in the final vehicle in the convoy—the bright red, uncomfortably conspicuous post van.

Donna sat in the driver's seat with Jack Baxter on the passenger side and Clare wedged between them. Behind them were the two surviving soldiers with yet more supplies packed around them. Donna looked at them in her rearview mirror. Kelly Harcourt seemed genuinely afraid and wasn't a concern. Her male colleague, however, was far more unpredictable. His name, she'd just discovered, was Kilgore. A short, wiry-framed and nervous man, he was too jittery and agitated for her liking.

A few minutes earlier Richard and Karen had left in the helicopter, taking with them the four children. The remaining group of people had crowded around and watched in awe as the powerful machine lifted up into the clear blue, early morning sky. Having spent weeks underground and cowering away in the silent shadows, to witness the aircraft rising up into the sun with such majesty, strength, and sheer bloody noise had been strangely emotional; a two-fingered "up yours" salute to the rest of the dead world. As the helicopter disappeared, however, the sounds being made by the horde of rabid bodies smashing themselves furiously against the metal fence had suddenly seemed louder than ever. The closeness and anger of the corpses was a reminder to each of them of the relentless danger they faced.

Before leaving, Cooper and Peter had gathered the other drivers around them to run through the proposed route in detail one last time. It was crucial that they all knew the route and the potential problems they might face along the way. Using road atlases he had found in the store, Peter had highlighted the directions they needed to take on maps and produced a handwritten set of notes for each vehicle. He was desperately keen to share with the others the information which Richard Lawrence had earlier given him.

"You see," he explained, talking with unprecedented energy, "they've obviously not needed to spend much time on the ground and so this was the most direct route they were able to come up with. Now I've not personally spent a lot of time in this part of the country so I'm not completely sure where we're—"

"Do me a favor," Steve Armitage interrupted. "Just shut up and let me have my bloody map, will you?"

Undeterred, Peter continued. "Richard Lawrence told me they've not seen any particularly large gatherings of bodies between here and Bigginford."

"What's 'large' supposed to mean?" asked Cooper. "Twenty-five of them? Two thousand? Half a million?"

"Not sure," he quickly admitted, keen to continue with his explanation. "Anyway it looks like we'll be able to stick to the motorways for a good part of the journey. They're probably not going to be completely clear, but from what they've seen from the air they think we should be able to work our way through."

"What about cities?" Jack Baxter asked anxiously. "We're going to stay away from the cities as best we can, aren't we?"

"We'd like to," Cooper answered, deliberately denying Peter the opportunity to respond, "but we've got to try and balance out safety and risk. To get to Bigginford we're going to have to get pretty close to the center of Rowley."

"What does 'pretty close' mean?"

"Like I said, it's going to be about balancing safety with risk. If we bypass Rowley then you're right, we'll probably avoid a whole load of potential trouble spots. The problem is, we'll also end up adding a hell of a lot of distance and time onto the length of the journey. Obviously we'll be in a better position to make a final decision when we get nearer, but my feeling is we'll be better off following this route. I'd rather take a chance and go for the quicker option than risk running out of fuel because we've driven further than we needed to. We could end up stuck out in the middle of nowhere."

"I don't like it," Jack complained.

"No one likes any of this," Cooper sighed, "but that's how it is. Let's just see how the land lies when we get there, okay? Chances are no one's been anywhere near Rowley for weeks. Most of the bodies will probably have drifted away."

"Suppose."

Peter seized on a momentary lull in the conversation to start talking again.

"Cooper's right, Rowley might be a problem, but once we're through it should pretty much be plain sailing until we get to the airfield."

"Plain sailing?" Steve grunted. "Bloody hell, when was the last time anything was plain sailing?"

"Did Richard tell you much about the airfield?" Jack asked.

"He said it used to be a private commercial site," Cooper answered. "He said it was pretty small with just the one runway and a few buildings. There's supposed to be a fence running all the way around to keep trespassers and plane spotters out."

"But does it keep bodies out?"

"At the moment."

"And what do you mean by that?"

"Sounds like they've got the same kind of problems we had at the base and back in the city."

"Such as?"

"Hundreds of bodies. Probably thousands."

The positivity and excitement of the helicopter's arrival had all but disappeared. Now they were crammed into their respective vehicles, facing the prospect of lurching headlong into the unknown once more, every last person—military and civilian alike—felt sick to the stomach with nerves.

Cooper, Donna, and Steve started their engines and slowly moved toward the exit. Michael undid the latch and let the gate swing open. No longer restrained, noxious cadavers immediately began to spill toward him on unsteady feet, reaching out with flailing arms. He sprinted around to the back of the personnel carrier, climbed inside, and slammed the door shut. Cooper began to edge forward, buffeting bodies out of the way and leading the convoy back out into the dead world.

16

Good fortune and sensible planning combined to their advantage and the three-vehicle convoy reached the first section of motorway less than half an hour after leaving the industrial estate. It was midmorning when they joined the main road, and in the hours they'd been traveling, the earlier bright sun had steadily been swallowed up and hidden by impenetrable dark clouds. A light autumn mist had begun to fall, barely noticeable but soaking everything.

Peter Guest, navigating for Cooper, had again become withdrawn and quiet, reverting to his more familiar demeanor and losing the sudden confidence, energy, and interest he had temporarily found. No one was surprised. Cooper had anticipated having problems with him, as had Michael.

"Junction twenty-three," Cooper said. Peter looked up, then anxiously checked his map again, frantically trying to confirm they were still on the right road. The fact that they hadn't taken any turns since he'd last checked didn't seem to matter. The farther they moved away from the warehouse, the more nervous he became.

"Everything all right, Cooper?" Michael asked, pushing his way closer to the driver and leaning over his seat.

"I'm okay," he replied, concentrating on the road ahead. Michael struggled to see out through the front of the personnel carrier. In the gloom it wasn't easy to see the direction the road took. The sudden mist obscured much of the landscape around them and the ground ahead was carpeted with a tangled layer of dead bodies and crumpled machinery. The vehicle Cooper controlled was powerful enough to simply push a path through the debris and decay, allowing the others to follow in its wake. Rowley, the second largest town in the county, was now less than ten miles away.

"Bloody grim, isn't it?" Michael grumbled unhelpfully from just behind Cooper's shoulder.

"This place was grim at the best of times."

Even allowing for traffic and other delays, on a clear day a few months ago, this journey would probably have taken two hours at the most. Today, however, it had taken double that time to reach the outskirts of the town. Although they had been relatively fortunate and had not come across many serious obstacles along the way, progress through the ruined landscape had been painfully slow. Cooper's head was thumping, aching with the effort of having to concentrate so hard for so long. He wanted to stop to rest and stretch his legs but he knew that wasn't possible. The personnel carrier's headlights seemed to be constantly illuminating random, fleeting movement on all sides. Lumbering, shadowy shapes seemed to continually emerge from the mist and then disappear back into the darkness again as the personnel carrier, prison truck, and van thundered past them.

"Which way, Peter?" Cooper asked, annoyed that he had to keep pressing the other man for directions. Peter was staring out of the window again, transfixed, and hadn't noticed they were rapidly approaching a fork in the road. Until a few seconds ago it had been hidden by the mist.

"Not sure . . ." Peter stammered unhelpfully. In sudden blustering, pointless panic his eyes darted around the map on his lap, which he'd been trying to follow by torchlight.

"Come on, you should be onto this," the ex-soldier snapped angrily at him, allowing his exhaustion and unease to show. "For Christ's sake, you're the one with the damn map in front of you!"

"Think I've got it," Peter said, looking up and squinting into the darkness to try and read a dirty, unlit road sign. "Take the 302."

Peter's indecision meant that Cooper had to yank the personnel carrier hard over to the left to change direction before they passed the junction. His unsuspecting passengers were thrown about in the back.

"Are you sure about this?" he asked as he drove down a dark roadway which curved round and down to the right and then snaked back under an elevated section of the carriageway which they'd just been following.

"This is right," Peter said quietly, trying his best to appease Cooper. "I'm sure it is. We need to follow this road for another couple of miles, cross the river, and then find the road to Huntridge. That way we'll have bypassed the city center."

Cooper swerved the personnel carrier around a crashed double-decker bus which had toppled over onto its side and which now straddled virtually the full width of the road. The prison truck followed close behind, then the post van.

"Bloody hell," Donna cursed as she forced the two off-side wheels of the van up the kerb and over a grass verge to squeeze past the wreck of the bus. Much smaller than the other vehicles, the post van didn't have the power to smash the remains of cars, bikes, trucks, and other obstacles out of the way like they did. Rather than clear a way through for her, as the other two drivers battered their way forward through the wreckage, the debris they disturbed was frequently dragged back out into the middle of the road behind them and left directly in her path.

Like Peter in the front of the first vehicle, Jack was also studying the maps.

"Not far now," he said, keeping his head down, preferring to look at the map rather than look outside. Whenever he did lift his eyes he could see the gray, constantly shifting silhouettes of bodies converging on the convoy. Jack knew they'd probably be okay as long as they kept moving, but the fact that they were so close to the dead again scared the hell out of him.

The road they were now following was a bypass which would eventually skirt around the main part of the city center. A wide and recently built expressway, it was covered with scattered remains of the people of Rowley and the surrounding districts. As their proximity to the lifeless heart of the city increased, so too did the amount of buckled metal and rotting flesh around them, threatening to block their way forward. Many, many people had fallen and died here on the city's outskirts when the rush hour crawl had been devastated by disease almost eight weeks ago. No one traveling through the decay today was surprised. It was nothing they hadn't seen before.

Donna's guide through the gray gloom outside was the bright rear brake lights of the two vehicles she followed. She simply matched their twists and turns rather than try to find the route of the road for herself. But then, without any warning, the brightness of the red lights increased as both the personnel carrier and the prison truck stopped suddenly. Her heart began to beat more quickly. Clare, who had managed to snatch a few precious seconds of sleep, sat up with a start when the van stopped too.

"What's wrong?" she demanded anxiously, frantically looking from side to side. "Why have we stopped?"

Neither Donna nor Jack said anything. Donna glanced into her wing mirror as a random corpse tripped out of the darkness and collided heavily with the side of the van. The two soldiers sitting in the back jumped up as the creature began to hammer its rotting fists against the metal side of the vehicle. A few seconds later and another four of them had appeared and were doing the same. Donna looked up again and saw that the same thing was happening up ahead, more dark and indistinct figures crowding and jostling around the back of the prison truck.

"What's happening?" Kilgore asked anxiously from behind her. He pressed his face mask against the window in the back door of the van and saw more corpses were emerging from the heavy mist all around them.

"What the hell are they doing, Donna?" Jack asked. Donna

was about to tell him that his guess was as good as hers when Michael suddenly appeared out of the back of the personnel carrier and ran around to the front, out of sight. Donna pulled the van farther forward so that they could get a better view of what was happening, stopping when they were level with the prison truck.

"Christ," she said when she saw what had happened. "What are we supposed to do now?"

A short distance in front of them was a narrow, one-lane road bridge. At either end of the bridge were traffic lights which had once controlled the flow of vehicles from either direction but were now as useless and dead as the rest of the world. Just over halfway across the single-lane bridge, a medium-sized truck had crashed and had somehow spun around almost ninety degrees, leaving it wedged awkwardly between the decorative concrete balustrades on either side. Twenty feet or so below the bridge was a wide river, its once relatively clear water now a stagnant, dirty, green-brown sludge, poisoned by the seeping decay it carried away from the nearby city.

"What now?" Clare asked. Jack looked down at the map on his lap again.

"There are another two bridges," he said. "One's about three miles further north, the other four or five miles back the way we came."

"Either way we'll add hours to the journey. Fuck, this isn't good."

Hidden from view of most of the nearby bodies by virtue of the mist, the confines of the narrow bridge and the various vehicles parked and abandoned around it, Michael surveyed the obstruction ahead, then ran back to the personnel carrier. Managing to somehow find a way to squirm through, a single corpse threw itself at him from out of nowhere, exploding furiously out of the shadows without warning. Caught by surprise, Michael took the full force of the impact head on and was slammed back against the side of the transport by the creature. The inescapable stench of rotting flesh filled his lungs, making him gag and spit. He instinctively lifted his arms to protect his face and recoiled in disgust as he grabbed hold of the decaying cadaver. Most of its ragged clothing having long since been ripped and torn away, his fingers squelched through the soft, greasy flesh which covered its bones. Michael closed the fingers of his right hand, wincing as dead skin flapped and the remains of putrefied organs began to dribble down his arms. He grabbed its partially exposed rib cage, then pushed back against the corpse, ran forward and forced it over the side of the bridge. Out of sight, the body fell for several seconds before landing in the murky water below. Pausing only to wipe his hands on a patch of wet grass at his feet, Michael scrambled back into the personnel carrier.

"You okay?" Emma asked. He nodded.

"Fine," he answered as he made his way forward back toward Cooper. "It looks like it's just the truck blocking the road, but it's pretty well wedged in. We won't be able to shift it by hand. You'll have to try and push it off the side of the bridge."

Cooper didn't waste any time discussing his options. Instead he accelerated slowly toward the blockage. The prison truck, now surrounded by somewhere between forty and fifty uncontrollable cadavers, all scrambling and fighting to get at the people

124

inside, also began to move. In the post van Donna, surrounded by a slightly smaller but no less animated or violent crowd, followed close behind.

"See where the corner of the bonnet's sticking out?" Michael said, still breathless, leaning over into the front of the personnel carrier and pointing at the crashed truck just ahead of them. "If you hit it there and give it a decent shove you should be able to push it through the wall." Again Cooper didn't respond, concentrating instead on trying to work out the physics of the situation in the few seconds remaining before they made contact. Michael seemed to be right, the truck looked like it was positioned in such a way that if he did manage to catch it properly, its back end would be forced through the concrete balustrade and out over the edge.

"What's that?" Sheri Newton asked. She was sitting next to Michael, peering over Cooper's shoulder and looking out through the front of the vehicle and across the bridge.

"What?" Cooper grunted, struggling to concentrate. Sheri lifted her finger and pointed ahead.

"Over there."

Michael looked up and saw that there was movement on the other side of the crashed truck. The mist was slightly thinner on the far side of the bridge. He stared into the dull grayness and realized he could see bodies. There were at least ten or twenty of them. No, wait, there were many more than that. Perfectly timed, the wind gently blew more of the drifting fog away, revealing for a moment a densely packed crowd of vacuous figures filling the narrow carriageway across the river, all trying to move in the direction of the light and noise coming toward them. As Michael watched the constantly shifting mass of decaying shapes, several of the creatures near to the front of the gathering began to rip and tear at those surrounding them, whipped into a frenzy by the approaching vehicles.

"Why are there so many of them?" Sheri asked nervously her voice little more than a whisper.

The answer to her question, although no one bothered to respond, was simple. The sound that the convoy had made had traveled and attracted the attention of just about every wandering corpse which happened to have been in the local area. The creatures on both sides of the river had been drawn to the sound. Those on the other side of the river had moved towards the disturbance with the narrow bridge being their only means of getting across. The growing crowd had been channeled forward by the sides of the bridge and in the same way that the wreck of the truck was preventing Cooper and the others from making progress, so it had also stopped the bodies from getting any closer. Oblivious to the obstruction, more and more of them had, as ever, continued to relentlessly herd toward the noise, packing themselves into a swollen bottleneck of diseased, decaying flesh.

Cooper was vaguely aware of the bodies, but he was concentrating on shifting the truck. Did he ram it or just push against it with slow and steady force? The machine he was driving was powerful and responsive. Rather than risk injuring his passengers by crashing into the blockage and trying to smash it out of the way, he instead elected to take the more cautious option. He increased his speed just slightly to give himself enough momentum and steered toward the truck's protruding front bumper, which Michael had pointed out. The people in the back of the personnel carrier lurched forward and then dropped back in their seats as the two vehicles made contact. Metal began to grind and strain against metal.

"Come on," Michael said under his breath as Cooper accelerated, willing the wreck in front of them to move. It shifted back a couple of inches but then stopped when the rear driver's-side wheel wedged up against the curb. Cooper accelerated again and pushed harder. No movement. He pushed harder again and then, after what felt like an endless wait and with his engine straining, the truck finally gave way to the force being exerted upon it. The back wheels jumped up into the air under pressure and the twisted chassis shot back a farther few inches. Another push from Cooper and he could feel the truck scrape against the wall. Peter Guest leaned out of his window and watched as showers of dust and huge lumps of broken masonry tumbled down into the polluted waters below.

"You've almost done it," he said nervously, keeping one eye on the bodies up ahead. "Give it another push and it'll be—"

Tired of waiting, Cooper accelerated again with force, shunting into the front of the truck again, this time sending it flying back through the hole in the wall. For a split second it remained balanced precariously, pivoting agonisingly and teetering on the edge before finally overbalancing and tipping back, flipping over and crashing down on its roof into the river. The moment his path was clear Cooper drove forward at speed, now powering into the crowd of advancing bodies with massive force, scything them down in a torrent of blood, bone, disease, and decay, obliterating each of them almost instantly.

Now free to move again, the convoy powered across the rest of the narrow bridge with ease and continued their journey skirting around the remains of the dead city.

17

Passage along the roads on the other side of the river was clear and relatively trouble free. Within a mile, the road they had been following opened up again into a dual carriageway, the city-bound lanes clogged with the disappointingly familiar sight of hundreds upon hundreds of ruined vehicles crashed nose-to-tail, some with the emaciated remains of their drivers and passengers still trapped inside, fighting to get out as the convoy neared. By comparison the two lanes running in the opposite direction were almost completely empty; far fewer vehicles had been traveling away from Rowley when the infection had first struck. Cooper led the convoy across the central reservation, smashing a hole through an already damaged section of metal barrier. Driving on the wrong side of the road felt annoyingly unnatural, but it was undoubtably quicker and easier.

A brief respite in the mist and rain increased the late October afternoon light levels for a short while. The road followed a long, gentle arc with woodland on one side and the shadows of the city of Rowley on the other. No matter how much time had elapsed since the germ—if that really was what had done all the damage—had struck and destroyed so much, the sight of a once busy and powerful city drenched in total darkness and without a single light on in any of its buildings was still unsettling. It was a stark reminder of the magnitude of what had happened to the world.

Peter Guest now seemed a little more composed again.

"In about half a mile we should reach a series of round-abouts on this road," he explained, carefully following every inch of their progress on his map and cross-referencing with his handwritten notes. "Keep going straight until we hit the fifth one, then it's left. Another twenty miles or so after that and we should just about be there."

Michael crouched on his knees on the floor in the back of the personnel carrier and washed his hands with strong disinfectant they'd taken from the store earlier, trying to get rid of the obnoxious smell of dead flesh. Emma sat at his side, watching him intently and occasionally looking up and glancing out of the window. Every couple of seconds the light from one of their vehicles would catch in a window of an empty building or on the windscreen of a motionless car, reflecting back for an instant, making her look twice and wonder whether there was anyone there. She knew there was no one, but she kept looking just in case.

His hands stinging and his eyes watering, Michael finished what he was doing and collapsed heavily into his seat beside her as the personnel carrier swerved around the first roundabout.

"You okay?" Emma asked.

"Fine."

"You stink."

"Thanks a lot."

She didn't know what was worse—the smell of dead flesh, or the acrid stench of the chemicals Michael had doused his hands with.

"I was thinking," he said, leaning against her and whispering quietly. "If this works out then I want to try and get over to that island as soon as I can. I think we both should."

"Why?" she asked, her voice equally quiet.

"Because if you believe everything we've heard then it could well be the place where we end up spending the rest of our lives. I want to make sure we've got everything we need out there."

"That's a bit selfish, isn't it? What about—"

"I'm not suggesting doing anything at the expense of any of the others," he explained quickly, keen to make it clear that he wasn't being completely self-centerd. "I just want to be sure we get what we need. And I'm not just talking about you and me either, I'm talking about all of this lot too."

He looked around the personnel carrier at the other people traveling with them. It was disheartening that even now after having spent so much time together, the group remained fragmented and disparate. The survivors generally seemed to fall into either one of two very distinct categories: those who talked about the future and did something about it, and those who didn't. Interesting, Michael thought, that he could name all those who had at least tried to look forward and make something of the little they had left. The others—those who still

spent each day silently wallowing in self-pity and despair—
remained nameless and faceless.

"All I'm saying," he said to Emma, keen to make his point,
"is that we need to make sure we stay in control here and not roll
over and take second best just because they've got a bloody helicopter. This little control is all we've got left."

Two vehicles behind, tempers were beginning to fray.

"Will you two just quit your fucking moaning?" Donna
shouted, looking over her shoulder at the two soldiers slumped
in the back of the van. "All you've done for the last hour is com-
plain. If you haven't got anything positive to say, don't say anything at all."

"I've got plenty to say," Kilgore shouted back. "Problem is
you won't listen."

"Just take your bloody mask off, then, so we can hear you
properly."

"Come on, Donna, that's a bit harsh isn't it?" Jack whispered across the front of the van. "Just let it go, he's not worth it.
He's just a bloody idiot who's scared to death. They both are,
you can see it in their eyes."

Donna watched in the mirror as Kilgore angrily slumped
back in his seat like a chastised child, crossing his arms and
turning his back on her, then looking out of the window.

"We should kick them both out now," Donna said out of
the corner of her mouth. "I don't know why we're even bothering to bring them with us. We should do what Cooper did to
the other two and—"

"Come on," he sighed, sounding disappointed, "you know

132

as well as I do why Cooper did what he did. This is different. At the end of the day they're just people like you and me."

"Whatever."

Jack shook his head sadly. He knew—he hoped—that she didn't mean what she was saying. Maybe it was just the tension and uncertainty of the day getting to her like it was getting to him. Not wanting to prolong the conversation any further, he returned his attention to his maps.

The convoy rapidly approached the third of the five roundabouts they expected to come across along the road to the airfield. Tired, Donna sat up straight in her seat and dropped the van back a little way to allow her to get a better view of the road ahead. In the center of the island in the middle of the carriageway was a tall, needlelike stone war memorial which she could see outlined against the darkening sky. At its base it had been hit by a juggernaut that had lost control when its driver had died. The huge lorry was twisted around awkwardly with its cab leaning over to one side and half its wheel-base lifted off the ground.

"Take it easy round here," Jack warned as the two vehicles ahead of them slowed down to navigate their way around the crash scene.

A body hurled itself out of the darkness and into the path of the personnel carrier, distracting Cooper and causing him to swerve. Steve Armitage, following too close behind and not paying enough attention, clipped the rear end of the beached juggernaut, shunting it farther forward into the base of the memorial. He glanced up in time to see that the tall stone monument had been disturbed. He increased his speed and drove quickly toward the exit that Cooper had just taken.

"Shit!" Donna yelled as she watched the truck and personnel carrier disentangle themselves and move on. From where she was she could see that the monument, already unsteady, had been seriously weakened by the impact and subsequent vibrations. As the prison truck powered away, the pointed top of the memorial began to sway. Its collapse was inevitable and rather than take any unnecessary risks, Donna slowed the van and they watched from a distance as the tall stone needle crashed to the ground, splitting into three large pieces. Even before the dust had settled it was obvious that the road ahead was blocked.

"Bloody typical," Donna said, banging her fist against the steering wheel in frustration.

"Doesn't matter, just go around the other way," Jack suggested, looking around anxiously at the bodies suddenly converging on them from the shadows. "Do anything, but for Christ's sake just keep moving."

Donna pulled forward again and began to steer counter-clockwise around the island, doing her best to concentrate on following the road and ignoring the swarming corpses.

"Which exit?" She was confused traveling around the roundabout in the opposite direction.

"Third," Jack told her, sounding less than sure. "No, wait, fourth."

His nervous indecision, coupled with the sudden intense pressure, the random movement of corpses all around her, and the various obstructions which littered the road caused Donna to take the wrong exit. Their mistake was immediately obvious.

"Damn," she cursed, slamming on the brake and stopping. She looked in her mirror and saw that the road behind was rapidly filling with bodies. It was impossible to reverse. Ahead, over to the left, she could see the taillights of the personnel carrier and prison truck rapidly moving farther away along the route they should have taken. "I can't turn around here," she said, desperately looking around for another way out.

"Keep going forward," Jack said as the first bodies began to slam against the sides of the van. "Just keep moving. I know where we are on the map. I'll get us back on track in a few minutes."

"They'll find us," Cooper said firmly, hoping to silence Peter Guest, who was already babbling nervously about the missing van.

"But they could be anywhere . . ."

"Listen, they've taken a wrong turn, that's all. They've got maps. They're not stupid. They'll find us."

"But what if—"

"They'll find us," he repeated. "And if they don't then they'll just have to make their way to the airfield like we agreed. They're going to expect us to keep following the route we've planned and not waste time looking for them. Stopping and turning around or leaving this road now will make things harder for everyone."

18

The situation in the van was deteriorating rapidly. Nervous recriminations and arguments had begun. More bad decisions had been made.

"You told me to go right!" Donna yelled at Jack.

"I said left! Tell her, Clare, I said left, didn't I?"

"I'm not getting involved," Clare answered, sinking down nervously into her seat, which was literally in the middle of the argument. "Anyway, it doesn't matter who said what, just get us out of here, will you?"

Whatever the instruction from Jack had or hadn't been, the fact remained they were now hopelessly lost. The light had almost completely gone and each dull and shadow-filled street now looked virtually the same as the next and as the last. It had only taken a couple of wrong turns for them to become completely disoriented.

"Haven't we been down here before?" Clare said.

"How could we have been here before?" Donna yelled angrily at her. "For God's sake, we've been driving straight for the last ten minutes. We haven't turned around. How the hell could we have been here before?"

"Sorry, I just thought—"

"Well, don't. We took two left turns and one right, remember? Since then I haven't done anything except drive straight. Now shut up and let me concentrate."

"Leave her alone," Jack said angrily. "She's only trying to help."

"If it wasn't for you and your bloody directions we wouldn't need help."

"Come on, Donna, we both screwed up. I got it wrong and you got it wrong and now we're—"

"Now we're in a real bloody mess because—"

"We should try and find somewhere to stop so we can work out where we've gone wrong," Kelly Harcourt suggested from the back, doing her best to end the pointless arguing. "All we need is—"

"We can't stop," Donna snapped, cutting across her. "Don't you understand? This place is crawling with bodies. We can't risk not moving."

"You think?" the soldier said, her voice calm and level in comparison to the others. "Seems to me we can either stop now and take a chance or just keep driving round in circles all bloody night until we run out of fuel and end up stopping anyway."

Donna didn't say anything.

"Maybe she's right," Jack cautiously suggested, wary of how Donna might react. "We should find somewhere to park the van until we're sure of where we are and where we're going. We don't have to get out or anything. Even if a hundred bodies manage to find us, if we keep quiet then they'll disappear off before long."

"Bloody hell, Jack," Donna said as she steered around the rubble of a shop frontage decimated by a crashed ambulance. "How naive are you? All it takes is for a couple of those things to start banging and hammering on the van and we'll have bloody hundreds of them around us in no time. They don't just lose interest and turn round and disappear anymore, remember?"

Jack didn't respond. He sat silent in his seat and looked out into the darkness around them feeling frightened, frustrated, and slightly humiliated. He returned his attention to the map and tried again to work out where they were.

"Find a landmark," Kelly suggested.

"What?" said Jack.

"I said we should find a landmark," she repeated, clinging onto the side of the van as Donna swerved down another road filled with wrecks. "We need to try and find something recognizable so that we can orientate ourselves to the map. Come on, this is basic stuff."

"It's pitch black," Donna yelled back at her. "How the hell are we supposed to find a fucking landmark when we can't fucking see anything?"

Desperate for inspiration, she turned left and drove down another narrow street. It was more residential than most that they had driven along so far and more cars seemed to be parked than crashed, perhaps indicating that it had not been a particularly busy throughway. On either side of the road were houses—very dark, ordinary, and unremarkable Victorian terraced houses.

The relative normality of the scene managed to momentarily silence the raised voices. It had been a long time since any of the survivors or soldiers had found themselves anywhere so inoffensive and reassuringly familiar. Jack's fear and nervousness gave way to a stinging, stabbing pain and a desperate sadness as the normality of the things which surrounded him made him remember all that he had lost.

"What about a church?" Kelly said, pointing out the silhouette of a large and imposing building nestled behind the row of houses to their right.

Donna took two turnings in quick succession and found the building surprisingly quickly. She steered the van down a narrow service road which bent around to the left then opened out into a small rectangular car park. In front of them, and slightly to the left, was the church, on the other side a school.

"We going to stop out here or take a chance inside?" Kilgore asked from the back. He looked out through the rear window and watched as a single corpse tripped awkwardly down the service road after them.

"Inside?" Jack suggested, looking at Donna. "In for a penny, in for a pound? Come on, this place looks pretty quiet and we've been driving for hours."

"Everywhere is quiet, you idiot," Donna said. She didn't want to move, but she didn't want to sit outside, exposed and vulnerable, either. She had to admit, it made sense to make the most of this unexpected break in the journey.

"We don't have much to lose," Jack said. "Our necks are on the line whatever we do. Let's do it."

"Okay," she reluctantly agreed as the solitary body approached the van. Exhausted, she pushed herself up out of her seat and clambered out, legs stiff and aching. The three survivors and two soldiers ran over to the dark school building, found an open door, and disappeared inside, leaving the corpse to clatter clumsily into the side of the van, then turn around and stumble after them.

19

The airfield was close now. Cooper knew they were near, not just because Peter Guest had been talking constantly and with renewed nervousness for the last ten minutes, but also because there were suddenly many more bodies around than there had been before. The city was behind them and the road they now followed ran between open, relatively featureless fields. He could see figures moving on either side. Some were distracted briefly by the noise of the trucks, but most continued to shuffle steadily forward in the same general direction. It was logical to assume that the living and the dead were all heading toward the same destination.

"How far?" Michael asked from the back of the personnel carrier.

"Just a couple of miles now, I think," Peter replied.

"And how are we going to get in when we get there?"

Michael's question was sensible but unanswerable. Peter and Cooper exchanged momentary glances before returning their attention to the maps and the road respectively. Michael slumped back in his seat next to Emma. He hadn't really expected any response. As foolish as it sounded, getting access to the airfield hadn't been something they had discussed at any great length with Richard Lawrence and Karen Chase. They'd been noncommittal and vague about this end of the journey, assuring Cooper and the others that they'd know when they arrived and that they'd make sure they had a clear passage to safety. From the distance and relative comfort of the warehouse hours earlier that had seemed reasonable to believe. Now, however, as they rapidly approached the airfield and the huge crowds of cadavers which would inevitably be waiting there for them, nerves and doubt were beginning to take hold.

Michael's concern increased tenfold as they took a sharp bend in the road and, for the first time, saw the airfield in the distance. Located in the middle of a wide plain, it was instantly recognizable for a number of reasons. Firstly, and most obviously, because of the light which shone out from what he presumed was an operations room or control tower of sorts. The only artificial light the survivors had seen since being out on the road, it burned brightly in the low gloom of the night. He saw that the building with the light stood just off-center in the middle of a vast fenced enclosure. The land around was clear for several hundred meters in all directions, and the entire estate was ringed by a tall chain-link fence. On the other side of the fence was the second, far more ominous indicator that the survivors were close. Around all of the perimeter of the site for as far as they could see in every direction, a dense, heaving crowd of thousands upon thousands of verminlike bodies had gathered.

From where he was sitting it was difficult to estimate with any degree of accuracy, but it seemed to Michael that in most places the crowd ahead of them was at least a hundred bodies deep, maybe deeper.

Toying with the idea of stopping short of the base and trying somehow to attract the other survivors from a distance, Cooper slowed the personnel carrier down.

"Something wrong?" Peter asked anxiously. Cooper shook his head.

"No," he replied quickly, his voice quiet as he gazed out into the distance, looking hopefully for some movement on the airfield.

"Are they really going to see us? Do you really think they're going to . . . ?"

Tired of his incessant chatter, the ex-soldier looked across at Peter, silencing his increasingly irritating babbling with his stare. Although conditioned by years in the forces and too professional to let his feelings show readily, Cooper was also beginning to feel nervous. If he could see the airfield, he reassured himself, then the people there could probably see him—if they were looking, that was. As bright and distinct as the light from their control tower was to him so, surely, the light from their vehicles would be also. As they got closer to the airfield, however, his doubts began to increase. He couldn't risk going much farther forward until he was sure they'd been seen. Driving too close to such an enormous crowd without an escape route would be tantamount to suicide.

"There!" Sheri Newton shouted from close behind him. "Look!"

Michael sat up and leaned forward to try and get a better view of what was happening. It was difficult to make out much from a distance, but their slightly elevated position on the approach road allowed him to see definite movement on the airfield. Several small lights—torches and lamps perhaps—were moving away from the control tower toward a dark shape at one end of an equally dark runway. After a delay of a few seconds the helicopter began to climb and then hovered some thirty or forty feet above the ground.

"This is it," said Cooper as he began to increase his speed again. The road continued its gentle descent toward the airfield. As they approached, the helicopter began to gracefully move through the sky to meet them, switching on its bright searchlight as it hovered over the road, illuminating the route they needed to follow. The brilliant burning light also illuminated a sizable section of the seething, volatile crowd which surrounded the airfield, the sudden incandescence causing their ferocity to increase massively.

"How are we supposed to get through that lot?" Peter sensibly asked as the personnel carrier made contact with the first few corpses, knocking them away to the side.

"Just drive straight through, I guess," Cooper answered, "same as always."

"But there are hundreds of them."

"There are always hundreds of them," he said, struggling to see the dark line of the road through the increasing crowds.

As they neared the airfield it became apparent that the helicopter was beginning to drop down again. When a gap of no more than a few meters remained between its landing skids and the heads of the corpses, it stopped moving. Hundreds of gnarled, grabbing hands reached up toward the powerful machine. Weakened by decay the bodies were like drunks, barely able to stand, thrown about and buffeted by the violent, swirling downwind from the helicopter's rotor blades.

"What the hell are they doing now?" Michael asked, craning his neck to get a clear view. He watched in confusion as someone in the back of the helicopter hung out over the side of the aircraft. Held safe by a rudimentary safety harness, two figures—one on either side—emptied large cans of liquid over the crowd directly below. Cooper hung back as the pilot gently swung the helicopter from side to side, ensuring that as many bodies as possible were drenched with the liquid. When the canisters were empty they were dropped into the enraged mass below, knocking down several of them at a time. The speed of the operation suddenly began to increase as the helicopter quickly flew higher.

One of the figures in the back of the helicopter lit something—a torch or flare or a bottle of something flammable— and casually let it drop into the crowd. The bright flame seemed to be falling forever, spinning over and over until it reached the cadavers below. In an instant the substance which had soaked many of them combusted, exploding in the night air and destroying scores of rotten bodies with remarkable speed.

"Here we go," Cooper announced as he slammed his foot back down and sent his vehicle careering at speed toward the airfield. The bodies which had been incinerated left a relatively clear area at the point where the road entered the enclosure. As the personnel carrier and the prison truck hurtled toward the fence, a group of six men and women pulled open a solid-looking gate that had previously been hidden by the mass of corpses swarming nearby.

More bodies were approaching, stumbling over the burning remains of those that had already fallen. The helicopter swooped and dived through the air above them like a giant bird of prey, distracting them from the two vehicles which disappeared quickly into the compound.

The gate was closed.

20

"I'm not sure," Jack said. "I don't see why we can't just wait here for a few hours longer and then try and get to the airfield. What difference is a couple of hours going to make, for God's sake?"

Donna was already beginning to regret their unscheduled stop. She wished they'd taken their chances and just kept driving until they'd got back on course. The others didn't seem that concerned. Clare, Jack, and the two soldiers were content to sit and wait for a while and then make their move.

"Let's forget it until morning," Clare suggested. "We might as well. We're pretty safe here and it's pitch-black out there now."

"She's got a point," Kelly Harcourt agreed. "It'll be easier to see where we're going in the morning."

"And it'll be easier for the bodies to find us," Donna argued. "We're vulnerable here. I think we should leave now."

"Seems to me we're vulnerable everywhere," Kelly said dejectedly, her voice distorted by her face mask. While Jack, Donna, and Clare stood and shivered in the cold, she and Kilgore were sweating under heavy layers of protective clothing. What she'd have given to feel the cold wind and rain on her face again . . .

"We've been here over an hour now," Jack continued, "and there are still hardly any bodies around out there."

He gestured for Donna and the others to look through the window he'd been staring out of. The group had hidden themselves away in a first-floor classroom in the small school, overlooking the imposing church where they'd originally planned to wait. Donna peered down into the car park below and saw that he was right, there were only a handful of bodies nearby. Most of them seemed to be wandering around as aimlessly as ever, either oblivious to the presence of the survivors in the school or unable to find a way through. A few of them had crowded around the van and were pressing their diseased faces against the glass. She could see several more around the edges of the car park. Strange how they seemed almost to be keeping their distance.

"It doesn't matter *when* we get to the airfield, as long as we get there," Jack continued, trying to convince himself as much as anyone else. "They're not going to be in a position to pack up and leave right away, are they? Richard Lawrence said they've only just started flying people out."

Clare sat on a child's desk a short distance away, tired of this conversation. She leaned down and picked up a book from where it had fallen on the wood-tiled floor. The name on the front was Abigail Peters who, she worked out from the school year she was in, had been nine or ten when she'd died. Jack had stopped talking but she hadn't noticed. He stood watching her flick through the pages of the book. Poor kid, he thought to himself. As hard as what had happened had been for any of them to deal with, it must have been infinitely harder for Clare. Everywhere Jack looked he could see evidence of young lives ended without justification or reason, the innocence of childhood shattered brutally and without explanation. Fortunately the school day hadn't quite started when the nightmare had begun. The building was virtually deserted. In the playground, however, there were thirty to fifty dead children. Around them lay the bodies of their parents and teachers. They'd all died waiting for the school day to begin.

"Where's Kilgore?" Donna asked, immediately concerned.

"What?" Jack mumbled, looking around. He could see Clare and Kelly, but not Kilgore.

"Did anyone see where he went?"

No one answered. Donna, followed close behind by Jack, left the classroom and ran down the long, straight staircase which led to the ground floor. The creak and slam of a classroom door at the far end of another corridor off to their right gave away Kilgore's location. Picking their way cautiously through the shadows, they ran down toward him.

"What the hell are you doing?" Baxter demanded as they entered the classroom and confronted the missing soldier. He was crouching down in front of a glass tank. The remains of several decomposing goldfish were floating on the top of six inches of stagnant water.

"All the animals are dead," he said. "Look." He gestured toward two more tanks adjacent to the first. At the bottom of one was the dehydrated husk of a lizard, and in the other three mounds of moldy fur which had once been gerbils, mice, or hamsters.

"Kilgore," Donna said angrily, incensed by the soldier's selfish stupidity, "get back upstairs, you bloody idiot."

"What's the problem? There's no one here to see me, is there? I'm just looking at—"

"We can't afford to take risks just because you fancy having a wander around. You're putting us all in danger by—"

"I'm not putting anyone in danger," he protested. "I'm not doing anything."

"Just get back upstairs, you stupid bastard."

Donna marched out of the room and back up to the classroom. Kilgore followed, not agreeing with her but knowing he was outnumbered and remembering what had happened to Stonehouse and his other colleague earlier. He couldn't understand why she had such a problem with what he'd been doing. He hadn't done anything wrong. He'd kept quiet and he wasn't putting anyone in danger. He was a skilled professional, for Christ's sake. He knew how to keep out of sight and under cover. He was damn sure Donna hadn't had the training he had. Vile bloody woman.

Jack watched the soldier as he traipsed out of the room. He was about to follow when something caught his eye on the ground over in the far corner of the classroom. It was a sudden, quick scuttling movement that was gone in less than a second. He walked back deeper into the classroom, peering into the darkness, and crouched down next to a shelf full of reading books. He could tell from the smell and debris on the floor around him that animals had been foraging in the building. A fox? Dogs? Rats perhaps? That must have been what he'd seen. Whatever it was, it was nothing worth worrying about.

He looked up and found himself face-to-face with the horrifically disfigured remains of what must once have been the class teacher. The corpse (which was so badly decayed that he couldn't tell whether it had been male or female) had laid sprawled across its desk for more than eight weeks. Whatever it was that had been scavenging in the classroom seemed to have taken much of its nourishment from the corpse. The face had been eaten away both by disease and by the sharp teeth and claws of vermin. A half-moon of yellow-white skull was exposed. In shock and surprise he tripped and fell backward, knocking over a cupboard full of basic percussion instruments. As triangles, drums, cymbals, maracas, and other assorted instruments crashed to the floor the school was filled with ugly noise. With cold sweat prickling his brow and his legs suddenly weak with nerves, Jack froze. As the godawful din finally faded away—it seemed to take forever—a body slammed angrily against the large window at the other end of the classroom and began beating and hammering on the glass. It seemed to be looking straight at him. He could see at least two more coming up through the shadows behind it.

"You fucking idiot!" Donna cursed as he dragged himself back upstairs, his heart still pounding. "Have you seen what you've done?"

Jack looked out through the first-floor window. There were corpses approaching the school from all directions.

21

Richard Lawrence flew back toward the dead city of Rowley in search of the missing van and its occupants. Bloody idiots, he thought to himself. How difficult was it for them to stay together and get to the airfield? This didn't bode well for the future. These were people who, inevitably, he was going to have to rely on in time, and how could he do that when they couldn't even get to the airfield in one piece? If it hadn't been for the fact that he'd already been airborne he wouldn't even have entertained the idea of going out again tonight. Dumb fuckers could have waited until morning.

Richard's journey—already unnecessary in his opinion—was further complicated by the number of people involved. The helicopter was designed to carry a maximum of five—the pilot and four passengers. As if the risks he was taking searching at night weren't enough, he now also faced the potential problem of trying to get back to the airfield with six on board and he was having to travel alone. He felt isolated and exposed, more vulnerable than usual. No one else could fly the helicopter but, for safety's sake, he'd always flown with at least one passenger before to navigate or help with the controls or to do whatever else he needed them to do so that he could concentrate on keeping the machine safely up in the air. If anything went wrong tonight, he was on his own: if he crashed and survived, the bodies would probably get him. He didn't even have the comfort of radio communication, the lack of power at the airfield making it impossible. Richard cursed the handful of idiots lost in the city beneath him.

From the air, Rowley appeared to be little more than a slightly darker stain on an already dark landscape; a featureless scar. Richard had trouble seeing where the city ended and where it began. Christ, he wished he'd gone with his instincts and waited until morning. The relentless blackness of the night made him feel like he was flying with his eyes closed and one hand tied behind his back. However difficult it proved to be he planned to fly directly across the city and then retrace the route he'd given the survivors earlier in the day, concentrating his search around the area where the missing five had become separated from the others. If they were still on the move he'd probably be able to spot them. His fuel supplies were sufficient, not endless, and he decided he'd search for no more than an hour before turning around and heading back to the airfield. If these people had any sense—and he was seriously beginning to wonder whether they did—then he hoped they'd get their heads down and keep themselves out of sight until they heard him.

Jack was looking out into the car park again.

"There are only about twenty of them out there," he said,

trying to make the best of a bad situation for which the others seemed to be holding him completely responsible. "We can deal with that many, can't we? We've done it before. We can get back to the van and get out of here."

"We don't have much choice," Donna said, still seething with anger. "I knew we should have kept moving. Bloody hell, we could have been there by now."

"Or we could still have been driving round in circles, using up our fuel," Kelly Harcourt reminded her.

"Okay," she said, struggling to stay focused and calm, "let's check the map again. We'll plot a route out of here and then make a break for it."

Jack spread out the map on one of the low desks and illuminated Rowley with his torch.

"That's where we are," he explained, circling the general area on the map with his finger, "and that's where we need to be. And around here," he continued, moving his finger back down the page toward the southern side of the city again, "is where I think we went wrong."

The map they were studying was too large a scale to be of any real use in helping them plot a route from their present location back to the road that would take them to the airfield. Jack took a book of town center street maps from the rucksack he'd been carrying. He flicked through until he found the right page.

"What's the name of this place?" he asked.

"Bleakdale," Kilgore said, holding up a child's exercise book which had the words BLEAKDALE CHURCH PRIMARY SCHOOL printed across the front cover.

"Bleakdale . . . got it," Jack mumbled. He began to run the

torch over the page again as he looked for a school and church in close proximity to each other.

"There," Donna said, peering over his shoulder and pointing at the map. "There's the school and there's the service road leading up to it. That's the turning we took to get in here."

"Right, so if we work our way back . . ." His words trailed away as he concentrated on finding his way back to the traffic island where they'd made their original mistake.

"Don't want to pressure you, but we need to get a move on," Kelly warned. She was standing next to the window with Clare, looking down into the car park. Although slow, a constant trickle of bodies continued to drag themselves toward the school building. Many of them seemed to be spilling out from around the corner, near to the classroom where Jack had first unwittingly attracted their attention. Some of them had grouped and become a small but animated crowd around the front of the van.

"More bodies?" Donna asked.

"Plenty more."

From their first-floor viewpoint Kelly could see along several of the streets surrounding the school. The longer she stared into the night, the more scrambling, stumbling creatures she saw. In the deep-blue darkness of evening, the figures looked like insects scuttling across the landscape, staggering along streets and alleyways, all converging on the source of the noise which had filled the air just minutes earlier. For the first time she witnessed the effect she'd previously been warned about: the nearest of the dead were themselves now causing enough of a disturbance to call more and more of them to the scene. Some stood still with their arms hanging heavily at their sides. Others tirelessly pummelled on the sides of the van and on the ground-floor windows and doors of the school building. The few of them gathered in the car park didn't bother her unduly, it was the mass approaching the school from all angles which posed the biggest threat.

Jack forced himself to concentrate. "I reckon we should just turn around and go back the way we came, sticking to the main roads," he suggested. "We turn left out of the car park and keep following the road until it loops back around onto the first road we drove up by mistake. Follow that back and . . ."

". . . and we should be on track again," Donna said, finishing his sentence for him.

"Why go backwards?" Kelly asked, moving away from the window and looking down at the maps with the others. "Why not just keep going forward?"

"We could," Jack replied, obviously unsure, "but that means going deeper into the city."

"So? Do you really think that matters now? According to this map we're close to the city center anyway. I don't think another couple of miles is going to make that much difference, do you?"

"I don't know . . ." Jack mumbled, not sure if he wanted to admit she had a point.

"Look," she explained, grabbing Donna's torch so she could show them what she was thinking. "We could go left as you suggested, Jack, but then turn left again at the next roundabout instead of going straight over. By the time that gets us onto the right road we'll only be a few miles short of the airfield."

The soldier's plan made sense—the risks they were facing were great whichever direction they chose, so surely it would be more sensible to leave the school and go forward, not back.

"I'm still not sure," Jack said.

"Well, you'd better make your minds up quickly," Clare said from by the window.

"Why?"

"Helicopter," she said, pointing up into the sky at the flashing lights on the tail of the aircraft high above them.

For a second no one moved. Then Kelly grabbed her stuff and started to run, followed quickly by the rest of the small group.

"How will they know where we are?" Clare asked as they thundered downstairs.

"We need to get moving," Donna said. "They'll have more chance of seeing us if we're in the van."

"You reckon?" Kilgore asked, pausing by the exit door.

"Hope so," she said as she pushed her way out and ran over to the van. It was surrounded by corpses and she ripped the first few of them away, glancing up to check she could still see the helicopter. She forced her hand through a gap between more of them and yanked open the van door. They were all immediately aware of huge swaths of movement around them as bodies turned from all directions and were now moving quickly toward them, lurching with ominous speed and purpose. The evening gloom was disorienting and made the perception of distance surprisingly difficult. One of the nearest cadavers reached out for Kilgore and caught hold of him before he even knew it was there.

157

"Get it off me!" he screamed in panic. "Get this fucking thing off me!"

He spun around, trying desperately to dislodge the emaciated creature or to somehow grab hold of it and drag it around in front of him. The corpse's slimy, rotting skin and constant writhing movements made it impossible for him to get a grip.

"I've got it," Kelly said calmly as she wrapped her arm around its neck and yanked the loathsome figure off him. She threw it angrily to the ground and stomped on its head with her standard-issue boots until it was still. There were many more of the dead around them now, too many to try and deal with. Kilgore, shocked by the sudden attack and not thinking straight, immediately began to check his suit for damage as the others bundled themselves into the van until Jack shoved him forward and he scrambled inside. Donna started the engine and pulled away, turning around in a tight circle, wheels skidding and corpses thumping against the bodywork. They roared out of the car park and along the service road, then swerved out onto the road, wiping out another advancing group.

"There!" Clare shouted as Donna threw the van around the second sharp turn. She pointed up at the helicopter, which was moving quickly through the sky ahead of them. "There it is!"

"Left here," Kelly ordered from the back, not about to let Donna screw up again. Donna did as she was told, guiding the van between the parallel wrecks of a car and a burned-out milk truck. The van's headlights lit up swarms of movement ahead of them as bodies emerged from all sides and stumbled toward the light and noise.

"He'll never see us," Kilgore moaned from the back.

"Of course he will," Jack said, sick of the soldier's pathetic defeatist attitude. "There's nothing else to see out here, is there?"

High above the streets, Richard Lawrence had completed his first sweep of the city center and was trying to find an excuse for giving up for the night when he caught sight of a momentary flash of light below. It was the only illumination in the whole of the dead city, making the van easy to pick out and follow. He took the helicopter down as far as he dared: low enough to keep track of the vehicle below, but still at a sufficient height to avoid any tall, blacked-out buildings, electricity pylons, or similar. He knew he probably wouldn't see such obstacles tonight until he hit them.

On the ground, the van had reached a blockage in the road. Nothing too serious, but the tangled wreckage of a three-car crash had covered enough of the carriageway to force Donna to slow down to little more than walking pace and drive on the pavement to negotiate the obstruction. Richard switched on the helicopter's searchlight, both to let them know he'd seen them and to provide extra illumination. Bodies stumbled into the light like moths.

To the right of the van was a row of buildings. On the other side of the road, however, perhaps another half mile farther ahead, Richard could see an expanse of open land—a park or playing fields perhaps? He eased the helicopter forward to hover above the grassland and saw that directly beneath him were two sets of football posts, and even if the pitch wasn't full size, he knew he probably had room to land. He moved the searchlight to point down at the pitch in a rudimentary attempt to signal to the people on the ground.

"What's the hell's he doing now?" Donna asked, concentrating on driving and relying on the others to tell her what was happening above them.

"He's moved over to our left," Jack replied. "And now he's hovering."

He stared up at the helicopter. Having now cleared the remains of the three-car pileup, the van sped up again and slammed into a random body, almost cutting it in two. Its head and shoulders thumped against the glass, leaving a bloody smear. Donna flicked on the wipers.

"He's definitely stopped moving now," he continued, struggling to see clearly through the dirty glass. "Try and get closer."

"I can only follow the bloody road," Donna said anxiously. "What do you want me to do?"

"Wait . . . he's dropping down."

"What?"

"I think he's landing."

Donna allowed herself to look up from the road. Jack was right.

"Stop the van," Kelly ordered from the back. "Quick! Stop the van and we'll find him on foot."

"Are you bloody stupid?" Kilgore protested.

"It's a park," Jack said as they passed a momentary gap in a tree-lined metal fence along the side of the road they'd been following. "Kelly's right, Donna, stop the van and let's make a run for it."

Donna didn't argue. She was cold and tired and frightened and she wanted this wild and pointless chase through nowhere to be over. She forced the van up onto the pavement and climbed out. A body threw itself at her, almost knocking her to the ground. She quickly regained her balance and shoved the corpse against the fence, then sprinted after Jack, Clare, and the two soldiers who were already up ahead, trying to find a way into the park.

Now that they were out of the van, the sound of the helicopter filled the air. With his legs already burning with effort, Jack forced himself to keep moving forward, trying to keep up with the others who were pulling away, all of them much younger and in far better physical condition than him. Being at the back of the pack terrified him but he couldn't move any faster. He allowed himself a momentary glance over his shoulder and saw bodies shuffling after them. There seemed to be hundreds of them dragging themselves out of the shadows from every direction, all gravitating toward him. He looked forward again and concentrated on following Donna, who had just overtaken him. He didn't dare look back a second time, but he was sure the bodies were gaining. How close were they now? Was one about to grab hold of him?

"Through here," Clare shouted as she reached an open wrought-iron gate and ducked through under the overgrown feelers of a wild bush. She ran into the park and was immediately able to see the helicopter in all its magnificent glory. Tonight, it was the most incredible thing she'd ever seen, hovering imperiously some ten feet above the ground and waiting for them.

"Has he seen us?" Donna yelled as she tripped through

overlong grass which had been left to grow wild for weeks. She began to wave her arms furiously, hoping that the pilot would see her and respond. At first nothing happened. The brilliant white searchlight lit up almost all of the park and illuminated crowds of shuffling cadavers swarming toward the helicopter from all sides. The relative speed and control of the survivors made them easy for Richard to pick out through the crowds but he didn't dare risk setting down until they were almost directly underneath him. At the last possible moment he dropped the final few feet to the ground.

"One in the front with me and the rest of you in the back," Richard yelled over the deafening engine and rotor blade roar as Kelly yanked the helicopter door open. "Strap yourselves in if you can, just hold on if you can't."

The pilot's voice was barely audible over the noise. Clare and the two soldiers climbed in, finally followed by Jack. Donna waited for him at the side of the helicopter and virtually had to push him up into his seat. Dizzy with exhaustion, he slumped back and sucked in long, cool mouthfuls of damp evening air as she slammed the door shut in his face.

"Come on," Richard urged. The bodies were damn close now. He could see the decayed faces of the nearest of the dead staring back at him. Donna scrambled into the front and pulled the door shut. By the time she'd buckled up they were airborne. Directly below, where the wind whipped the wild grass furiously, the bodies converged and tried pointlessly to reach up for the rapidly disappearing machine.

22

The flight to the airfield took under fifteen minutes. The silence and stillness which greeted them when they finally touched down was in stark contrast to the chaos they'd left behind. Oblivious to the thousands upon thousands of cold, dead eyes which stared at them from beyond the other side of the distant fence, Jack, Clare, Donna, Kelly, and Kilgore stumbled out of the helicopter, exhausted but relieved, and followed Richard Lawrence across the tarmac. He led them toward a collection of dark buildings: a large, half empty and skeletal hangar, a control tower, and several smaller buildings which had once been used as offices, waiting rooms, and public lounges. Jack was impressed. Even though it was dark, the place looked better equipped and more substantial than he'd dared imagine it might. It looked like it had been an unusual cross between a small commercial airport and a flying club and he guessed it had probably been used for private planes, chartered flights, and pilot training. He noticed the prison van and personnel carrier parked a short distance away. The presence of the other vehicles was an enormous relief. The rest of the group had made it safely to the airfield.

A dull light was shining out from the very top of the control tower. They followed Richard into the building, across a small open area and up two flights of steep, echoing metal stairs. The events of the last few hours had been physically and mentally exhausting; Jack in particular was struggling to keep moving forward. They finally reached the top of the building and entered a large room through a pair of heavy swinging double doors. Inside, the room was light and warm and was buzzing with noise and relaxed conversation. It couldn't have been more different from the cold, enforced silence of the outside world. The sight of familiar faces dotted around filled the new arrivals with a sudden surge of energy.

"You finally made it, then," Cooper shouted sarcastically from across the room. "Where the hell have you lot been?"

"Piss off!" Jack replied, managing a tired grin. "We took a couple of wrong turns, that was all!"

"Just a couple? Bloody hell, we'd almost given up on you. We've been here for hours!"

Donna stood in the doorway and soaked up the atmosphere. The mass of people around her—both those she knew and the twenty or so faces she didn't recognize—looked at ease. She too suddenly felt much calmer, as if the stresses and problems that had continually plagued her for almost eight weeks had finally begun to be stripped away. Was it because she'd reached the airfield that she felt that way, or was she just relieved that Cooper and the others were safe? Whatever the reason, she hadn't been in such a comfortable and welcoming environment for a long, long time. In fact, now she stopped to think about it, she hadn't felt free like this since before this nightmare had begun. For a few precious moments the relief was such that she couldn't move. The hell outside suddenly seemed a thousand miles away.

"You okay?" someone beside her asked. It was Emma.

"I'm fine," she answered quickly, suddenly self-conscious. "I'm sorry, I was just . . ."

Donna stopped midsentence, but Emma knew what she was trying to say. She'd experienced the same bewildering range of emotions herself when she'd first arrived at the airfield.

"This is great, Donna," she continued. "These people have really got themselves sorted out here."

"Looks that way . . ."

"You won't believe some of the things they've been telling us. You know, when we first saw the helicopter this morning I knew it was going to be important, but I didn't realize just how important. None of us had time to stop and think about it, did we? Christ, these people have been up and down the length of the whole bloody country. They've seen other bases like the one Cooper came from and—"

"I know, I heard Richard talking earlier. So how come there's so few of them?"

"Suppose they've just been taking the same approach to all this as we have," Emma answered. "Mike and I decided right from the start that we couldn't afford to spend all our time looking around for other survivors. We knew we had to forget about everyone else and concentrate on getting through this ourselves. Looks like these people have spent their time doing that too."

"So how many of them are there?"

"Not sure exactly. I think someone said there are about twenty or so of them here, with another six already on Cormansey."

"Cormansey?"

"The island, remember?"

Donna nodded. She was tired and her brain wasn't functioning properly. She looked drained and weak, a shadow of her normal self. Emma passed her a drink. It was a small bottle of lemonade. The sweet liquid was warm and gassy but very welcome.

"Much happened since you've been here, then?" Donna asked, wiping her mouth dry on the back of her sleeve.

"Not really," Emma answered. "We've just been waiting for you lot to turn up. What happened? Did you run into trouble?"

"Stupid cock up," she admitted. "We took the wrong exit on the roundabout where that bloody memorial came down, and then made more mistakes trying to get back on track and catch up with you."

"You're here now. That's all that matters."

A sudden loud burst of laughter came from the far side of the room. It was an unexpected and strangely startling noise. Donna looked up and saw that Michael, Cooper, and several others were talking to people she didn't recognize. At first she didn't question who these people might be, or what they might have found amusing. Instead her mind was preoccupied with the fact that she'd just heard laughter for the first time in weeks.

Whatever it was they were finding funny, it unexpectedly touched a nerve. Normally strong and determined to the point of sometimes seeming cold and uncaring, Donna now felt ready to crumble and burst into tears. She dismissed her feelings as just a passing moment of weakness, probably brought on by exhaustion. She turned and looked out a window behind her before Emma could see she was upset.

"See that woman sitting next to Mike?" Emma asked. Donna turned back around and nonchalantly wiped her eyes. The woman between Michael and Phil Croft was rotund, red-faced, and very loud. In a world where silence was now the key to staying alive, Donna wondered how the hell she'd managed to survive for so long.

"The big lady?" she replied, choosing her words carefully.

"That's right."

"Who is she?"

"Her name's Jackie Soames. I don't think anyone's officially in charge here, but she seems to get involved with most of the decision making."

"She doesn't look . . ." Donna began.

"She doesn't look like the kind of person who'd be sat in a place like this dishing out advice," Emma interrupted, successfully anticipating what Donna had been about to say. "She's got a lot of respect here, though. I've spoken to a few people and they've only got good things to say about her. Apparently she used to run a pub. Story is she slept through everything that happened on the first day. Went to bed with a hangover then woke up at midday and found her husband dead behind the bar."

"Nice. Who else is there?"

"See the young lad on his own with his back to us?"

"Yes."

"That's Martin Smith. He's the one who—"

"Who reckons he found out how all this happened?"

"That's him. And the bloke standing looking out of the window over there," she continued, nodding across to the diagonally opposite corner of the square room.

"The one with the jacket and the hair?"

"That's the one," she replied, "I think his name's Gary Keele. He calls himself Tuggie."

Donna looked at the man and felt a strange combination of emotions. While just about every other survivor she'd seen wore whatever clothes they'd been able to salvage, this man's appearance seemed to suggest that, for some inexplicable reason, he still considered it important to be well-dressed and presentable. His hair—in contrast to just about everyone else—was surprisingly well-groomed. He looked conspicuously out of place and out on a limb, somehow distant and separate from the others. But was it because he'd chosen not to mix with them, or did the rest of the group not want to associate with him? Whatever the reason, in a room full of people he was very much alone.

"So what does he do around here?" she asked, guessing that the man must have had some relevance to the group for Emma to have pointed him out.

"Apparently he's the one who's going to fly the plane and get everyone to the island."

"Why do you say it like that? What do you mean, 'apparently'?"

"Girl over there called Jo Francis told me that he used to fly little tug planes at a gliding club."

"Hence the nickname."

"That's right. Anyway, she says he's not flown anything as big as the plane they've got here yet."

"Does he need to? They've got the helicopter, haven't they?"

"The plan is to keep sending people over to the island in threes and fours to make it safe. When it's all clear they'll load up the plane and take everyone and everything else over."

Donna nodded and finished her drink. "So what's the problem?"

"Richard Lawrence told me he found him hiding under a table in an office at another airfield when he stopped to refuel the helicopter. The guy's a bloody nervous wreck. I'm not convinced he's going to be able to fly anyone anywhere."

"Great," Donna mumbled.

Jack Baxter crossed her line of vision and began to walk toward her. The tension and fear so evident in his face earlier had now disappeared and been replaced with a relaxed, almost disbelieving grin.

"You two all right?"

"Fine," Donna answered. "You?"

"Bloody fantastic!"

"That good, eh?" she mumbled, unable to match his enthusiasm.

"Yep, that good."

"And what are you so happy about?"

"Can't you feel it?"

"Feel what? We've only been here a few minutes, Jack. I haven't had a chance to feel anything yet."

"This is going to work out," he grinned. "I can feel it in my bones. I tell you, it won't be long now before we're out of this mess."

23

The control tower had become the focal point of the airfield. The strongest and safest building, it was where the people sheltering there ate, talked, slept, planned, argued, cried, and did pretty much everything else. The first people to arrive there had naturally gravitated toward it, as its relative height and its distance from the perimeter fence and the decaying hordes beyond provided a little welcome security. With the unexpected arrival of Cooper, Donna, Michael, and more than thirty others, however, space was suddenly at a premium. Michael and Emma found a small, dark room at the foot of the stairs opposite the main entrance, where they sat together, draped in blankets to protect against the bitter cold. Winter was still a couple of months away, but the average temperature seemed to be dropping daily.

Michael had something on his mind. He'd wanted to talk to Emma about it since an earlier conversation he'd had with Cooper and Jackie Soames, but she seemed more relaxed today than he'd ever seen her and he found it difficult to talk when he knew that what he was going to say would inevitably upset her.

After skirting around the subject for what felt like the hundredth time, Michael took a deep breath.

"Em," he began slowly, choosing his words with care, "I was talking to Cooper earlier . . ."

"I know," she replied, "I saw you. The pair of you were as thick as thieves."

"Remember the conversation we had on the way here?" he continued. "When we talked about the island? I said I wanted to try and get over there pretty quickly so we could make sure we get everything we needed."

"I remember," Emma said, already anticipating what he was about to say next.

"I'm going to go over on the next flight," he told her, forcing the words out as quickly as he could. Emma nodded but she didn't say anything. In the dark it was difficult for him to gauge her reaction. As the uncomfortable, prolonged silence dragged on, Michael felt compelled to explain himself. "There are a couple of damn good reasons why I should go. Most important is that I really do want to get over there to try and make sure that this island is everything we need it to be. Second—"

"What happens if it's not?" Emma interrupted. "What are you going to do? Ask them if they wouldn't mind just dropping you back so you can start looking for somewhere else?"

"Second," he continued, ignoring her anger, "have you looked at the people left around here, Em?"

"What about them?"

"Just go back upstairs and have a look around. Most of the

people here are empty. There's more life in half the bodies out-side than in some of them up there. It's not their fault, they just can't handle what's happened."

"What point are you trying to make?"

"Jackie Soames says they've already sent some of their stron-gest people over there but they need more. They're planning to try and clear out the village in the next couple of days and they're going to need as much manpower as they can get."

"I know that, but why you? Why not send Cooper or some of the others?"

"Cooper's a hard bastard. He'll be more use here keeping this lot moving in the right direction. And if I'm honest, I want to do this, Emma. I want to go."

"So when do you think you'll be leaving?" she asked, not sure she really wanted to hear his answer.

"They're planning the next flight for sometime tomorrow. Probably early afternoon."

She didn't say anything, and her silence concerned Michael. He knew he was doing the right thing—hell, he was sure they *both* knew—but that didn't make it any easier.

"It'll be okay," he said, his voice soft and quiet. "This place seems secure and—"

"You say that every time we find somewhere new to shelter and within days we're on the run again," she snapped at him. "You and your bloody chaos theory."

"This place seems secure," he repeated, "but we both know it probably won't last. The bodies will keep coming—"

"So you thought you'd leave now before we're overrun?"

"Come on, that's not fair. I want to go over to the island to make sure things are moving, that's all. The place could be cleared of bodies in a couple of days. By this time next week we could all be over there standing out in the open without a hundred thousand bloody corpses watching our every move."

Emma regretted what she'd said. He was right, it had been unfair and unnecessary. "Sorry."

"It's okay."

"It's just that I don't want you to go," she continued. "I don't want to be here on my own."

"But you're not going to be on your own, are you? There are more people here now than we've been with since this all started."

"No, that's not what I meant. You and I have been together since this started and I don't want that to change. I've been okay as long as I've been with you. We've had some pretty bloody awful times, but we've got through them all. I guess I'm just frightened that you'll leave here and things will go wrong. Something will happen to you, or you won't come back, or . . ."

"Shh . . ." he soothed. "Come on, now you're just being stupid."

"Am I?"

"Yes. Look, this is nothing. I'll go over there in the helicopter tomorrow and the job'll be done and you'll be over there with me before you know it."

"You make it sound easy."

"It is easy."

"Is it? Is it really? Wake up, Mike. In case you hadn't noticed, nothing's easy anymore. Finding the next meal isn't easy. Keeping warm and dry and out of sight isn't easy. Keeping quiet isn't easy. Driving around the country running from place to place isn't easy so please don't patronize me by telling me that getting in a frigging helicopter with a man we hardly know and flying God knows how many bloody miles to wipe out this island's already dead population is going to be easy either."

"Look," Michael said, becoming irritated by her negativity, "I've got a chance to do something tomorrow that might guarantee a future for both of us. And if I'm honest, I think I have to do it because I don't trust any of those other fuckers upstairs to do it properly. We can't afford to take any chances with this."

"I know all that," Emma replied, sounding equally emotional. "I know why you're going and I know what has to be done, but none of that makes it any easier to deal with. I just don't want you to go, that's all. You're all I've got left."

24

"You okay?" Jack Baxter asked. Kelly Harcourt looked up and nodded. She was slumped in a seat in the shadows of the farthest, quietest corner of the room at the top of the control tower. Kilgore was asleep, curled up in a ball on the ground at her feet like a faithful dog. Unlike him, Kelly couldn't switch off. Her head was spinning, filled with dark and frequently painful thoughts. The hard and bloody fight outside the bunker and the subsequent journey which had brought them to this place had been a long and difficult distraction. But now, sitting here in the silence and calm, there was nothing to think about except the grim inevitability of her immediate future.

"No, I'm not okay," she said to Jack with what he thought was admirable honesty. "Are you?"

"I'm all right," he replied, pulling up a chair and sitting down next to her. He glanced across at the soldier who stared impassively ahead, out of the window and into the darkness. For the first time since leaving the base Jack thought she looked odd and out of place in her heavy protective suit. In the chaos of the last day and a half he had become used to seeing soldiers, guns, and helicopters, but Kelly Harcourt and Kilgore suddenly didn't seem to fit in with their surroundings. He could see her dark, melancholy eyes behind her visor. The poor kid could only have been in her early twenties. He felt desperately sorry for her but he was already regretting sitting down next to her. There was absolutely nothing that he or anyone else could do to help her, or even soften the blow of what was almost certainly going to happen to her in the near future. He'd sat down with the intention of trying to start a conversation, but now he didn't know what to say.

Jack was about to get up and walk away again when she spoke. She'd realized she didn't want to be alone.

"My dad," she said, her voice flat and empty, "he would have liked it here. He loved planes. He was turning into a proper old-fashioned granddad. He used to take my sister's boys to the airport and they'd spend the whole day watching the planes taking off and landing."

"Never appealed to me," Jack admitted.

"Me neither. Dad loved it, though. Should have seen him at my passing out parade. Mum told me she had to keep reminding him to watch me. He spent the whole time looking around the base and admiring the kit instead of looking at me."

The conversation faltered. Feeling slightly more comfortable Jack spoke again. "So tell me, how did you end up in uniform?"

"I had two older brothers in the forces. Like I said, Dad was always interested in the military, so I guess I just grew up surrounded by it. Didn't know what I wanted to do when I left school, so I just sort of stumbled into it. I figured what was good enough for my brothers was good enough for me too."

"Glad you did it?"

"I had some good times. I knew some good people."

"You talk about it as if it's over."

She sighed. "Come on, Jack. Cut the bullshit. You know it is."

"But doesn't this feel like it did every time you went out to fight? What I mean is," he said groping for the right words, "you knew that you were putting your life on the line every time you picked up your weapon, didn't you?"

"This is different," she explained. "At least on the battlefield you had a chance. Here I'm just sitting and waiting for it to happen, and that's what makes it so bloody hard to deal with. There's nothing I can do about it. Nothing anyone can do."

"I'm sorry, I shouldn't have . . ."

"Forget it. It's not your fault."

Jack wondered whether it would be better for both of them if he just got up and walked away now. Or perhaps he owed it to her to stay and try to talk some more and repair some of the damage he was sure he was doing? The pity he suddenly felt for this young woman was both overpowering and humbling. He couldn't even begin to imagine how she must have been feeling.

"If I could have my time again," she said quietly, "then I never would have signed up." Her voice, although muffled by her breathing apparatus, suddenly sounded tearful and full of regret. "I probably would have left school and got myself a normal job like all my friends did."

"Why do you say that?"

"Because, if I hadn't signed up then I wouldn't be sitting here now, talking to you and waiting to die. If I hadn't signed up then I'd probably have died on the first day like I should have. I'd have died next to my mum or my dad or my boyfriend, not on my own out here."

"You're not on your own."

"I don't know anyone, other than Cooper and this idiot," she sighed, gently nudging the soldier on the ground with the toe of her boot. "Honestly, Jack, it would have been so much easier that way."

"But you don't know. You might—"

"Please don't try to make me feel better with bullshit. There's no point."

"You might be able to breathe," he continued. "There are almost fifty of us here who can."

"And there are millions of dead people out there who couldn't. I think there's a pretty good chance I'm not immune, don't you?"

"But you've made it this far, why stop and give up now?"

"Because now that I have stopped I can see that there's no point. I'm just prolonging the inevitable. It's going to happen sooner or later."

"So why not later?"

"There's nothing to hang on for. You'll all be gone soon anyway."

"So come with us."

"Why? It might as well happen here as anywhere. If you've got any sense then you won't bother taking me and Kilgore over to your island. We'd be taking up precious cargo space. Might as well use it to take something that's going to be useful."

"There might be somewhere on the island that we can adapt so that—"

"Shut up, Jack, it's not working. I appreciate the thought, but you're just digging a bigger hole for yourself now. Honestly, what are you going to do? There's only one village on the island, for Christ's sake. I don't even know if there's a hospital. There won't be anywhere for me. Are you planning to bubble-wrap a house so that we can live in a fucking oxygen tent? Thanks for your concern, but it's not going to happen."

Jack finally realized that it really was time to stop talking. He'd meant well but she was right, he wasn't helping. "So what are you going to do?" he asked after a while.

Silence.

"Nothing," she eventually replied. "I'll just sit here in this bloody suit until I can't take it anymore. Then I'll end it."

25

Michael woke up in agony next morning. He and Emma had spent the night sleeping on the floor together in the little room they'd found. He'd been lying on hard concrete and Emma had been lying on him. Every bone in his body ached. He opened his eyes and looked around. Their difficult conversation still echoed around his head. His heart sank when he remembered that he would be leaving her today.

Emma was still asleep. Michael carefully eased himself out from underneath her and made sure that she was comfortable and warm before going out of the room and walking down to the main entrance. He pushed the door open and stepped out into a bright and cool morning. The sky was clear and blue, the sun strong. A gusting wind blew across the airfield, the cold breeze waking him fully. A short distance ahead of him was the helicopter, the sun glinting on its curved surfaces and reflecting back at him. He stood and stared at it for a moment, before remembering what he'd actually come outside for. He found a less exposed corner of the building, leaned against the wall, and began to empty his bladder.

"Morning, Mike," a voice suddenly said, making him jump. He looked around and saw that it was Donna. She was sitting on a fold-up chair at the edge of the runway, staring out across the airfield at the bodies on the other side of the distant fence. A couple of months ago Michael would have been mortified being caught urinating publicly like this. Today he didn't care.

"Morning," he said nonchalantly as he shook himself dry, then did up his fly and wiped his hands on wet grass. "You all right?"

"Fine," she replied, shielding her eyes from the sun as he walked toward her.

"What you doing out here?"

"Originally the same as you," she answered factually. "Other than that, not a lot. I just wanted to get some air. I still can't get used to being able to be outside like this."

"Bloody cold, though, isn't it?"

Donna looked up at him. He seemed distracted.

"You okay?"

He crouched down next to her but didn't immediately answer. From here the bodies on the other side of the fence looked miles away. From this distance he couldn't make out individual figures anymore, just a constantly shifting mass of gray-green decay. Phil Croft had mentioned that he thought the corpses might not be able to see the survivors for much longer because of the steady deterioration of their faces and eyes. Their limited eyesight may have reduced, but the fact that they remained on the other side of the fence in such vast numbers seemed to be proving the doctor's theory wrong.

"Cooper tells me you're leaving us," Donna said.

"You make it sound like I'm going for good. I think we're planning to leave later today. All depends on Richard being able to fly in this wind, I suppose."

"And how does Emma feel about it?"

"She's ecstatic," he answered sarcastically. "Yes, she's really pleased."

"I bet."

"She understands."

"What happens on Cormansey is important."

"I know."

"Do you realize *how* important? This could be the difference between living and just existing, Mike. This is the best chance we've had, and it's probably the best chance we're going to get."

"I know," he said again.

Michael stood up, brushed himself down, and walked out onto the runway. He thought about what Donna had just said, and the sudden gravity and importance of the day were suddenly humbling. Until now he hadn't stopped to think about what he was going to do in any great detail. Sure, he'd considered the practicalities of getting over to the island and he'd paid lip service to helping slaughter the dead and starting to build a future for the group. Standing outside, however, with the biting wind blowing into his face and the smell of death still hanging in the air, he began to fully appreciate the enormity of the task ahead. Behind him Richard Lawrence emerged from the door at the base of the control tower and walked over to where Donna was sitting.

"You two all right out here?" he asked.

"Just taking in the air," she replied, giving him the same answer she'd given Michael minutes earlier. "It's been a long time since we've been able to do this."

Michael turned around when he heard the pilot's voice.

"We'll be looking to leave around midday, okay?" said Richard.

"Will we be all right with this wind?"

"Believe me, this is nothing," he answered, laughing. "I've been up in far worse than this recently. Trust me, mate, this is a good day for flying. A little breezy, perhaps, but nothing I can't handle."

Michael had been quietly hoping for a delay. Events were suddenly unfolding at an uncomfortable speed and he wanted to spend some time with Emma before he left. They'd spent just about every minute of the last eight weeks together and now that they were going to be apart, every remaining second suddenly felt more precious. He turned and jogged back to the control tower to find her.

26

The morning disappeared in minutes. For the first time in recent memory Michael prayed that time would slow down. Takeoff had been delayed by an hour but that wasn't enough. He'd wanted longer.

The helicopter's powerful rotor blades sliced through the air above their heads as Richard flew Michael, Peter Guest, and a teenage boy called Danny Talbot across the dead land. The spare seat between Michael and Peter was piled high with their belongings and supplies, every scrap of space taken.

What was quickly becoming a regular, almost run-of-the-mill journey for Richard was far more of an unsettling experience for his passengers. As well as being used to flying, Richard had also grown accustomed to the view of the scarred landscape from the air. For Michael, Peter, and Danny, the turbulent journey was a harsh education—a painful reminder of the almost incomprehensible scale of the devastation down at ground level.

For the first half of the journey Michael had been preoccupied with thoughts of Emma. He hadn't been able to get her tearful face out of his mind for even a second. Now that he'd left her he felt hollow and alone. He'd looked down from the air and watched her grow smaller and smaller until she'd disappeared from view. He tried to comfort himself with the thought that if everything went according to plan they would be back together in less than a week, but there was a lot of work to do before then, and these days things rarely seemed to go according to plan. Michael was already bitterly regretting having left her. It was like she'd said in the early hours of the morning just passed, so far they'd struggled through almost every second of the nightmare together. Being away from her now just didn't feel right.

Forcing himself to try and clear his mind and focus on what was ahead, he looked across the interior of the helicopter at Peter Guest. Peter was sitting with his head resting against the glass and he was staring down. Transfixed, almost unblinking, he watched the ground rush by beneath them at a furious speed. Michael turned back and looked out of his side. The bright sun of early morning had long gone and the late-autumn sky was now dull, gray, and filled with rain. He peered down and watched as they flew over a small town. It might have been the speed or his imagination, but everything below looked blurred and undefined. It was almost as if the buildings and roads were being swallowed up, melting back into the land.

Danny Talbot—a short, acne-ridden teenager who had arrived at the airfield in the back of the prison truck—found himself instinctively looking out for survivors amongst the ruination. But almost everything was still, and he saw nothing. *If I was down there on my own*, he thought, *when I heard the helicopter I'd go outside and I'd made damn sure they saw me.* So why couldn't he see anyone down there now? Why could he see only rotting bodies shuffling painfully across the silent landscape? Was it because any survivors who heard the helicopter were too scared, too slow, or too vulnerable to react? Or was it just because there were no more survivors? That seemed the most probable explanation.

"Cormansey," Richard Lawrence announced just over twenty minutes later when he spotted the island on the misty horizon. The mainland was behind them now, and the helicopter raced out over the ocean. Michael had closed his eyes and had been on the brink of falling asleep when the pilot's words had made him quickly sit up again. He felt nervous as he stared out of the rain-streaked window. The longer the journey had gone on, the more he had become used to the feeling of protection the helicopter gave him and the thought that they would soon be back down at ground level and in the midst of the mayhem again was disconcerting.

The helicopter soared over the deceptively smooth and steady ocean, dropping closer to the waves. The frothing surf was just a few feet below them and, for the first time, Michael and the others were able to fully appreciate the speed at which they were traveling. The dull, dark blur on the horizon quickly grew in size and definition and in a few minutes more they were over the island.

"This is it, then," mumbled Peter as he looked down at the rough, unwelcoming landscape beneath them. It looked just as

Michael had imagined—cold and bleak, with gray rock giving way to lush green grassland with the occasional patches of russet-red and orange-brown vegetation. The sea was relentlessly battering the island's coastline. Tall waves crashed against the rocks, sending huge plumes of surf and froth high up into the air. Below them now was the village, little more than the intersection of several short roads lined with buildings, as yet untouched by the people who now inhabited this small pocket of land. Bodies lay motionless in the middle of the street where they had fallen months earlier. Although they were only over the tomblike place for a matter of seconds, it was time enough for them to spot several corpses, shuffling ominously between the buildings. Strange, Michael thought, that they still seemed to gravitate there.

Richard flew farther along the length of the island. Michael continued to stare at the land they passed over, the rich colors below a stark contrast with the black and gray sky. He could see narrow roads and gravel tracks leading up to the doors of isolated small cottages and houses. Virtually every home on the island, although often in view of one or two other buildings, stood a distance apart from even its nearest neighbor. Some looked even more remote than Penn Farm.

"Almost there," Richard shouted as the helicopter climbed again, rising quickly to clear a sudden elevation in the level of the otherwise fairly flat landscape. They passed over a rocky scar which seemed to run across almost the entire width of Cormansey. Once over the rocks, the helicopter and its passengers had a clear view of the rest of the island. In the distance just ahead, Michael could make out a short landing strip cut into a large expanse of relatively flat grassland. A little farther still and he could see more buildings. From behind a small, whitewashed cottage, a plume of white-gray smoke rose up into the squally air. Unperturbed by the swirling winds, Richard skillfully touched the helicopter down in the middle of the runway. Neither Michael, Peter, nor Danny moved at first, not even to unbuckle their safety belts.

"They'll be here in a couple of minutes," Richard said, lowering his voice as the powerful engine slowed and died.

"Who will?" asked Peter, panicking. Did he mean the bodies?

"The others," he explained. "Brigid, Harry, and the rest of them."

Michael wiped a section of window clear so that he could see outside. Now that the helicopter had landed they could hear and feel the full strength of the fierce wind. It whistled through the rotor blades, buffeting and battering the aircraft so hard it felt as if it was being shunted back along the runway. Michael had felt safer up in the air.

"So where are these people coming from?" Peter asked. "Not that it really matters, I suppose. Can't take long to get from one place to the other here."

"Takes fifteen minutes to drive from one end of the island to the other," Richard said. "We drove a quick circuit when we first got here to get our bearings. We based ourselves at this end because of the airstrip and the hill. Figured the bodies would struggle to get over the rocks so they'd mostly stay around the village at the other end. Hang on, here they are."

Richard opened his door, climbed down onto the runway,

then helped the others out. As he stepped down onto the tarmac Michael saw a pair of bright headlights moving along the airstrip toward them. As the vehicle approached he could see that it was a strong, modern-looking jeep. It stopped a short distance from them and a large, stocky woman climbed out of the driver's seat.

"You okay, Richard? Good flight over?"

"Not bad," he replied. "How've things been here?"

"Quiet," she answered. "Quieter than I'd expected, actually."

The woman looked at the three new arrivals.

"Brigid, this is Michael, Peter, and Danny," Richard said, introducing them. Each of them acknowledged her, struggling to stay standing in the wind. "They were with a group that joined us yesterday," he explained. "Remember I told you about the crowd of bodies we saw on our way over here last time? That was these guys. They'd been holed up for a while in some military installation or other. Had some trouble and ended up having to make a break for it."

"You can say that again," Peter said.

"Karen and I managed to track them down."

Michael stood next to the helicopter with his arms folded across his chest, looking around anxiously, only half-listening to the conversation. It still didn't feel right to be standing out in the open like this, exposed and defenseless. Were there really so few bodies around here that it didn't matter?

"Come on," said Brigid, "let's get in the warm."

The men unloaded the supplies from the helicopter and threw them into the Jeep. Michael, Peter, and Danny crammed themselves into the back of the vehicle. Suddenly overloaded with questions, emotions, random thoughts, and sheer mental exhaustion, they sat in silence as Brigid turned around and drove back down the runway.

"Been keeping yourself busy then, Brig?" Richard asked.

"You know me, Rich, I always do," she replied. "What about you? Everything all right back on the mainland?"

"The same as when you left, really. There are a few more of us now, that's all."

"And are you going to be able to get Keele to fly that plane over here soon?"

"I bloody well hope so. I'm sick of doing all the donkey work. Christ, the number of times I've flown backwards and forwards between the airfield and this bloody island."

"Don't make it sound like such an ordeal." She laughed, leaning forward and wiping condensation from the windscreen with the back of her hand. "You love it when you're here."

"I do," he agreed. "It's going back to that dead place that I can't stand."

A narrow dirt track curved away from the end of the airstrip and disappeared between two low, dunelike hills. Brigid drove onto the rough track and followed it around to the right. Sandwiched uncomfortably between Peter and Danny, Michael looked out through the windscreen and saw that they were approaching the billowing cloud of smoke he'd seen from the other end of the runway. They rounded another corner and pulled up behind the whitewashed cottage which had been visible from the air where a short, athletic-looking man was standing, pumping up the tires of another car. He stopped what he was doing and looked up as the jeep approached.

"Here we go, home," Brigid announced as she turned off the engine. "What you doing, Richard? Coming in or going straight back?"

"I'm knackered. I've told the others I'm stopping here tonight," he answered. "There's not a lot of point trying to get back until morning. I'd rather stay here anyway."

Once Peter was out, Michael was also able to get out of the jeep. He stretched his legs. Although short, the drive had been cramped and uncomfortable. The man who had been working on the other car walked over to him and held out his hand. Michael shook it. His grip was unexpectedly strong.

"Harry Stayt," the man said brightly. "How you doing?"

"Good, I think," he replied, feeling slightly overwhelmed. "I'm Michael. This looks like quite a place you've found here. I didn't think that I'd get to see anywhere like this again."

To his embarrassment Michael found that talking coherently had suddenly become stupidly difficult. This was such a quiet, and unremarkable place and yet he was struggling to take everything in. It wasn't the location that had affected him or the physical appearance of the island, which was at once very different to the decayed land he'd left behind and at the same time not at all what he'd expected. It was the atmosphere and the attitude of the people he'd met so far that had taken him by surprise. They seemed to be amazingly relaxed and at ease. They were standing outside, talking freely, unconcerned by the level of their voices and not looking constantly over their shoulders.

"I'll tell you something," Harry said, "this place is the business. As soon as we got here I knew it. Once we get it cleared up and get everyone else out here we'll be set for life."

Michael didn't respond. He just stood still and listened to the wind and breathed in the air. Apart from the occasional waft of smoke from the fire nearby, everything smelled relatively pure and fresh. The sickly stench of death and decay which tainted the rest of the country was far less prevalent here. There was still a trace of it in the air, but it was much weaker than he'd become used to.

"Is there much left to do?" he asked.

"Not really," he replied. "All that's left now is the big one."

"The big one?"

"Danvers Lye."

"What the hell's that?"

"The village. They have told you about the village, haven't they? We're going to start clearing it."

"They told us about it. When?"

"Next couple of days, probably. We might even try and make a start tomorrow now there's a few more of us here."

Michael heard another engine approaching. He took a few steps to his right to look around the side of the cottage where another road stretched out away from the front of the building. A pickup truck was moving toward them, but it drove past the cottage and carried on toward the plume of the smoke rising a short distance away.

"Who's that?" he asked.

"Bruce Fry and Jim Harper," Harry answered. "They've been cleaning up."

"Cleaning up?"

Harry walked after the truck and toward the smoke and Michael followed him. They reached the top of another low hill and looked down into a natural hollow. There was a bonfire burning at the bottom of the dip, and the truck was parked on the other side.

"It's the only sensible way of doing this, really," Harry explained as they watched the two men climb out of the truck. Both of them were dressed in protective overalls, fishing waders, and rubber gloves.

"Doing what?"

One of the two men acknowledged Michael and Harry, then went around to the rear of the truck and dropped the back down. Between them they began to drag bodies from a pile on the bed of the vehicle and dumped them unceremoniously into the flames.

"These are mostly just the ones we've found lying around. We've got rid of about thirty so far," Harry explained as he turned around and began to walk back toward the cottage. "Only another few hundred to go!"

Michael stood and watched the fire for a while longer, staring deep into the flames. If he looked carefully he could definitely make out charred bones—skulls, hands, and feet were particularly distinct—and there were scraps of partially burned clothing around the edges of the pyre. Eventually he turned away and jogged after Harry.

"There are six of you here, aren't there?" he asked as he caught up with him.

"That's right."

"So where are the other two, in the cottage?"

"No, they're out. They'll be back in a while. They're scouting around somewhere."

"Doing what?"

"Just checking the place over. Don't forget we've not been here that long," he said as he reached the back door of the small building. "We've managed to get quite a bit done already, but we wanted to get a little more muscle behind us before we tried anything too risky."

"Risky?" Michael repeated as he followed him into the dark kitchen of the cottage. The room was cramped and cluttered and the ceiling low. Through an open door he could see Danny and Peter sitting in an equally gloomy living room talking to Richard and Brigid.

"We've been taking things steady," Harry continued. "We need to be completely sure of what we're doing before we do anything we might regret."

"Such as?"

"Such as walking into Danvers Lye and getting our arses kicked by a hundred corpses."

"Point taken."

Michael walked into the living room. Although as poorly lit as the kitchen, the room was dry and relatively warm and was considerably more inviting and appealing than pretty much anywhere else he'd been in the last two months. It still didn't feel right, standing here in full view of the rest of the world like this and talking without a care as if nothing had ever happened. He felt nervous and on edge. What if there were bodies nearby?

"You okay, Mike?" Richard asked, noticing him standing in the corner.

"Fine," he replied. "I'm just a little . . ."

"Tired?"

Michael shook his head and struggled to think of the right word to properly convey how he was suddenly feeling. "Disorientated."

"You'll get used to it," Brigid smiled. "It won't take long."

Michael sat down on a comfortable armchair next to an unlit fire. Christ, it felt good to be able to sit down like this, he thought. He leaned back and stretched his legs out in front of him as he looked around at the others who were continuing to talk. At first he was content to sit and listen without taking an active part in the discussion. He'd been too active for too long now.

After a couple of minutes the conversation changed direction and tone. Another car pulled up outside and the final two island inhabitants entered the cottage, introducing themselves to the new arrivals as Tony Hyde and Gayle Spencer. The two of them had been out on reconnaissance all afternoon. They'd driven to the outskirts of Danvers Lye to check out the situation there in readiness for the cull of corpses which was inevitably going to begin at some point soon. They'd explained that they had been able to get closer to the village than they'd expected. Michael was confused.

"I don't understand," he said, looking up at Tony and Gayle, who were sitting opposite him. "How did you manage to get anywhere near the village, and why were you risking your necks out there anyway? Surely the bodies would have reacted to you just being that close to them?"

Gayle shook her head. "We think the behavior of some of the bodies here is changing."

"Changing?"

"We first noticed it yesterday," she said. "When we first arrived here everything was pretty much as we expected—we only had to cough and most of the bodies that were near started swarming around us."

"So what's different now?"

"When we got up yesterday we were expecting to have been surrounded by bodies because of the noise we'd made and the fire, and we'd pretty much decided to play it that way so we could try and get rid of a few of them. We figured we might as well try and draw them out gradually . . . you know, bring them to us rather than us running around after them? Anyway, when we got outside there was only a handful of them about. We got rid of them quick and we assumed that the rest just hadn't made it over to this side of the island yet."

Tony took over the story.

"Midmorning, three of us drove over to the village. We just wanted to see what we were up against and get an idea of the lay of the land. We stopped the car at the end of the main street and waited."

"What happened?"

"Now this is the weird part," Gayle continued. "The bloody things weren't reacting to us. At least, they weren't reacting how we thought they would. Some of them did and they came straight for us, but most of the others stayed out of the way. We managed to get a little closer and we could see them. But this is the weird part: it was like they were waiting for us. Hiding from us almost."

"Bullshit."

"I swear, we could see them waiting in the shadows and inside buildings that had been left open, but keeping out of our way."

"So what did you do?"

"Nothing," Tony said. "Christ, we didn't want to get too close. The last thing we wanted to do was antagonize them."

"Antagonize them? You don't think these things are about to roll over and give up?"

Brigid shook her head. "I think there's plenty of fight left in them."

"So what's changed?" Peter Guest asked.

"I've been thinking about this a lot," she replied, suddenly the focus of all attention. "I don't know what the rest of you have seen, but I've watched these things changing since the day they first got up and started walking around again. In the beginning they were just able to move, then they could hear and see, then they became more aggressive and now it looks like they've started to . . ."

"Think?" Michael anticipated when she paused.

"I suppose so. They've gained another level of control. It's a logical progression, if you can call any of this madness logical."

Michael looked around the room.

"I've seen something similar happening, but not to the extent you have. We've got a doctor with us and he told me that he thinks part of their brains survived the infection. It's like they're gradually coming around again, despite the fact that their bodies are falling apart. It's like they've been sedated, and now the drugs are starting to wear off."

"That's good then, isn't it?" Peter said. His mouth was dry

with nerves and he swallowed hard before speaking again. "Problem solved, eh? If they're going to be able to think and control themselves, then they're not going to be a threat to us, are they? They'll see it's not a fair contest and just sit there and rot."

"Possibly," Michael said cautiously, "but I don't think that them being a threat to us is the issue anymore."

"What are you talking about?"

"I've said all along that the bodies are driven by instinct. It's like they're being motivated and controlled at the most basic level. Each time there's been a noticeable change in their behavior, it's as if they've gained another layer of self-awareness."

"I don't know what you're on about," Peter complained.

"Have you seen how they sometimes fight with each other? It always seems to be completely unprovoked, doesn't it? But have you ever stopped and wondered why they do it? What have they got to gain from fighting? There's no class or status or other division among them, is there? They don't eat, they don't want shelter, they're not fighting over food or possessions."

"So what are you saying?" Brigid asked. "Why do they do it?"

"I think the only thing they've got left to fight for is survival. They're fighting just to continue to exist. It's self-preservation, and that's what we're seeing here. In a crowd of thousands, they'll take any number of us on. When they're in the minority, they'll hold back."

"I don't buy any of this," Peter said. "Just listen to yourself, will you? Can you hear what you're saying? Can you hear how stupid it sounds?"

"What I'm saying is the bodies aren't a threat to us, it's more that they're seeing us as a threat to them. And if they really are driven by instinct, then they'll do whatever they have to do to make sure they continue to survive."

27

Kelly had had enough. She'd been at the airfield for almost a day and couldn't take anymore. She'd listened to everything the others had said and she'd tried to understand and see things from their perspectives, but it was impossible. She knew there was no point holding on and that no matter what they promised they'd try and do for her and Kilgore, it was never going to happen. They were going to have enough trouble trying to look after themselves.

It was the waiting that hurt the most.

Kelly had been through fair share of hard times before. She'd cried her way through the first half of basic training like a bloody baby and she'd been stuck out on the battlefield staring down the barrel of the enemy's gun. She'd handled all of that and dealt with it well. As hard as it had been, she'd managed to get through it all, no matter how bad things got.

The difference today, she decided, was that everything was out of her control. She knew she couldn't fight or negotiate her way out of this situation. The end was a foregone conclusion and all she was doing was putting it off. She couldn't even close her eyes anymore without replaying the memory of all that had happened and remembering everything she'd lost.

Things had changed since she'd arrived at the airfield. It felt like she'd reached the end of the road. She'd watched the helicopter leave this afternoon and had realized that events were moving on without her now. She was an outsider, neither living nor dead. She couldn't go on like this.

Standing a little way short of the perimeter fence, she stared into the dead faces which stared back at her. The longer she stood there, the more violent and animated they became. They reached out for her, poked their bony fingers through the fence to get closer to her, ripped and tore at the other corpses getting in their way . . . but Kelly didn't care. She ripped off her face mask. And for a few precious moments the relief was overpowering.

Cool, fresh-tasting air flooded her lungs, making her feel stronger and more human than she'd felt in weeks. She could smell the grass again and the autumn air tasted a thousand times better than she remembered. The seconds ticked by, and it began to seem that the impossible might have happened. Was she immune? By some incredible chance, did she share the same physical traits which had allowed the people in the building behind her to survive? She didn't dare believe it at first. What were the odds against her managing to survive like this? In a delirious instant her mind was filled with visions of actually making it to the island and living again . . .

And then it started.

From out of nowhere the pain gripped hold of her like a

hand wrapped tight around her neck. The inside of her throat began to swell. She stayed standing for as long as she could until, with her eyes bulging, she fell back onto the grass and stared deep into the heavy gray sky overhead, seeing nothing.

Thirty seconds later it was over.

28

The fact that he found himself lying in a warm and comfortable bed for the first time in weeks wasn't helping Michael sleep. Danny Talbot, in comparison, was snoring away in his narrow bunk on the other side of the small, square bedroom. It was almost midnight. Michael's head was pounding and he wished that he could find a way to switch off and disconnect for a while. It was impossible. If he wasn't being distracted by the noise coming from the others talking downstairs then he was thinking about the island and how he had finally managed to get there. When he stopped thinking about the island he found himself thinking about the changing behavior of the bodies, and when he stopped thinking about that, he started to think about Emma. Once he'd started he couldn't stop thinking about her. The distance between them felt immense, almost immeasurable in the circumstances, and it hurt. He knew that she was more than capable of looking after herself—Christ, she'd looked after *him* enough recently—but that didn't make it any easier. He felt responsible for her. More than that, he knew that he loved her, although he hadn't yet dared tell her, and he was reasonably confident that she loved him too, as much as anyone could love anyone else in this fucked-up, emotionally starved world. The distance between them made him realize the full depth and strength of the feelings he had for Emma which, for the most part, he'd kept subdued.

Lying on the bed in the dark was pointless. He obviously wasn't going to be able to sleep. Already fully dressed, he got up and crept back down the narrow staircase to where Brigid, Peter, Jim, and Gayle were sitting in the kitchen.

"You all right?" Brigid asked.

"I'm okay. Couldn't sleep."

"Coffee?"

He nodded. The kettle was already boiling on a portable gas stove, filling the room with steam and heat.

"Where are the others?" he asked, looking around and trying not to yawn.

"Danny, Tony, and Richard are upstairs; Harry and Bruce are outside."

"Outside? What the hell are they doing out there?"

"Keeping watch."

"Why? Has something happened?"

"No, we're just not taking any chances, that's all."

"Bloody hell, just being outside would have been taking a chance where I've just come from."

"It's different here, you'll get used to it."

Michael stepped over to the window and looked out. He could make out movement a few meters up ahead. It was too quick and purposeful to be anything other than one of the others.

"Here you go," Brigid said, handing him a mug of coffee.

"Cheers," he said, turning back to the window. He could clearly see one of the men outside now. Whichever one of them it was, he was walking back toward the cottage. The door creaked open and Harry Stayt leaned inside.

"Okay, Harry?" Gayle asked.

"Bloody cold," he complained.

"Anything happening out there?"

"Saw a couple of bodies about half an hour ago, that's all."

"Give you any trouble?" Michael wondered. "I mean, did they go for you or were they like the others earlier?"

"They went for us."

"I don't understand. Why do some of them still react like that when others don't?" asked Jim. A young man, tonight he looked aged beyond his years.

"Who knows," Michael replied. "My guess is it depends on what condition their brains and bodies are in. Some of them are more decayed than others, so it follows some will be in a worse mental state than others."

"Bloody hell, they're all in a bad mental state, aren't they? They're dead!" Harry grinned. "Look, sorry to spoil the party, but I saw the windows steaming up and guessed you'd put the kettle on. Any chance of a drink?"

Brigid stood up and spooned coffee into two more mugs. She poured on boiling water, stirred the drinks, and then pushed them over toward Harry, who picked them up with one hand.

He was carrying a blade of some description in the other hand. Harry noticed Michael looking at it.

"Bloody useful this is," he explained as he lifted the weapon up into the dull light. It was a long and ornately decorated sword. The other survivors watched him raise it with cautious eyes. "I nicked it from a museum a few weeks back. It's the best thing I've found for getting rid of bodies."

"Put that damn thing down, will you?" Brigid said, scolding him like she was his mother. "You're like a bloody kid with a new toy. I used to spend half my time locking up idiots who carried things like that."

Michael looked puzzled. Harry explained.

"Brigid was a copper," he said as he turned and walked back out. "And she still thinks she's on duty!"

"Mind if I come out with you?" Michael asked, surprising Harry.

"You can if you want. If you'd rather spend your first night here out in the dark with me and Bruce instead of tucked up here in a warm bed then be my guest!"

"Can't sleep anyway," Michael grumbled as he zipped up his jacket and followed Harry out into the darkness.

"I don't know why they get so wound up about this sword," Harry said as they walked away from the cottage. "I don't know about you, but I'd rather carry a weapon like this than a gun."

"I've never got on with guns," Michael agreed. "They're too bloody noisy and you have to be a damn good shot to take the bodies out. Miss the head and they'll just keep coming at you."

"Damn right, and by the time you've got rid of one of

them there'll be another couple of hundred following close behind trying to see what all the noise was about."

"You stick to your sword, mate."

"Bruce," Harry shouted into the darkness. "Oi, Bruce, where
are you?"

"Over here," a disembodied voice replied from the direction of the small hill which overlooked the pyre Michael had
seen earlier. The remains of the fire were still smoldering. He
could see the faintest orange glow in the darkness.

"Two of us coming over," Harry shouted back. He lowered
his voice again to whisper to Michael. "Didn't want him thinking you were one of them and trying to take you out!"

Michael managed half a smile. "Cheers."

They found Bruce crouched over the embers of the fire,
warming his hands. Earlier in the evening they'd stoked up the
flames with wood and other general rubbish but the remains of
the fire's original fuel could still clearly be seen. Michael found
it a little unnerving to see so many charred bones. It looked like
the mass graves he'd seen in history books.

"How you doing, Mike?" Bruce asked cheerfully as they
approached.

"I'm good," he answered. "Just sick of sitting in there and
staring at the walls."

"I know what you mean. Guess we've all done enough of
that recently to last a lifetime."

"That's why we keep volunteering to come out here," Harry
explained. "I'm not going to be able to relax until I know we've
got rid of all the bodies here and the rest of our people are on
their way over from the mainland. I just want to get it done now."

"How were they all doing when you saw them?" Bruce asked. "Jackie still keeping them in line?"

"She seemed to be."

"Give them a week or so and I reckon they'll all be over here," Harry said, yawning.

"Why should it take that long?" Michael asked. "I'm with you two, I'd rather sit around drinking coffee *after* we've got rid of the bodies."

"We just need to get the village cleared," Bruce said.

"So we should start tomorrow, shouldn't we? There are enough of us here now, surely."

Bruce sounded less confident now. "I'm not sure. Maybe we should—"

"Let's be honest," Michael interrupted. "We all instinctively make excuses and try to put things off. The sooner we do this and get it done, the sooner we get on with our lives."

"I know that, but clearing the village is going to be a big job and there's a lot riding on it. We need to make sure we get it right the first time."

"I agree, so we make sure we plan it right. We should get in there quick and strike, then get out again. After that we'll regroup then go back in and do the same again. And again and again until the job's done."

"So why are you so keen all of a sudden?" Harry asked.

"Partly because I just want it done, also because of what I heard today," Michael answered, kicking at the ashes on the ground next to his feet, sending a shower of sparks up into the air. "I've watched those things steadily changing, almost from day to day. I know there's going to come a time when they've rotted down to nothing and they don't get in our way, but everything I've seen and heard has made me think things might get more difficult before they get any easier. The dead are starting to watch us and pay attention to what we're doing."

"What exactly are you getting at?"

"I think that if we don't make a move now, then it might be the bodies hunting us out, not the other way round."

29

The first light of morning crept across the airfield painfully slow, almost as if it didn't want to be seen. From the top of the control tower Clare stood and watched the darkness gradually disappear. It looked blustery and cold outside but the building isolated her from the brunt of the almost wintry conditions. From where she was standing she could see right across to the fence and the hordes of constantly moving corpses beyond. As the light improved she was able to make out the body of Kelly Harcourt lying on its back in the overgrown grass, just meters away from the dead.

"You can understand why she did it, can't you?" Emma said, standing just behind her.

"Such a shame, though," Clare answered quietly, her voice disconsolate and low. "I liked her. She was nice, much nicer than Kilgore."

"You can't even begin to imagine what the poor girl was

going through. You don't know how you'd react if you were in that position, do you?"

"Makes you realize how lucky you are, doesn't it?"

"Suppose so."

"We are lucky, aren't we?"

Emma couldn't answer. On the face of it, they had survived where millions had fallen and that had to make them lucky, didn't it? But every day things seemed to be getting harder, and she couldn't help thinking that in many ways it would have been easier just to have died on the first morning and not known anything.

"Of course we're lucky," she said. "We're lucky to be here, and we're lucky to have a chance of getting away from all this."

Clare was only half-listening. "So are we just going to leave her there?" she asked, staring at Kelly's body on the ground. "Shouldn't we move her?"

The sudden arrival of Cooper and Jackie Soames bursting into the room interrupted the conversation. Emma could tell from the expressions on their faces that they were not happy.

"Has anyone seen Keele?" Jackie asked, looking around the room hopefully. Her already red face looked even redder and more flushed than usual.

"I saw him earlier," Emma said.

"Do you know where he is now?"

"No, have you tried looking . . . ?"

She didn't bother finishing her sentence, Jackie and Cooper were already walking away. Donna, coming the other way, unintentionally blocked their way.

"Any luck?" Cooper asked her.

"Not yet," she replied. "He's not in here, then?"

"He's probably hiding in the outbuildings somewhere," Jackie suggested. "He's done that before, the cowardly little bastard."

Jackie and Cooper bustled out of the room again leaving Donna standing alone by the open door. Emma was confused.

"What the hell's going on?"

"Gary Keele's done a runner," Donna explained. "We can't find him."

"What's he running from?"

"Cooper wants him to try and get the plane moving."

"And?"

"And that's it. Fucker's had a panic attack. He suffers with his nerves apparently. Pathetic. I hate blokes like him, I really do. They're all bloody talk and no action. Apparently he's spent the last couple of weeks making noises to some of this lot about how he's going to be the big hero and fly them all to safety, but now the time's come he's bottled it."

"But he can't have left the airfield, can he?"

"Not without getting himself ripped apart or letting a couple of thousand bodies in here he can't."

"So what happens if they can't get him to fly the plane?" Clare asked. It was a sensible question.

"Then we'll have to try and get to the island by helicopter, I suppose. Richard will end up making loads more flights and we'll be limited on the amount of stuff we can take over with us. We'll still get there, it'll just take a lot longer and be a lot more complicated, that's all."

"But what if—?"

"We'll get there," Donna assured her.

"What the hell are you doing in here?" Phil Croft asked. Smoking one of his last few precious cigarettes and limping slowly through the shadows between the empty airfield buildings, the doctor had stumbled across Keele sitting alone in the corner of a musty waiting room. By chance, Croft had spotted him moving as he'd walked past a cobweb-covered window.

Keele didn't answer. He kept still, hoping the doctor would get the message and disappear, but Croft wasn't going anywhere.

"I'm just trying to get some space," Keele answered eventually keeping his eyes fixed on the ground in front of him.

"Christ," Croft laughed, "the population of this country has been reduced from millions to probably less than a few hundred people and you're trying to get some space! Bloody hell, mate, if you want space there's plenty of it out there. You don't need to hide away in here to be on your own."

"Just piss off."

"Fine."

Croft was about to leave when he glanced out of the window and noticed Cooper and a number of other people moving from building to building. He put two and two together and reached the obvious conclusion that they were looking for the man he'd just found. Out of the corner of his eye he noticed that Keele was watching him anxiously.

"So how long were you planning to hide in here for?" the doctor asked, still looking out of the window.

"I'm not hiding. I told you, I—"

"Come on, cut the crap. They're looking for you, aren't they?"

Keele didn't want to say anything, but he forced himself to spit out an answer. "I'm not hiding."

"Yes, you are. So I guess what I heard someone saying last night is true—you're too scared to fly the plane."

"I'm not scared."

"Oh, right," Croft sneered. "So let me see if I've got this right, you're here sitting in the dark, on your own, in the corner of this dusty shit-hole because you want some space, and you're not hiding from the others, you're just choosing not to let them know where you are, is that it?"

"Piss off," Keele said again.

"Keele," Croft continued, turning away from the window to face the man in the corner, "let me just tell you something, and I want to make sure you understand what I'm saying, okay? I'm a doctor and I've spent years looking after other people and making sure they get better when they're sick. Things have changed now and if I'm completely honest, I'm not that bothered about anyone else anymore. I'm only really interested in myself and I tell you now, you'll do whatever you have to do to get us out of here because if you don't I'll break your fucking legs."

"You don't scare me—"

"You *will* fly the plane to the island because if you don't, I swear I will kill you," the doctor said in a calm and emotionless voice. "I haven't come this far to have my chances blown by some stupid, cowardly little fucker like you. Understand? Is that clear enough for you?"

Keele didn't respond. Croft glared at him, then turned and

walked out of the building, slamming the door behind him. Still smoking his cigarette he began the slow and painful walk back to the observation tower. He passed Donna on the way.

"Have you seen . . . ?" she started to ask.

"He's in there," he replied, pointing back toward the building he'd just left.

30

Richard Lawrence took off from Cormansey just after ten o'clock. The nine survivors remaining on the island stood at the end of the runway and watched the helicopter until its bright lights had disappeared into the gray morning gloom. They hoped it would return later in the day as planned, bringing with it the plane and at least another fifteen people. Michael hoped that Emma would be one of them.

During the long watch the previous night he had managed to convince Harry and Bruce to listen seriously to his concerns about the changing condition of the bodies. So much remained unpredictable and it made sense to take action sooner rather than later. Never one for diplomacy, Michael had expressed his opinions in blunt, direct, and honest terms to the rest of them over breakfast and, apart from some initial nervous reluctance, they had been largely receptive. Harry had pointed out the immediate practicalities of their situation, and that proved to be the deciding factor. With the arrival yesterday of Michael and the others there were already too many of them on the island to continue to shelter comfortably in the single small cottage. Clearing the bodies away now would make their lives immeasurably easier.

Armed with sticks, axes, clubs, and blades of varying descriptions, the small group traveled from the cottage toward the village of Danvers Lye in a convoy of two cars and the pickup truck. This was the first real opportunity since arriving that Michael, Danny, and Peter had had to see anything of the island. Much of it was barren and rocky, covered in patchy grass and bracken. The ocean was almost always in view on one side or the other and plumes of cold gray water seemed to constantly be shooting into the air as waves pounded the shore. Trees were few and far between and the wind howled across the weather-beaten landscape. A basic network of rudimentary roads connected the various buildings, most of which were small cottages and houses; some made of old gray stone, others more modern in appearance. There was a one-classroom school, a farm over on the southwest of the island, and he'd seen a few abandoned fishing boats dotted along the shore, but other than that Michael struggled to imagine how the inhabitants of Cormansey might have earned a living. This land was harsh and unforgiving and life would surely have been difficult at the best of times.

Michael felt increasingly nervous as they reached the village. He stared at the motley collection of unkempt buildings and his unease increased when he realized that this was the first time he'd ever gone out actively looking for bodies to destroy. Until now his time had been spent either hiding from them or defending himself and Emma against them. Although he knew the corpses would probably offer very little in the way of serious resistance, the trepidation he felt was substantial. And, judging from the expressions around him, he wasn't the only one who felt that way.

Michael traveled in the jeep at the front of the convoy with Brigid and Jim. He was hot. Everyone was dressed in boots and gloves and either boiler suits or strong waterproofs taken from the empty homes of long-dead fishermen. The advanced decay of the bodies had now reached such a stage that their destruction, removal, and disposal was inevitably going to be a bloody, greasy, and gruesome, germ-filled affair. The rotting shells would be ripe with disease. No one relished the prospect of close physical contact.

"Stop here," he said when they were just short of the turn onto the road which ran through the heart of Danvers Lye. "I think we're better off leaving the vehicles here. We don't want to go too far in and find we've got ourselves cut off."

Brigid stopped the jeep. The other car pulled up behind her and the truck stopped alongside it. They all got out of their vehicles and regrouped in the middle of the road.

"So what now? Do we just go marching in there?" Jim asked. Michael shook his head.

"No, I don't think so. Maybe we should take it slow and try and clear the buildings one at a time?"

"Sounds sensible."

"Look," Gayle Spencer whispered, "a welcoming party."

Alerted by the sound of the engines, a number of bodies had already dragged themselves out into the open and were moving along the street toward the group with obvious intent. Harry Stayt readied his sword.

"We knew there were going to be a few like this, didn't we?" he said as he anxiously swapped the blade from hand to hand.

"We should try and flush these out," suggested Bruce. "Let's make a bit of noise and get all of the bodies that are still reacting like this out into the open."

"Makes sense," agreed Brigid. "What have you got in mind?"

Bruce ducked into the front of the pickup truck and reached across and leaned on the horn. The ugly, unexpected noise echoed across the otherwise quiet island, so loud that for a moment it seemed even to silence the relentless sound of the waves crashing against the gray-stone walls of the rudimentary harbor just a couple of hundred meters away.

"I'll make a start," Harry said purposefully. He strode forward to head off the gangly bodies staggering the other way, his sword gripped tightly in his hand and raised ready to strike.

"Does anyone else get the impression he actually enjoys this?" Jim said quietly. "Sick bastard."

"At least he's trying," Gayle snapped. "We're just stood here looking at him."

Michael watched as Harry neared the first two bodies. Like an expert swordsman—which he clearly was not—he lifted the blade above his head and swung it round in a long and surprisingly graceful arc, managing somehow to effortlessly sever the head of the nearest cadaver. The body crumbled to the ground instantly, its decapitated head thumping down onto the tarmac at his feet like a rotten peach. Another flash of the blade and the second corpse was also felled, its head removed with equal speed but far less precision.

"I'm behind you, Harry," Jim shouted as Harry marched forward with steadily increasing confidence. He jogged down the street after his sword-wielding friend, keeping a safe distance back from the razor-sharp blade. Ahead of them were six more figures, and Harry quickly hacked them down. Jim, Michael, and Gayle began to collect up the bloody remains of his handiwork which lay scattered around the street. Moving quickly they dragged the corpses over to an area of scrubland on the other side of the road and began to pile them up.

The emaciated remains of Cormansey's most senior police officer took Harry by surprise, lurching out from behind a high wooden fence and knocking him off-balance momentarily. With one gloved hand he pushed the body away, sending it stumbling backward. It tripped over the twitching torso of another dead islander and fell heavily on its backside. Seizing the opportunity Harry lifted his sword and chopped down at the corpse, slicing the top of its head clean off, the blade following through and hitting the ground. He winced as the vibration of the impact of the tip of the sword on the tarmac traveled the length of his aching arms. Breathless, he moved on to the next body and then the next and then the next, driven on by a curious combination of adrenaline and revulsion. Bruce and Brigid stood together and watched from a distance, listening as Harry's blade whistled and sliced through the cold air.

"That's it, Harry," Jim shouted. Suddenly aware that the clumsy movement around him had stopped, Harry stood still and looked up and down the street, panting hard with effort.

The previously unremarkable gray village street was now awash with blood and gore, littered with fallen corpses. That seemed to be all of them for now. He couldn't see any other moving bodies.

"So where are the rest?" he asked, still looking around. "This can't be it, surely. There should have been about a hundred of them at least."

Michael walked over to where the other man stood, staring into the shadowy buildings on either side of the street as he moved slowly along. "They're hiding from you and your bloody sword."

"You've got to be kidding," Harry laughed. "They're not hiding!"

Michael pointed into the nearest building, a small, glass-fronted shop.

"Well, some of them are," he said. "Look."

Christ, Harry thought, Michael was right. He could see several bodies inside the building, gathered together at the other end from the door. Were they actively trying to keep out of sight? The door was open so they weren't trapped. What the hell was going on?

"So what do we do?"

"Go in there and flush them out, I suppose."

Michael was momentarily distracted by a sudden burst of light and noise which came from the scrubland behind them. Brigid had doused the pile of body parts with fuel and had set light to them. Bright orange flames pierced the gray gloom.

"That might drag a few more of them out into the open,"

he said. Harry walked across the road and pressed his face to the window of a butcher's shop.

"There are only a couple of them in here," he said. He could see at least two dark figures shuffling behind a counter which was still piled high with rancid, maggot-ridden meat.

"Let's see what happens, then," Michael said. He pushed the stiff door open and the bodies immediately began to move. Unexpectedly, they were retreating farther back into the shadows.

"Are they becoming territorial?" Harry asked. Michael shook his head.

"I doubt it. Do you think that's what's left of the butcher and his wife?"

"No." Harry scowled. "That's not what I meant. I just wonder if they're aware of their surroundings. Are they really just keeping out of our way or are they standing their ground? Are they just sheltering in there?

"I don't think they're sheltering," he said as he shoved his way through the door. "Christ, look at them. They're not interested in keeping warm or keeping dry."

Michael stopped before going any farther inside.

"What's the matter?" Harry asked, immediately concerned.

"Look."

Harry saw that the two bodies had suddenly stopped their clumsy retreat. "What the hell's going on?"

"Like I said yesterday, on their own they might not be much of a threat to us anymore, but it looks like we're still a threat to them."

"Come on, let's just get this done."

"Hold on," Michael said, grabbing hold of Harry's arm. "Take it easy. We've got them cornered. We don't know how they'll react if we just—"

"I've had enough of this," Harry said, shrugging him off and pushing his way into the shop. The two bodies shuffled forward slightly, then stopped again.

"Careful," Michael said, just behind him. Harry wasn't listening. He marched toward the back of the shop and the nearest of the two bodies immediately launched itself at him. Taken by surprise, he managed to impale the creature on his sword, its putrefied innards dripping out onto the floor from the gash in its gut. Oblivious to the wound, it grabbed hold of Harry's shoulders and pulled itself forward, dragging itself farther onto the antique weapon and forcing the blade out through the small of its back. Surprised by its speed, Harry didn't fully realize what was happening until his right hand and forearm had disappeared into the grotesque cadaver's decaying chest cavity. He began to gag and choke. The stench was overpowering.

"Get this fucking thing off me," he wailed as he pushed the body away with his left hand and struggled to free the right. The creature was flailing its arms around his face, trying to grab hold of him again. The other rotting figure pushed its way past the first and rushed toward Michael. As Harry squirmed free from his attacker and kicked the empty shell back across the room and into the window, Michael began to repeatedly punch the face of the body now attacking him. Each hard contact made the corpse's head rock back on weak shoulders before instantly rebounding and drooping forward again. Again and again he struck out, and each time the condition of the head deteriorated further. Its features gradually became unrecognizable as cold, congealed blood, dripping flesh, and brittle bone were ground together. Splits in the weak and rotten skin exposed the cheek and jaw bones and Michael hoped that the continuous beating would eventually smash and mangle what remained of the despicable thing's brain as it rattled round its head. Harry managed to push the first body to the ground and stomped on its head, crushing its skull, then grabbed the second corpse by the scruff of the neck and pulled it away from Michael.

"I'll sort it," he said as he lifted the sword, then plunged it down into one of its eyes.

As quickly as it had begun, the sudden frenetic activity in the shop ended. Breathing hard, Harry and Michael stood side by side and looked down at the gruesome pile of remains at their feet.

"Answers a few questions, doesn't it?" Michael panted. "They're not just going to give up and roll over, are they? Those two went for us with as much force as ever. Difference was they had more about them. They definitely had more control than usual. They were keeping out of our way until we took away their options and backed them into a corner. It was attack us or be attacked."

31

By midafternoon Cormansey was again shrouded in heavy mist. Working their way building by building through the dark streets of Danvers Lye, the nine survivors made good progress with their impromptu cull. The group had naturally divided into three sets of three; two of the trios concentrated on emptying buildings while the third, with Brigid taking charge, followed behind and cleared the bodies, picking them up from where they'd been unceremoniously dumped in the street and driving them back in the truck to the roaring fire still burning at the entrance to the village.

Michael, Harry, and Peter Guest had reached one of the larger, more modern buildings, three-quarters of the way along the otherwise quaint and traditional street. An unusual but practical combination of village stores, post office, gift shop, hardware store, and supermarket, the shop had almost certainly been one of the focal points of the island's small community before it had been destroyed. And on that first morning some eight weeks ago, it had clearly been a busy place. Michael stood and leaned against the dirty glass, covered his eyes, and peered into the building. He could see several corpses lying still on the ground, and others moving nearby.

"Problem?" Peter asked, trying to look over his shoulder without getting too close.

"There are a few of them in there," Michael replied, his face pressed hard against the window. "I can see them hovering around the back."

Harry tried the door. He pushed it open slightly, then it jammed. The slender opening allowed the fermented stench inside the building to seep out like a noxious cloud. He turned his head away in disgust at the sickly sweet, overpowering smell of death which filled his nostrils.

"Bloody hell," he complained, screwing up his face.

"Well, what do you expect?" Michael asked. "Christ, that door's not been opened in two months. It's full of bodies in there."

"The light's fading," Peter said anxiously, stating the blatantly obvious. "We need to get a move on."

Michael wouldn't be rushed. He was struggling to see what was happening inside the shop. The place was fairly large and he wanted to get a basic appreciation of its layout before he risked going inside.

"Pete," he said, looking over his shoulder, "do me a favor, will you? Go and bring one of the cars over here."

Glad to have been given something relatively easy and safe to do, Peter jogged back over to where they'd left the cars. The keys had been left in the ignition of an old but well-maintained silver hatchback. He climbed in and started the engine, then moved slowly through the misty rain until he was level again with the building where Michael and Harry were waiting. Under instruction from Michael, in a few clumsy movements he managed to turn the car around almost ninety degrees, leaving the lights shining into the shop on full-beam. Michael pressed his face against the glass again. Because of the dirt and dust much of the light was immediately reflected back but there was some improvement.

"Better?" Harry asked, also struggling to see inside.

"A little," Michael answered. "I can see at least six bodies moving, but I think there are more. Can't be sure how many."

"Where?"

"Right at the back. Bloody things are keeping themselves out of sight again."

As he spoke a single corpse broke ranks and slammed against the glass, smashing its fists against the window. Surprised, Michael tripped back and caught his breath, his heart thumping furiously. The sound the creature was making was curious and unexpected. One hand thumped against the glass like moldy fruit, leaving a greasy residue behind. The flesh on the other hand had deteriorated away to nothing, bare bone clattering against the window.

"Come on," Harry muttered as he watched the pitiful figure, holding his sword ready again. "Let's get this done."

He shoved the door open and the three of them went inside. They stood just inside the entrance to the shop, illuminated from behind by the car's headlights. The body by the window immediately began to move toward them, tripping through the rubbish on the ground. Grabbing its diseased head in one gloved hand, Michael rammed it up against the nearest wall, managing to wedge it awkwardly between a tall drinks dispenser and a metal magazine rack. He plunged the end of an already bloody crowbar he'd been carrying all afternoon into its left temple, pulled it quickly out again, then watched as the corpse slid to the ground.

"Just look at this, will you?" Peter whispered nervously, pointing straight ahead. The far end of the building was full of constant, shuffling movement. In the half-light it was impossible to be sure how many bodies they now faced.

"So what do you think?" Harry wondered. "Should we just go for it or—"

The movement of the bodies rendered his question unnecessary before he could finish asking it. One of the them started moving toward him and then, spurred on by the actions of the first, others followed. The corpses began to stumble towards them *en masse,* moving almost like a pack, filling the building with sudden noise as the clumsy dead collided with fixtures, fittings, and each other as they dragged themselves toward the three men.

"Spread out!" Michael yelled, concerned that he might be caught by Harry's sword in the melee which was inevitably about to unfold. "Spread out and hit the damn things until there's nothing left standing but us!"

He lifted the crowbar again and ran deeper into the building until he reached the first body coming their way. In one swift movement he swung the crowbar up and forced it into the creature's head, shoving it up through its chin and deep into its decaying brain.

To Michael's right Harry was cutting his way through the crowd with his now familiar ferocity and style. Behind and to

229

his left, however, Peter was struggling. He'd so far managed to avoid just about all direct confrontation with the bodies but now there was no escape. He carried with him a cricket bat, and now he cursed his stupid and inappropriate choice of weapon.

"What do I do?" he screamed as the nearest body lashed out at him with clawlike hands. He didn't really expect an answer, but in the midst of the close-confined chaos and mayhem he got two.

"Hit them, you fucking idiot!" Harry shouted at him.

"And keep hitting them until they stop moving," Michael added between striking out at another two bodies. "Just do it!"

Trembling with nerves, Peter instinctively held the cricket bat as if he were at the crease in a Sunday afternoon match. Anticipating the lurching speed of the hideous body which stumbled toward him, he took two steps down an imaginary wicket and swung the bat as if he was trying to hit the ball back over the bowler's head toward the boundary rope. The wood connected with the underside of the creature's jaw, severing the remains of its spinal cord and practically knocking its head off its shoulders. It flew back into a freezer full of spoiled food and lay still.

More through luck than judgment, Peter eventually managed to dispose of another body. In the time it took him, Harry had cut down four more and Michael another two. A total of thirteen of the wretched things had been destroyed.

After dragging more than twenty bodies out of the foul-smelling building Michael, Harry, and Peter allowed themselves a short break. The long day's work so far had been physically and mentally exhausting. Their eyes had adjusted to the low light indoors and, with the car still providing limited illumination, they searched through the remains of the shop, picking through the wreckage as if they were high street shoppers on a Saturday afternoon looking for bargains.

Michael leaned against a wall and flicked through the faded pages of a lifestyle magazine filled with images of beautiful, immaculately presented men and women. Stupidly and pointlessly, for a second he was aware of his own scruffy, blood-soaked appearance.

"Look at this," he mumbled to anyone who would listen. "Just look at this."

Harry stood nearby drinking a can of beer and eating a bar of chocolate which was only out of date by a couple of weeks.

"What?" he asked, his mouth full of food.

"All of this shit," Michael replied, turning the magazine slightly so that Harry could see what he'd been looking at. It was a double-page spread of photographs from some celebrity wedding or other. He recognized some of the faces in the pictures, but he struggled for a second to remember their names or what it was they used to do.

"What about it?"

"Just hard to believe, isn't it? Hard to believe that this kind of thing used to matter. Christ, thousands of people used to buy this crap every week, now there's probably not even a thousand people left alive."

Harry stepped through the rubbish to stand closer to Michael and get a better view of the pictures.

"She was beautiful, wasn't she?" he said quietly, pointing at

231

the face of a television actress he remembered. "I had a thing for her."

"She's probably like that lot now," Michael half-joked, gesturing toward the pile of corpses in the middle of the street that Brigid and the others were busy carting away. "Hey, remember this?" he asked as he flicked back a few pages to a film review section he'd just passed.

"Bloody hell, yes," Harry answered, his eyes darting around the spread of photographs from a long-forgotten film. "Never got round to seeing that."

"It wasn't that good," Michael volunteered. "I saw it about a week before everything went tits-up. Anyway, you might still get to see it. If we can get the electricity supply working here we could fetch a projector from the mainland and show as many films as we can get our hands on. We'll paint the side of one of the buildings white and we'll project against it. It'll be like a drive in, but without the cars. We'll—"

"No we won't," Harry sighed, shaking his head. "Nice idea, mate, but it's never going to happen, is it? If we're lucky we'll get something set up so that we can watch videos or DVDs if we really want to." He took another magazine from the rack and began to leaf through its pages. He wiped an unexpected tear away from the corner of his eye. "Jesus," he said quietly, "I'd forgotten about all of this. I hadn't thought about any of it until now."

Michael continued to look through his magazine as he thought about Harry's words. He understood completely what he was saying. He'd spent the last two months either running at breakneck speed or sitting still and hiding in terrified silence.

This was the first time they'd been able to move around freely. This was the first time that any of them had been afforded the luxury of being able to stop and think and remember without having to constantly look over their shoulders in fear of attack from the seemingly endless hordes of bodies which plagued them.

Looking back was painful. It hurt more than any of them might have expected it to, but now that they had suddenly been allowed to remember, all three of them found it was impossible to stop. They picked through the musty contents of the shop with mixed feelings of warm nostalgia and heavy, heartbreaking sadness and grief. For weeks the speed and magnitude of the events unfolding around them had prevented them from dwelling on the memories of what they'd lost. Since arriving on the island the fear had reduced and the pace and urgency of life had slowed down. They finally had a chance to grieve.

On the other side of the room Peter was sitting on a counter, crying. Not just sobbing or sniffing quietly to himself, he was wailing with pain, almost screaming with the sudden release of previously pent-up and suppressed emotions. Tony Hyde was walking past the front of the shop. The noise which Peter was making was so loud that it made him stop and walk toward the building. Concerned, he leaned inside.

"Everything okay?"

Harry nodded. Michael walked over to Peter.

"All right, Pete?" he asked pointlessly. Peter looked up with tears pouring down his face. In his hands Michael saw that he was holding a small toy. He couldn't see exactly what it was. A car perhaps? Some kind of spinning top or model spaceship?

Whatever it was, he was staring at it as if it was suddenly the most important thing in the world. He wouldn't put it down. He wouldn't let it go.

It was almost an hour later before Peter had composed himself enough to be able to talk to the others again. Even now, as he sat next to Michael on the bonnet of the pickup truck and stared into the mass of burning bodies a short distance away, occasional tears still rolled down his cheeks.

"It's like when you shake a bottle of beer, isn't it?" he said suddenly.

"What is?" Michael asked, confused.

"How it feels today," he explained. "I know you feel the same, I can see it in your face. I can see it in everyone's faces."

"Still don't know what you're talking about."

"I've been through so much stuff. There are things I can't bring myself to think about because they hurt too much. Things that are too painful. I've wanted to try and sort them out, but I haven't been able to do it yet."

"So what's that got to do with a bottle of beer?"

"I feel like everything inside me's been shaken up but my top's been screwed down tight. Until you take the top off, nothing can get out. Being here today has been like a release. I just wasn't expecting it."

"So how do you feel now?"

"Half-empty and flat." Peter smiled sadly.

Michael nodded thoughtfully as he considered his unusual, but accurate, analogy. He understood completely. "What was that business with the toy earlier?" he asked. He could tell from the sudden change in Peter's body language that his nerves were still raw. Peter took the toy from his pocket and stared at it again.

"On the first morning," he explained, his voice cracking with emotion, "I was supposed to go and see my lad Joe at school. It was his first class assembly . . ." He stopped talking when the pain threatened to overwhelm him again. Although he'd thought about Joe constantly, he hadn't talked about his son, not once in more than eight weeks.

"What happened?" Michael pressed, although he thought he already knew.

"I wasn't anywhere near the school when it happened. I was on my way to work. There was a meeting I couldn't get out of and if I'd missed it I would have . . ."

"Would have what?"

"Would have got the sack."

"Was it that important?"

"Obviously not, but I thought it was at the time. We'd been working for weeks to close a major deal. My bonus and an almost guaranteed promotion hinged on getting the papers signed at that meeting. I would have lost a hell of a lot of cash if things hadn't worked out."

"But looking back now, did it matter? What good would your bonus have been to you now?"

Peter shuffled awkwardly. He knew the answers to Michael's questions already but the admission was still not an easy one to make.

"I know now that none of it really mattered. The job, the

money, the car, the house—none of it. I should have given the whole fucking lot up months earlier but I thought I was doing the right thing. Saddest thing is I'd probably have done it again too. My priorities were all screwed up. I should have been there when it happened. I should have been there with my wife and my boy when they . . ."

"We've all got regrets," Michael said. "I bet everyone here could tell you at least a hundred things they wish they'd done differently. I don't think we'll ever get over it. I just hope these feelings get easier to live with, that's all."

"I loved Joe, you know. That kid was everything to me. Just wish I'd told him."

"You'd only have embarrassed him." Michael smiled. "He wouldn't have understood."

"Oh, I know that. I just wish I'd spent more time with him," Peter said, correcting himself. "I just wish I could have been there for him when it happened."

The two men stared into the fire again, and for a while the cracking and popping of the flames was all that could be heard.

"So what was with the toy?" Michael asked again, remembering that his question hadn't been properly answered.

"Oh, that," Peter replied. "It's silly, really. Jenny, and I went shopping with Joe on the Sunday afternoon before it happened. We were walking around town for hours and Joe was getting tired and fed up like kids tend to do. I told him that if he behaved himself and if everything worked out at the office over the next few days then I'd get him a present when we next went out, whatever he wanted. I asked him what he'd like, expecting him to go for the biggest and most expensive thing he could think of.

Anyway, he dragged his mum and me into this shop and showed us this toy like the one I found today. It wasn't much and it wasn't expensive, but all his mates had one and I was going to get it for him. That was all he wanted. Christ, Mike, I wish I could see him again. Just once more."

32

Cooper stood outside the control tower and looked around with satisfaction. Things were moving in the right direction. Richard had returned safely from the island and, perhaps even more importantly, they'd finally got Keele behind the controls of the plane. Okay, so he'd only got as far as moving it out of the hangar and down to the end of the airstrip, but it was a start. Suddenly their chances of getting everyone over to Cormansey in the next few days seemed to have dramatically improved.

The day so far had been spent trying to coordinate the evacuation of the airfield. They'd calculated that Keele would only need to make two flights to the island, three at most, and that had been a relief to everyone, not least the pilot himself. He hadn't got as far as thinking about what would happen when they reached the island, but that didn't matter. For now all that was important was getting away from this godforsaken place.

A sudden flurry of noise and activity on the other side of the chain-link fence momentarily distracted him. He peered into the distance but couldn't see anything unusual. He kept watching for a second longer, feeling uneasy. Jack had said something earlier which had been troubling him. He'd said he'd been watching with Croft and the two of them had decided that the behavior of the dead was changing again. Croft had been walking, trying to exercise his injured leg, and without thinking he'd found himself a little too close to a section of the perimeter fence. Many of the bodies had reacted to him as they normally did—ripping and tearing at each other's flesh and trying to push themselves ever closer—but others had behaved very differently. Some of the dead, Jack had told Cooper, stood still, almost as if they were watching he and Croft. Richard Lawrence had confirmed that the people over on the island had noticed something similar. He didn't know what it meant, but he didn't like it. Were the bodies about to finally give up and drop? Or was this change in their behavior the first sign of something worse to come?

"You okay?" Emma asked, surprising Cooper as she walked past.

"Fine," he grunted. He'd been concentrating on the corpses and hadn't noticed her approaching.

"It's too cold to be stood out here," she said over her shoulder as she disappeared inside. The control tower was dark but it was a relief to be out of the wind at last. She ran up the stairs and let herself into the main room where she found Jackie Soames trying unsuccessfully to coordinate the emptying of the building.

"So what's the plan?" Emma asked. Things had stepped up a gear since the helicopter had returned. She could see a few people moving around with apparent purpose, but she could also see many, many more sitting still and staring into space as they always did. They'd have to make an effort soon or they risked being left behind.

"There is no plan," Jackie replied dejectedly. "I just thought it would be sensible to get as much stuff out of here as we could before morning."

"So what exactly do we need to take? Do you know what's already on the island?"

"Not really."

"Didn't someone say there used to be about five hundred people living there? So there should be plenty of clothing and beds and the like?"

"Suppose so."

"So all we really need to take with us from here is any food we've got and any specialist stuff that we know we won't find there. That's not going to be very much."

"I know," Jackie admitted. "You're right, love. I'm just trying to keep myself busy, that's all. I don't know about you, but I can't stand all this bloody waiting around. It's starting to get to me. I just want to get on, get things done, and get out of here."

"We've all done more than enough waiting around," Emma agreed.

Realizing that it was pointless trying to motivate herself or anyone else at the tail end of this long and trying day, Jackie slumped heavily in a chair. Emma sat down next to her. She thought the large, red-faced woman looked unusually troubled.

"What's on your mind?"

Jackie shrugged her shoulders and lit a cigarette. She only

had a couple left in the box she carried with her. The one she'd just put in her mouth had already been half-smoked.

"This just about sums it up," she said as she blew out a match.

"What does?"

"These bloody cigarettes."

"I don't understand."

"I used to run a pub," Jackie explained, taking a deep, tired breath. "I used to smoke like a bloody chimney. I used to like having a good time first, then worrying about it afterwards. Now I'm down to my last box of cigarettes and I'm hoping there's going to be some on this bloody island when I get there because the last thing I want to do now is give up. Bloody hell, I want to smoke more than ever now."

"I don't understand. What point are you making?"

Jackie didn't—or couldn't—give Emma a direct answer.

"And drinking," she continued. "I never used to get a hangover because I never stopped drinking. I used to drink every day but there's hardly a drop of alcohol left here now. I need booze."

"I still don't understand."

Jackie laughed sadly to herself and shook her head. She flicked ash from the end of her cigarette and watched as it fluttered down onto the floor.

"Sometimes," she said, "I really have to think hard to remind myself why we're bothering to do all of this. You and Michael have got each other and you're bloody lucky because that's more than the rest of us have got. From now on we're going to have to fight for everything we want or need. And okay, the bodies might eventually disappear, but we're still going to be out on our own, aren't we? We're going to have to be self-sufficient, for Christ's sake! Bloody hell, I've never been self-sufficient in my life! I've never had anything handed to me on a plate, but I've always been able to go out and get what I want, whenever I've wanted it. It's all different now. I'm never going to be able to nip down to the shops to get myself a packet of cigarettes or a bottle of gin again, am I?"

"No."

Emma felt she should say more, but there was nothing else to say. Jackie was right.

"Sorry, Emma," she mumbled apologetically, "I didn't mean to go off like that."

"That's okay," she insisted. "Really, I understand how you're feeling."

"Thing is," Jackie added, "I know how lucky I am to still be here and to still be in one piece, but sometimes that's not enough. I can handle this most of the time, but now and then I just want my life back."

33

Wrapped up in a thick winter coat to protect him from the cold and wearing a baseball cap to keep off the intermittent rain, Michael sat on a low stone wall in the darkness and stared into the distance. He was alone, and at that moment that was just how he wanted to be. The only other person he wanted to be with tonight was miles away. He'd left the eight other survivors celebrating their day's work and drinking themselves stupid in the shadow-filled lounge bar of The Fox, Cormansey's only pub.

The sound of the ocean filled the evening air. The constant crashing of the waves on the beach just ahead of him was a welcome and relaxing sound. He felt safe being out on his own tonight. Last night he wouldn't have risked being out in the open like this but today the group had worked hard to clear the village and a large number of bodies had been slaughtered and accounted for. From where he was sitting he could still see the bright glow of the huge pyre they'd lit just outside Danvers Lye. If there were any other bodies nearby tonight—and he guessed there probably would be—then he knew he'd be able to deal with them quickly and easily. His trusty crowbar remained slung at his side in constant readiness.

Michael was keen to escape from the dead village, and had chosen to walk down the twisting coastal road which led back toward the far end of the island. Suddenly feeling the cold, he jumped up from the stone wall where he'd been sitting and ambled down toward the sea, his feet grinding through the shingle. The waves drowned out the sound of his footsteps.

He'd been busy and preoccupied all day but now that he'd finally stopped working, he was struggling again. He walked farther along the beach which, unlike most of the coastline of Cormansey that he'd seen so far, was fairly even and flat. The wreck of a fishing boat had been washed up onto the shore near to where he was walking. He had no way of knowing whether this was a vessel which had originally set sail from Cormansey or whether it had simply drifted over and crashed into the rocks here by chance. Wherever it had come from, it had ended its working life stranded on this beach, tipped over onto one side like a dead whale. As he got nearer, Michael saw that the captain of the boat—if that was who it had been—was still on board. Caught up in the rusted winch machinery, the body was particularly badly deteriorated, almost skeletal in places, no doubt because of its exposure to the harsh and relentless ocean conditions. Almost all of the visible flesh had been stripped away by the salty sea water, leaving yellow-white bone exposed.

Months ago the discovery of a body like this would have mattered. The lives of many people would have been affected by the repercussions of the death—the family, police, the man's employers . . . the list went on. Today it didn't mean anything to anyone. Michael pitied the poor sod who had died. What would have been headline news in the days before the world had been turned upside down was now little more than an unimportant piece of driftwood. It was getting harder to remember that all of these bodies had each been someone once. Someone with a personality, a name, a history, and a life. Once he'd forgotten about it, Michael knew this man would be gone forever.

Today had been difficult, but not for the reasons he'd expected. Michael, along with the rest of the unprepared men and women on the island, had been given a sudden opportunity to look back and remember all they'd lost. As Michael ambled farther down the beach, with the driving wind whipping up off the ocean and gusting furiously into his face, he thought back even further, remembering the life he'd lived before this nightmare had begun. He thought about his family and friends. He thought about his home. He pictured his house in his mind as he'd left it, and then tried to drag that image into the present. He pictured the street where he used to live, now overrun with weeds and decay, the pavements littered with the remains of the people he used to know.

As the shingle gave way to larger, more dangerous rocks, Michael turned his attention to the more immediate past. He remembered finding the farmhouse with Emma and Carl. Christ, they should have done better there. He should have been stronger. But maybe what had happened at the farmhouse had been inevitable. He thought about the military base and how somewhere so safe, strong, and secure had been exposed and compromised so quickly and disastrously. Would the island prove to be any different? He had to believe it would be. In principle the dangers here were less, but these days the gulf between predictability and reality was hard to gauge.

All he wanted was security and shelter. A quiet, simple life with his basic needs satisfied. A roof over his head and Emma by his side were all it boiled down to.

34

Just after six the following morning, Gary Keele stood between two of the disused buildings on the airfield, out of sight of the numerous survivors who were now shuffling to and fro between the control tower, the office buildings, and the helicopter and plane. This time he wasn't hiding from them, he just didn't want them to see him. He was literally sick with nerves. He'd already thrown up twice and the sudden mouth watering and cramps in his gut indicated that he was about to vomit for a third time. He hadn't eaten anything since late yesterday evening and his stomach was completely empty, but the thought of flying that plane instantly made the bile rise again. He retched and belched and then threw up.

His legs shaking, Keele crouched down and spat into the overgrown weeds at his feet, trying to clear the sour taste of vomit from his mouth. This was stupid, he thought to himself. He had hundreds of flying hours under his belt, why was he so worked up about making this flight now? If anything, flying to the island should be easier than most of his previous flights—apart from the helicopter the skies were otherwise completely empty. Was it the responsibility of carrying so many passengers and having them rely on him that was causing his nervousness? That could well have been the reason. In his job as a tug plane pilot at a gliding center he'd almost always flown alone and had no one else to worry about once the pilot behind him had released. On the first morning he'd been alone, tugging the fourth out of five gliders into the air, when they'd started falling like stones, dropping out of the air around him.

Get a fucking grip, he thought to himself. Suddenly determined he took a deep breath and marched to the edge of the building but then stopped and turned back when he saw the plane. He pushed himself flat against the wall, a cold, nervous sweat prickling his brow again. He *had* to do this. He had to make himself do this. He didn't have any choice. Never mind the rest of them, if he didn't get in that bloody plane and fly it then he was stuck at the airfield too.

"Finally!" Richard Lawrence grinned as Keele marched past him purposefully. "Here he comes. You feeling all right, Tuggie?"

Keele didn't hear him, concentrating instead on trying to rise above his fear and focus on the job at hand. Richard looked over at Cooper and shrugged his shoulders.

"Don't knock it," Cooper said, "at least he's here. As long as he gets that bloody plane up in the air I don't care what state he's in."

They stood and watched as Keele climbed up into the cockpit of the plane and began to run nervously through his preflight checks. In the back of the aircraft twelve equally nervous survivors sat strapped in their seats, surrounded—as they had been for more than half an hour now—by all the bags and boxes of useful supplies they'd been able to cram safely inside. Five more people, Donna and Clare included, emerged from the office building. With her arm wrapped around the shoulder of Dean McFarlane, at only eight years old the youngest person left alive, Clare made her way over to the plane.

"You take care when you get there," Jack shouted to her from where he stood at the edge of the runway.

"I will," she grinned, hiding her nerves. "I'll send you a postcard. Let you know what the place is like!"

"Don't bother," he replied. "I'll be over there with you before the postcard gets delivered!"

Keele emerged from the cockpit of the plane. He climbed out onto the runway again and looked up and down the length of the aircraft and then up into the sky, obviously psyching himself for the flight. Richard Lawrence turned and spoke to Donna.

"Looks like we're ready," he said, taking hold of her arm and gently ushering her forward. "Get yourself on board."

Donna made her way over to the helicopter where three other survivors were waiting. Cooper watched as she walked away. Richard sensed his concern.

"It'll be fine," he said. "I reckon as soon as Keele's off the ground he'll get his nerve back."

"Either that or he'll go to pieces. What if he loses it?"

"Then it'll be a short flight, won't it? And I'll end up spending the next week flying backwards and forwards between this hole and the frigging island."

Keele was walking toward them.

249

"Ready?" Cooper asked him.

"Suppose," he replied, his voice sounding less than sure.

"You know where you're going, don't you, Keele?" Richard checked for the umpteenth time. Better to be safe than sorry.

"I know."

"You shouldn't have any trouble finding the place. If the worse comes to the worst just head for the east coast and then follow it north until you find the island. You'll see the smoke and the people and they'll see you before you can—"

"I know," Keele interrupted. "You already told me."

Cooper and Richard exchanged quick glances, both of them still dubious about the pilot's mental condition and his ability to fly.

"Get going," Cooper urged. Keele jogged back to the plane.

"We should be back later today," Richard shouted over his shoulder as he walked away towards the helicopter. He stopped and turned around to face Cooper and Jack. "I'm aiming for midafternoon. Just do me a favor and make sure everyone's ready to go first thing tomorrow. I want to get this done quickly, okay?"

"Okay," he replied.

Jack and Cooper, suddenly the only two left standing out in the open, moved away from the runway as first Richard and then Keele started the engines of their respective aircrafts. A sudden increase in wind and noise accompanied the takeoff of the helicopter, which rose up and then gently circled the airfield, driving the rotting masses beyond the perimeter fence into a frenzy. Keele began to taxi down the runway and then increased his speed. Richard hovered high above the ground and watched as the other pilot cautiously coaxed the plane off the ground and lifted it into the air. A few nervous rabbit hops and then it climbed quickly and powerfully towards the gray clouds.

At the edge of the airfield, Kelly Harcourt's body began to move. The dead soldier had remained where she'd fallen for almost two days. Now, beginning deep inside the brain of the corpse, and showing itself first at the very tips of its cold, numb fingers, the change was starting.

It spread throughout the body quickly, the movement building gradually until its dead, clouded eyes flickered open slowly and its torso and clumsy arms and legs became animated again. With awkward, uncoordinated movements the body hauled itself onto all fours and then stood up and began to stumble forward. It tripped through the long grass and kept moving until it clattered into the border fence.

In common with the basic reactions of the thousands upon thousands of other bodies which had previously dragged themselves up from the ground and begun to move in this way, the shell that had once been Kelly Harcourt turned and tried to walk away. But it couldn't move. It was trapped, held tightly from behind by the grabbing hands of numerous rotting bodies on the other side of the fence. Already agitated by the noise of the plane and the helicopter flying low overhead just moments earlier, the resurrection of the dead soldier provoked more of the same basic, brutal reactions. The most dexterous of the creatures managed to poke their decaying fingers through the wire mesh and grasped the cadaver's hair, clothing and whatever else they could grab onto. The bodies pulled and tugged at the soldier's remains, trying to drag them back through the fence, not understanding that the wire barrier was stopping them. Eventually the numb fingers lost their grip and slipped away, allowing the corpse to stumble off again in the opposite direction.

On the other side of the fence, just to the right of where Kelly's body had been briefly trapped, another body was reacting in a different way. Eight weeks ago this creature had been a young and intelligent clothing store department manager with a bright future ahead of her. Now it was a mud-splattered, half-naked, emaciated collection of brittle bone and rotting flesh. Unlike the majority of the huge, seething crowd, however, this one was beginning to exhibit signs of real control and determination. Unlike those which simply stood there vacantly or those which ripped and tore at the other corpses immediately around them, this body was beginning to think. Pressed hard against the fence and surrounded by many thousands of creatures on either side and a similar number behind, it knew that it needed to move to survive. On the other side of the mesh it could just about make out the dark blur of Harcourt's body tripping away and it decided that was what it needed to do too. It grabbed the wire fence with cold, bony hands and began to shake it. All around it other bodies began to do the same.

35

With Danvers Lye now almost completely cleared and the majority of Cormansey's dead population eradicated, the group on the island set about moving from building to building, uncovering the last remaining corpses and then beginning to clean and disinfect the houses.

Michael, Danny, and Bruce had taken the Jeep down to the southernmost tip of the island and were beginning to slowly make their way back north along the simple road network. They had cleared and emptied one house already and were now getting ready to start on the second. In comparison to the gloom of the previous day, this morning was bright, dry, and warm. Conditions were good and they could see the next building from a fair distance away. Its redbrick frontage contrasted with the rest of its predominantly green, brown, and gray surroundings.

Michael stopped the Jeep outside the house, which had a small, square-fenced garden. The three men crossed the road and walked up the short garden path to the front door. They paused to assess the situation before barging inside. It didn't matter how many corpses they had previously found and disposed of, each new discovery was different from the last and was almost always unsettling. Michael found it especially difficult dealing with the bodies he found in their own homes, perhaps because the corpses in the streets had a peculiar anonymity and detachment from their surroundings. Conversely, when he came across a body which had died surrounded by its own belongings, he instinctively tried to piece together the details of its abruptly truncated life. Seeing what these people had once been made it immeasurably more difficult to think of them just as lumps of cold, dead flesh.

"Listen," he whispered as they stood at the door. Danny moved a little closer. They could hear something moving inside the house. Bruce peered in through the front windows, first the kitchen and then the living room. He could see the remains of a body lying on the ground next to an armchair, and he could also see shadows and faint signs of movement in a doorway behind it. If there was a corpse moving through the house, then it was in the hallway, no doubt attracted by their sudden noisy arrival.

"Can't see a lot, Mike," Bruce said from a short distance away. "There's only going to be one or two in there. Might as well just go for it."

Michael pushed the door and it opened inward with ease. He instinctively took a step back as the single moving occupant of the house shuffled and tripped out of the shadows and lurched toward him. His heart sank. This was one of those devastating occasions when he found it almost impossible to think of the bodies as objects. Sometimes the scale of the tragedy still took him by surprise. Sometimes it still hurt. He stood to one side as the emaciated remains of a small child stumbled toward him. Half his height, the poor kid could only have been five or six when he'd died. That was if it was a boy—the body had deteriorated so much that he wasn't even sure. It continued to move closer with the familiar awkward gait and pointless intent of the dead. It fixed him with its cold, vacant eyes. Funny, he thought, how death had stripped away all individuality from the remains of the population. This thing looked and behaved no differently than those bodies which had been twice its size and many more years older.

Danny Talbot stepped forward and, with a sudden grunt of effort and aggression, chopped down at the body's slender neck with a hand axe. It took five good, hard swipes before the head and spinal cord had been sufficiently damaged to stop the corpse from moving. It fell at Michael's feet and he knelt down next to it.

"Okay?" asked Bruce. Michael nodded. Holding his breath, trying hard to ignore the suffocating smell of the insect-infested body, he picked it up and carried it out of the garden and over to the roadside. He placed it down on the grass verge, ready to be collected and cremated later. That was all this poor child had left now, he thought sadly as he stared into what was left of its face. Maggots crawled under its flesh, making its expression appear to change. This kid would never finish school. He'd never go through adolescence. Never experience his first kiss or leave home or get a job or become a parent. No successes. No failures. Nothing.

By the time Michael had gotten up again, Bruce and Danny had already gone inside. He followed them indoors.

"Anything else in here?" he asked. The smell in the confined house was typically obnoxious and overpowering.

"Just this one, I think," answered Bruce. He was pointing at the body on the living room carpet that he'd seen from outside. He could hear Danny upstairs checking out the bedrooms. A few seconds later, he came crashing back down, his face flushed red with sudden effort.

"Clear," he gasped.

Bruce grabbed the bony wrists of the corpse in the living room and dragged it down the hall. Presumably the mother of the dead child, it had been comparatively well preserved in a dry and relatively constant environment. It left behind a dark and sticky outline of decomposition on the carpet.

The cold, echoing house was modest and traditional. The musty smell and lack of fresh air gave the building an antique, museumlike atmosphere. Michael stood and looked around.

"You sure you're okay?" Bruce asked him as he came back indoors after dumping the body next to the child's corpse. "You're miles away this morning."

"Wishing I was," he replied quickly. He did feel different today, there was no denying it. He felt a strange sense of anticlimax and disappointment. He wondered whether it was because he was gradually becoming aware of the limitations of the island. As safe and protected a place as it would no doubt eventually prove to be, he could also see it becoming a restricted and stifling environment. Their isolation and remote location would inevitably make it difficult for them to grow and expand their small community easily. It was already obvious that Cormansey was never going to be the haven that he and the others had naively dreamt it might be. Nothing was going to be easy here, that much was for sure, but then again, nothing was going to be easy anywhere. Maybe everything looked worse today because he'd spent too long yesterday thinking about everything he'd lost.

Their brief this morning had been simply to clear the bodies from the homes they visited. Looking around this particular small and unimposing property, however, it was obvious that there was going to be much more work to do to make each building habitable again. In the kitchen, the fridge and cupboards were filled with rotten food. Dust, mold, and decay were everywhere. Nothing was salvageable. There were traces of insect and rodent infestations. An open window in one of the bedrooms had allowed in several nesting birds and two months' worth of rainwater. Damp was spreading across the walls.

The implications of what he saw around him, although he chose not to share them with the others, were immense. What he saw today was a world slowly being reclaimed. No doubt the arrival of the survivors on Cormansey would prolong the life and usefulness of this building and others on the island but elsewhere, back on the mainland, the process of decay and deterioration would continue unchecked. The disappearance of man from the face of the planet was inevitably going to cause a massive change and imbalance to the ecosystem. Crops would no longer be grown or harvested. Vermin would be allowed to breed and consume. The decay of millions of bodies would result in a huge increase in the numbers of insects, germs, and disease. The ramifications were endless, too much for him to think about. When he'd arrived on the island he'd felt strong, determined, and full of hope. Today, however, those feelings had started to fade. In comparison to the almost unimaginable scale of the changes the infection had brought to the entire planet, the minor achievements of this small group of survivors meant nothing. Disheartened, Michael dragged himself back out to the jeep with the other two men.

"Where to next?" he asked.

"Road splits in a while," Bruce replied. "We'll keep west. Harper said he was sticking to the east side."

"Okay."

Michael sat back in the driver's seat and readied himself for the next building. He stared into the wing mirror and looked at the bodies of the child and its mother for a couple of seconds before turning the key in the ignition, starting the engine, and driving away.

"Did that kid get to you?" Danny asked from the backseat with clumsiness but a surprising degree of perception.

"Everything's getting to me today," he grunted back.

"Decent weather, though!" Bruce said cheerfully, doing his best to lighten the increasingly dark and sombre mood. "Just imagine what this place is going to be like in the summer. Plenty of coastline, good fishing waters—"

"Just got to get through the winter first," Danny reminded him.

"I know, you killjoy, but that doesn't mean . . ." He stopped speaking, leaned forward, and peered up into the sky. "What's that?"

Michael slowed the jeep and looked up. He could see the helicopter, scurrying across the deep blue like a small black spider.

"Bloody brilliant," Bruce sighed with relief. "Here comes some help. Wonder who he's brought with him? Hope it's someone who's going to pull their weight. The last thing we need here is—"

"The plane," Danny interrupted. "I can hear it."

All eyes switched from staring at the helicopter to scouring the sky, looking for the plane. Bruce spotted it first and pointed it out to Michael. It looked like it was following the exact same course the helicopter had taken. Suddenly feeling more alive and invigorated than he had since he'd arrived here, Michael put his foot down and accelerated again.

"Where are you going?" Bruce asked as they sped past the front of the next house and carried on down the narrow road.

"I need to see who's here," Michael answered, his pulse racing with sudden nervousness and anticipation.

By the time they'd reached the airstrip, both the plane and the helicopter had already landed. The passengers were being unloaded from the back of the plane. They staggered onto the tarmac strip and wandered toward Brigid and Gayle, who ran toward them from the far end of the runway. The new arrivals stared at their surroundings in awe like tourists arriving at some long-awaited and much anticipated holiday destination. Gary Keele ran in the opposite direction and stopped when he reached a patch of long grass. He bent over double, put his hands on his knees, and threw up into the clump of weeds at his feet. Landing

259

the plane had proved to be even more nerve-racking than taking off.

Michael stopped the jeep, jumped out, and started to look around hopefully. He could see several faces that he recognized immediately. He could see Donna, Clare, and Karen Chase among others.

There was no sign of Emma.

36

With the first sizable tranche of people now gone, the control tower had suddenly become a hollow and empty place. Where Emma had quickly become used to seeing people, she could now only see empty spaces. Several of those who had gone had done little more than sit in the same spot and wait since they'd first arrived at the airfield. It annoyed her that some of those who had done nothing to help the group had been among the first to get away, but she understood it had to be this way. She wished they had a way of knowing if the plane had reached the island safely. For an hour or two after they'd left she'd half-expected to look up and see Keele bringing the plane limping home, still full of passengers. She didn't have much faith in him, either as a pilot or a human being. But, come to think of it, she didn't have much faith in anything anymore. If she was perfectly honest with herself, the truth was that she wanted the plane back so that she could go. She wanted to get away from this place and the thousands of bodies surrounding it, and she wanted to get away now, not tomorrow. Whatever had happened they would know if the pilots had been successful in a few hours' time. The plan had been to get back to the airfield as quickly as they could. They'd planned to travel there and back within the day and had hoped to return to the mainland by three o'clock. It was already almost that time.

Emma had earlier counted just over thirty people left at the airfield. That included herself and Kilgore, who had disappeared several hours ago, heading toward one of the outbuildings close to the control tower. Exhausted, dehydrated, and starving, the soldier knew that his time would soon be up but he didn't have the strength or courage to do what Kelly Harcourt had done. Instead he stayed where he was and festered. The rest of the group kept their distance from him. Their most recent approaches had been met with either anger and hostility or with equally unpalatable outpourings of self-pity and grief from the weak little man. With enough confusion, disorientation, and doubt of their own to deal with, they each did their best to forget about him. Most of them could now be found in the office building, waiting impatiently for the helicopter and plane to return.

Emma tripped down the control tower staircase and stepped out into the cold but bright afternoon. She found Cooper standing outside, scanning the perimeter fence and occasionally the skies with a pair of binoculars.

"See anything yet?" she asked hopefully.

"Nothing," he answered. Emma watched him as he shifted his attention from the sky to closer to the ground. "I doubt they'll be back for another hour or so."

"What are you looking for then?"

"Nothing really," he replied. "Just keeping an eye on them."

Emma shielded her eyes from the low sun and looked toward the fence. Without the benefit of the binoculars she could see little more than a constantly moving and apparently endless mass of dead flesh. The immense crowd didn't look any different today than how it had appeared yesterday or the day before.

"I don't like the look of that," Cooper said suddenly, focusing his attention on one particular section of fence.

"What?" Emma asked, anxiously.

"Bloody things down there look like they're trying to pull the fence down."

"What?" she said again, unable to believe what she'd heard. Cooper handed her the binoculars and she lifted them to her eyes. She quickly focused on the fence and then scanned along to her left until she came to the section that Cooper had been watching. "Bloody hell," she gasped. He was right. In the distance a tightly packed group of figures had grabbed hold of the wire mesh. Together they were pulling it toward them and then pushing it back the other way as if they were trying to work the posts out of the ground. They looked barely uncoordinated, but their intent was clear.

"They won't do it, will they?"

"I don't know if they've got the strength, but . . ."

"But . . . ?"

"But there are thousands of them out there. Give them enough time and enough numbers and who knows what they might do."

Emma looked deep into the mass of bodies again. The entire

crowd seemed to be writhing and squirming constantly. "What do we do about them?"

"Don't think there's anything we can do," Cooper replied, "except what we're already doing. The number of bodies still following us around is going to cause us problems whatever happens. We should be out of here by tomorrow, the day after at the latest. We'll just have to ride our luck until then."

"We've been riding our luck since all of this started."

"True, so a couple more days shouldn't make much difference. We could go down to that part of the fence, soak the bloody things in fuel and torch the lot of them if we wanted to, but what good's that going to do? It might make us feel a bit better, and it might get rid of a few hundred of them, but will it make us any safer or get us out of here any quicker? And if they really are starting to think logically again, then they might see what we're doing as an act of aggression and try and fight back."

"You are joking, aren't you?"

"I've seen stranger things happen recently."

Emma passed him the binoculars, then turned and walked to the control tower, suddenly anxious to get indoors. Cooper continued to look along the fence. There was another small pocket of activity by the main entrance gate, where more bodies were pushing against the barrier. He headed for the office building. He needed to keep people indoors and out of sight. He didn't want to risk antagonizing the bodies unnecessarily. They needed to keep the crowds on the other side of the chain-link fence under control, and the best way of doing that was to keep their distance.

37

Kilgore lay on a dust-covered sofa in a shadow-filled waiting room. He closed his eyes and tried to ignore the pain. He couldn't remember when he'd last eaten, and he hadn't drunk anything for more than a day and a half. He felt so weak that he couldn't sit upright anymore. He could barely lift his arms. Everything felt heavy and leaden. He couldn't bring himself to move his head and so lay facing in one direction, staring out of the windows on the opposite side of the room. The relentless physical discomfort had been hard enough to deal with, but the mental anguish he was now having to endure was much, much worse.

Kilgore had come to the conclusion that today—or possibly tomorrow if he was really unlucky—would be his final day alive. His mouth was dry and he struggled even to find enough saliva to lick his chapped lips. His head ached and all that he could hear was the sound of his own labored, rasping breathing echoing around his face mask, and the constant hum and buzz of insects which, in his disorientated state, seemed to swarm around the room like circling vultures, waiting for him to die. The end had to be close now, didn't it?

Lying there and waiting for the inevitable was, bizarrely, beginning to get easier in some ways. The first hours he'd spent in this quiet little room had been difficult, and confusing. When he'd first shut himself away in here he'd still been able to believe that there was some slight ray of hope for him. In his tired mind he'd explored every escape route and potential outcome. He'd thought about trying to get back to the underground base he'd originally come from and had started to make plans to take one of the trucks and drive back there alone. But he didn't know whether any of the vehicles had enough fuel and he didn't know how he'd get the gate open and get through the bodies and . . . and he came up with a multitude of reasons why every plan he considered would be impossible to follow through. He could still have gone with the others to the island, but what would have happened to him there? He could have done what Kelly Harcourt had done and enjoyed one final breath of fresh air but he knew that he had neither the physical nor the mental strength to take that final step and remove his mask, no matter how desperate he became.

Kilgore was tired. He'd had enough. He wanted it to stop now. He wanted to fall asleep and not wake up again. He'd been hallucinating since early morning, and there'd been a sudden and dramatic increase in the strength of the freakish sights which surrounded him. About half an hour ago he thought he'd been visited by his dead mother and father and one of his teachers from school. In his confused mind the three of them had stood over him and critically discussed his general lack of progress in life. An hour before that and the room he was lying in had appeared to lose all structure and form. The ceiling above him had drooped and dripped down until it had almost touched the floor and the windows on the wall opposite had seemed to close up until they'd disappeared and the room had become dark as night.

The windows were clear again now.

Another hallucination.

He could see Kelly Harcourt.

Kilgore watched as she came closer. He could tell that it was her because she was wearing the same kind of protective suit that he still wore. He could see her long blond hair being blown in the wind. She didn't have her face mask on, he realized. Christ, she could breathe! And if she could breathe, he thought, then maybe he could too? Groaning with effort he slowly sat up and lifted his hand to his mask. Then he stopped.

Kelly continued to come closer. She walked slowly and awkwardly with her head listing over to one side and her arms and legs inflexible. She must have been hurt. She was dragging her feet, not even able to lift them. And then the sun illuminated her face: a cold and lifeless mask with swollen, bloodstained lips and dark eyes. Her mouth moved constantly as she approached, seeming to form silent words and moans. Despite his lack of energy, Kilgore forced himself to stand up and walk toward her. He hobbled across the room and leaned against the window exhausted. Kelly's body clattered against the other side of the glass and for a split second he stood face-to-face with her before the sudden noise and vibration sent both of them reeling backward.

Swaying unsteadily for a moment, he watched as the corpse turned and began to walk away.

Each step forward took huge amounts of effort, but Kilgore found himself instinctively following the cadaver out onto the airfield. He wasn't sure why; was it fear, inquisitiveness, or nervousness which drove him to do it? Was it that he wanted to see properly what he might still become? He waited in the doorway for a moment to catch his breath before leaving the building where he'd presumed he'd die. Just ahead of him Kelly's body continued to stagger away, silhouetted against the low, late-afternoon sun. The sky above Kilgore, so clear and blue for much of the long day now ending, was beginning to darken and was tinged with hints of deep reds and purples and trailing wisps of clouds. Away from the horizon the moon and the first few bright stars could be seen. He followed Kelly along the runway, past the front of the control tower and then out toward the perimeter fence.

Kilgore stopped. He couldn't keep up. He'd not gone far but the effort of moving was already too much. He put his hands on his knees and sucked in a long, slow mouthful of purified air. Another hallucination was beginning now. More powerful than any of the others he'd had, this one seemed to surround and swallow him. It began with a noise. Starting quietly and initially seeming to be without direction, it quickly built to a deafening roar, accompanied by a fierce and angry wind. Exhausted, he lifted his head and saw the helicopter above him beginning a rapid descent. Wrong footed by the sudden distraction, his weak legs buckled and folded underneath him and he fell onto his backside. Shooting pains ran the entire length of his emaciated body and he winced with sudden agony. Just over ten meters from the perimeter fence he sat in the long grass and watched as the powerful machine hovered in the air above the heads of thousands of seething bodies. Then another sound from out of nowhere and a sudden, sweeping movement as the plane glided over him before touching down and bouncing along the runway, finally coming to an undignified, lurching halt at the far end of the strip.

Kilgore watched from his collapsed position at the edge of the airfield as people began to emerge from the control tower. He didn't recognize any of them anymore. They were just dark, featureless figures now, as faceless as the thousands of corpses surrounding the airfield.

Too tired to stay sitting up, he lay on his back and stared up into the darkening sky. The relentless noise of the helicopter changed direction and faded away.

Once he was sure that the plane had safely touched down, Richard Lawrence began to bring the helicopter in to land. He looked down into the mass of diseased cadavers below as he hovered above the perimeter fence. Bloody hell, he thought, the bodies were more incensed and animated than he'd ever seen them before. Some still slashed at each other and fought with those nearest to them. Others were pushing against the fence, being crushed, no doubt, by the weight of hundreds more corpses behind them. But now there were many more who were standing their ground as best they could, looking up at him defiantly with cold, unblinking eyes. Forcing himself to look away and concentrate again, he flew toward the control tower and the other buildings.

Cooper was waiting for him. The rotor blades were still spinning as the pilot ducked down and ran over to the ex-soldier. Together they jogged toward the plane. Keele was sitting in the cockpit trying to recover from the trauma of the flight. He'd managed to turn the plane around to face back down the runway but he hadn't yet moved from his seat.

"Everything go all right?" Cooper asked Richard as they stood and waited for Keele to move.

"Like clockwork," he replied.

"And you're both still okay for fuel?"

"Just about."

"You've got enough to make another flight?"

"Plenty. I should have enough for a good few crossings yet, and I think Keele's got similar."

"So we'll try and get another load over there first thing tomorrow morning, okay?"

Richard sighed with exhaustion. "Bloody hell, mate," he protested, "give me a chance to get my breath back first, won't you? It's been a long day."

"Get this lot over there and you can spend the rest of your life relaxing."

"Everything all right, Richard?" Jackie Soames asked from behind them. She was walking toward them from the office building, and the look of relief on her tired face was clear.

"Everything's fine," he replied.

Keele had finally composed himself enough to be able to get out of the plane. He walked along the runway toward the others, relieved that his ordeal was over for one day.

"Well done, son," Richard said when he was close enough to hear him. "Told you we'd be all right, didn't I?"

Keele nodded. He was still breathing heavily and his shirt was soaked with sweat. His usually neatly coiffured hair was unkempt. The effort of landing had exhausted him.

"You did well," Jackie said, wrapping her arm around him. "If I still ran the pub I'd buy you a drink!"

"There's a pub on Cormansey. You can buy me a drink when you get there."

The four of them stopped outside the office building. Inside Richard could see many faces staring back at him expectantly. For once they seemed to be positive and happy faces too, all of them sharing a common desire to get away from this unwelcoming, dangerous place. The responsibility he shared with Keele to get these people to safety was humbling. Light from the bright orange sun setting on the horizon reflected off the glass and obscured his view momentarily.

"So they're all okay over there?" Jackie asked.

"What?"

"The people over on the island, are they okay?" she repeated.

"Looks like it," he replied. "They've cleared the village and they've managed to get rid of most of the bodies. We left them emptying out houses."

"So they'll have a place ready for me by the time I get over there?" she joked.

"I doubt it. I was talking to Brigid earlier. She reckons it's going to take us weeks to get the place cleaned up properly."

"Doesn't matter," Cooper said, yawning and stretching his

arms up into the cool evening air. "The one thing we should have plenty of is time. Won't matter if it takes us weeks or months to get everything done, will it? As long as we can get hold of enough food and we're relatively comfortable then who cares how long it take us to—"

He stopped talking.

Emma had appeared from the doorway of the control tower just a short distance away from where they were standing. Breathless from the effort of the sprint downstairs, her face looked ashen with fear. Her unexpected appearance and terrified expression immediately silenced the chatter. In the sudden quiet they became aware of another noise coming from the edge of the airfield.

"They've brought the fence down," she said.

There was a moment of shock and disbelief.

"What?" Jackie demanded.

"The bodies," she said, shaking. "They've brought part of the fence down."

Cooper was the first to react. He turned and sprinted back down the runway, instinctively concentrating his attention on the section of the rotting crowd that had concerned him earlier in the afternoon. The fading light made it difficult to clearly see what was happening from a distance, but he could already see bodies spilling onto the field, falling over a short section of fallen fence then picking themselves up and moving towards the buildings. The sudden, deafening noise made by the returning helicopter and plane had whipped the dead into a frenzy, he decided, and that hysteria had given them enough impetus to hurl themselves forward and bring down the fence. Cooper could see that one of the metal posts had been pushed over until it was almost lying flat on the ground, and now the combined weight of surging crowd of bodies was threatening to collapse another section of the barrier.

"Fucking things are going to tear the whole fence down," Jack Baxter desperately shouted as he ran from the control tower toward the others. "What the fucking hell are we going to do?"

"Block it," someone suggested. "Get one of the trucks over there and block it off."

"Where's Steve Armitage?" Emma demanded, but Jack was one step ahead of her. He ran over to the office building and dragged the truck driver outside. Steve pounded over to the truck, already panting and wheezing. He wasted precious seconds staring out toward the perimeter of the airfield in disbelief. Already weakened by the collapse of the first, a second section of fence was falling. They were still several hundred meters away and were moving as slowly and awkwardly as ever, but an unstoppable deluge of dead bodies was spilling across the airfield.

"Too late for that," Cooper screamed to Steve as he sprinted past him, heading back toward the control tower. "Keele, get that fucking plane back in the air. Get out of here now or we'll never get off the ground again."

The farthest advanced of the bodies were close to reaching the end of the runway. Cooper was right. If the pilot didn't act quickly and get the plane airborne in the next few minutes, the runway would be swarming with corpses and takeoff would be impossible. Keele's earlier nerves were suddenly replaced by sheer bloody fear. He scrambled back into his still warm seat in the cockpit and restarted the engine. Phil Croft tried to control the flow of people from the office building toward the plane but gave up when they surged forward in terrified panic. The breach in the fence had been visible from the back of the building and word of what happened had spread quickly. People pushed, jostled, and fought each other for position. Cooper tried to head off the crowd, using all his strength to limit the numbers getting onto the plane. Forced to make a decision that was as selfish as it was selfless, Jack came around behind him, pushed his way inside and pulled the door shut, knowing that there were already enough people on board.

"Out of my fucking way," Jacob Flynn, an obnoxious bully, screamed as the plane door closed in his face. He threw himself at Cooper, almost knocking him to the ground, but he quickly regained his footing and charged at Flynn, pushing him back toward the office building.

"Get back, you stupid bastard," he pleaded with him as Flynn began to race forward again. "The rest of you get back. It's too late."

Flynn stopped and looked around. Beyond the terrified faces which surrounded him he could see the dark, shapes of the dead continuing their unstoppable advance. He turned and ran back into the building behind him.

Cooper slammed his hand against the side of the plane and Keele began to taxi forward. "Get back inside," he screamed again at the sea of terrified people who still hoped to get onto the plane. "Stay calm and we'll all still get away from here. Get out of sight."

Croft looked back over his shoulder and realized how close

the first bodies were. He limped back toward the office building as quickly as his damaged body would allow. A short distance away Richard Lawrence was pushing Jackie into the back of the helicopter before grabbing the three nearest survivors and bundling them into the aircraft. He jumped back into his seat, started the engine, and took off.

Emma watched tearfully from the door of the control tower. She screamed something to Steve Armitage on the other side of the runway but her words were drowned out by the roar of the plane. She watched helplessly as it powered along the concrete strip and lifted into the air, its wheels missing the heads of the farthest advanced cadavers by little more than a meter.

Cooper pushed the final few survivors through the door of the office building and slammed it shut, then sprinted back to the control tower.

"Upstairs," he yelled to Emma and Steve as the overweight truck driver dragged himself across the runway, swerving around some of the closest bodies, smashing into others. There were corpses all around them now. Some slammed into the sides of the office building, trying to reach the group of terrified people trapped inside, others lurched toward the base of the control tower where Cooper was scrambling to shut and bar the door. Two lumbering cadavers managed to slip inside, only to find themselves face-to-face with Steve, who picked up a metal chair and swung it repeatedly at the desperate creatures until they had been reduced to a pile of rotten flesh and smashed bone. He moved out of the way as Cooper dragged tables out from a small ground-floor room to block the entrance.

At the top of the staircase Emma collided heavily with another body. Instinctively she scrambled around in the semidarkness for something to destroy it with. She grabbed the corpse's leg to try and prevent it from getting away, and it kicked out at her with surprising strength.

"Don't," a mousy woman protested. "Please don't hurt me."

Emma relaxed and pulled her to her feet. She recognized her as Juliet Appleby, one of the silent majority who had spent their time hidden in the control tower. As Cooper and Steve rushed past them both she shoved Juliet forward. The terrified, shaking woman stumbled across the room to the window directly opposite and looked down over the airfield. The damage to the fence was obscured now by hundreds of bodies. More of them still scrambled through the gap, advancing relentlessly toward the center of the airfield. An unstoppable tidal wave of dead flesh surged forward. Already there were thousands of them inside the perimeter fence and an incalculable number followed behind.

The airfield was lost.

Kilgore lay on the ground and looked up at the sky.

He was aware of movement all around him and sometimes on top of him. All of the earlier noise had stopped. The plane had gone again. The helicopter had gone too.

It was getting darker.

Too tired to react or fight or even to take off his face mask, he lay there helplessly as the bodies trampled him into the ground.

38

"So what the hell do we do now, Cooper?" Steve Armitage demanded angrily. Cooper didn't answer. He walked over to stand next to Emma and Juliet, who were staring out at the desperate scene outside. Tears of fear and frustration were flooding down Emma's face.

"For Christ's sake," she sobbed, "this isn't fair. We were so close to getting out of here."

"We can still get out."

"How are we going to get past that lot?" she asked, pointing out of the window and down at the ground. Cooper took a few steps farther forward and peered down. From their high vantage point the hopelessness of the situation was painfully apparent. They could see right across the wide expanse of the airfield. In the distance bodies continued to push their way through the now sizable gap in the fence, fighting with each other to get through, following each other like a plague of rats. In the rapidly darkening sky above them the lights of the helicopter and plane could be seen disappearing into the distance.

"Richard will come back," he said, turning away from the window and massaging his temples. His head was pounding. He couldn't think straight.

"And what's going to happen then?" Steve demanded. "Do you think those fucking things are going to stand to one side so that he can land and pick us up? For fuck's sake, just admit it Cooper, we've had it."

Cooper wondered whether he might be right. The bodies below them were congregating around the base of the control tower and other nearby buildings. He moved around so that he had a better view of the small office block where the rest of the group were. By his calculations there were between ten and fifteen people trapped there. Jesus, they were surrounded too.

"How are we going to get them out?" Emma asked. "We have to get them out. We can't just leave them there, can we? We have to—"

"Come on, Emma," Cooper said. "We're as trapped as they are. There's nothing any of us can do."

"What do they want?" Juliet Appleby asked. She had gradually moved away from the window and was now standing in the middle of the room, too afraid to look out.

"Haven't you ever seen them like this before?"

"No," she replied, shaking her head. "I've been here for weeks. I've seen the crowds, but never anything like this. I've never been this close to so many of them."

"Chances are you're going to get a lot closer yet," Emma interrupted. "And in answer to your question, I don't know what they want and neither do they. Those damn things don't know who they were or what they are now. They don't know who or what we are or what they want from us. They don't know a fucking thing and all that I know is they've probably just taken away our last chance of ever getting away from here."

"We can still get out!" Cooper shouted instinctively.

"You keep saying that," she yelled back at him, sobbing again, "but how?"

Dejected and demoralized she sat down heavily and held her head in her hands. Cooper turned away from the window.

"They're crowding around us because we're a distraction," he said. "More to the point, were the *only* distraction. They're here because we're different, and I don't know if they do it because they want help from us or because they're scared of us or because they want to rip us to fucking pieces or—"

"It doesn't matter why they do it," Steve said, his voice strained and hoarse. "You're right, though, the only thing left for them to do is to try and get to us. They won't stop until we're gone."

"I think," Cooper continued, "that all we can do for now is keep out of sight and not make a bloody sound. If they don't know we're up here then we should be okay for a while. We'll wait for the helicopter to come back."

"Come on," Emma protested, "they already know we're up here. Even if just one of them knows and tries to get inside then hundreds more will copy and try to do the same. And Richard's not coming back."

"Yes, he will, and until he does all we can do is shut up, sit tight, and wait."

39

"Just get down, shut your fucking mouth, and keep out of sight," Phil Croft ordered Jacob Flynn. Croft was crouching behind a desk. Flynn was standing in the middle of the room, in full view of every window. He was a volatile, selfish bastard who'd generally kept himself to himself for as long as he'd been at the airfield. He was different now, desperate and frightened, and his fear had forced him into action. He was furious that he'd been left behind, angrier with those who had got away than any of the dead outside. As far as he was concerned it was every man, woman, and child for themselves now, and he was damn sure that he wasn't going to end his time trapped in this fucking building with these stupid fucking people.

"What good is keeping out of sight, you frigging idiot?" he yelled. "They already know we're in here. The only chance we've got is to open the fucking door and fight our way out."

"Fight your way out to where?" Croft asked. "Can't you see? There's nowhere left to go."

One of the people cowering in the darkness behind Croft let out a sudden wail of fear. The doctor turned around but he couldn't see who'd cried out. From his position low on the ground, however, he could see into several of the nearby office rooms. Thick, angry crowds of rotting bodies were pressed against every window, trying to push and force their way inside. Even if Flynn was right and they tried to make a run for it, he thought, the sheer number of cadavers outside would prevent them from getting anywhere. Sensing that his time was running out, he dragged himself back up onto his unsteady feet and walked over to Flynn, who was still standing ranting in the middle of the room.

"Open any of these doors," he said quietly, his face just inches from Flynn's so that no one else could hear, "and this place will be full of them in seconds. You won't survive and I won't survive. Open the door and we're all dead."

Flynn glared at Croft. He was a good six inches taller than the doctor, his presence imposing and threatening. He grabbed hold of Croft by the scruff of his neck and pulled him even closer.

"I want to get out of here," he hissed, more than a hint of terrified desperation in his voice. "You've got to help me get out of here, understand?"

"You can't," Croft replied, struggling to keep his balance and his nerve. "All we can do is wait."

"Wait for what?"

When Croft didn't answer, Flynn shoved him away and he fell back onto a nearby chair. The sudden movement caused searing pain to shoot up the length of his injured leg from ankle to hip. He gasped at the shock.

"We should all get into one room," he said, his heart racing, struggling to keep calm and find focus. "Let's get everyone together and out of sight. We need to limit what they can see of us."

Flynn grunted reluctant agreement and looked around the dark building. He pushed open a door to his right.

"In there," he said, gesturing toward a small bathroom which contained a single cubicle and a basin. More importantly, the only window in the room was a narrow strip which was above head height. Flynn made sure he was in first, then another nine people crowded in after him. The space was desperately limited. Apart from the toilet in the cubicle there wasn't room for any of them to sit or lie down. Phil Croft, the last man in, pulled the door shut behind him.

Someone was crying. He couldn't see who it was or where they were standing. It might even have been more than one person. Whoever it was, they needed to shut up fast if they were going to have any chance of getting out of here alive.

"Whoever that is, you've got to please be quiet," he whispered. He winced in pain and leaned back against the door. His leg was hurting badly again. He didn't know how long he'd be able to stay standing like this. "I know it's hard but please, just be quiet."

He could still hear muffled crying and sniffing. Someone else was crying now too.

Wedged tightly up against each other and hardly able to move, the eleven desperate people stood and waited.

40

An hour and twenty minutes later the helicopter appeared in the dark sky over Cormansey.

"What the hell's he doing back here?" Donna asked. She'd been walking down the road which ran through the middle of Danvers Lye with Michael and Karen Chase, trying to get used to her sudden freedom.

"No idea," Michael answered, immediately concerned. He stood still and watched the helicopter's blinking lights for a moment.

"Well, either he didn't make it back to the airfield or they've decided to bring the rest of them over here early," Karen suggested.

"But why would they do that?" Donna asked, trying to make sense of the situation. "Christ, something must have happened, mustn't it? Something's gone wrong."

"Come on," Michael said, turning and running back to the jeep.

"Let's not jump to conclusions," Karen continued optimistically as she climbed into the backseat, trying not to show that she shared Michael's unease. "They might have just decided to make a move tonight rather than wait for morning. Let's face it, if it was you flying and you had the energy, then you'd probably want to get the job over and done with too."

"So where's the plane, then?" Michael asked as he started the engine and turned the vehicle round to drive toward the airstrip.

"There," Donna replied, pointing to the left. She could see the lights on the plane's wings and tail flashing intermittently. Michael slammed his foot down.

"Take it easy, will you?" Karen complained from the backseat as the car jolted forward. Michael ignored her. There were any number of plausible reasons why the plane and helicopter might have returned to the island so soon, but until he heard otherwise, he couldn't help but presume the worst.

Driving at such speed, the jeep arrived at the airstrip before the plane. The helicopter was just touching down as Michael pulled on the brakes.

"What's happened?" he demanded as people began to emerge from the back of the helicopter. He didn't recognize the first woman who appeared. She looked around the airstrip, disoriented and frightened. The noise of the engine and rotor blades made it difficult for her to hear what was happening. She knew someone was shouting at her, but she couldn't see who or where they were. "What's happened?" Michael yelled again, grabbing hold of her and spinning her around. He stared desperately into her pale, bewildered face.

"Fence came down," she gasped. Her breathing was wheezy and asthmatic. Michael relaxed his grip, realising that he was frightening her. "Fence came down and they got in," she repeated. "Hundreds of them."

Michael turned and looked at Richard, who walked towards him.

"It must have been the noise we made when we landed back there," he explained. "The bloody things went wild and managed to pull down part of the fence. It's been brewing for weeks. All our noise today pushed them over the edge."

"Did you manage to get everyone away?" Donna asked. Michael closed his eyes and dropped his head, almost too afraid to listen to the answer. He knew that there wouldn't have been room in the plane for everyone.

"We had to leave some people behind," Richard admitted quietly. "There just wasn't enough room. We'd never have been able to get off the ground if we'd brought any more over with us."

"We always said we'd need another flight over after this one," Jackie Soames said tearfully, walking around the helicopter to stand with the others.

"I'll try and get back there tomorrow," Richard continued. "Christ knows how I'm going to land with thousands of those damn things swarming all over the place, though . . ."

His voice was drowned out by the deafening noise from the plane as it swooped down behind him. Keele's already fragile nerves had been shattered by the events of the last couple of hours, and now he was struggling to keep control. His descent was too steep and too fast. The plane hit the ground and bounced back up off the runway before crashing down again, finally stopping at an awkward angle in the grass almost twenty meters over the end of the tarmac strip. After a brief pause the door opened. Keele half-jumped, half-fell down and then stumbled away as his passengers poured out after him.

"It was a fucking nightmare back there," Jack Baxter shouted into the whipping wind as he ran back along the runway toward Michael and the others. "Christ, we didn't have a fucking chance. They were all over us before we knew what had happened."

Michael wasn't listening. He pushed past Jack to get closer to the plane, having to fight his way through the stream of frightened people coming the other way. More still were climbing out onto the runway—Jean Taylor, Stephen Carter, several others—but there was no sign of Emma. He stood less than a meter from the door and watched and waited. Still more people—Sheri Newton, Jo Francis—and then the flow of survivors stopped. He moved farther forward and leaned inside, desperate to see her. She had to be there, didn't she? But the plane was empty. Now beginning to panic he turned around again and began to run back toward the area where the frightened survivors had grouped farther down the runway. Maybe he'd missed her. He must have done. She must have walked straight past him.

Donna noticed Michael approaching and tugged Richard Lawrence's arm to attract his attention.

"Where the hell is she?" Michael demanded. "Where's Emma?"

"Sorry, mate," Richard said, swallowing hard, "she's still at the airfield. We couldn't get everyone over here without—"

"Go back tonight."

"I can't. You don't understand, Mike, the whole place is swarming with them."

"I'll come with you," Michael said, distraught, not listening to what Richard was saying. "We'll go now."

"No, Michael," Donna said, trying to hold him. He pulled away from her. "You can't go. You have to stay here."

"I'll come with you," he said to Richard again, ignoring her. He stared at the pilot with desperate, unblinking eyes.

"Listen, mate, she's right," Richard said. "There isn't room. There's at least fifteen people left back there. If I manage to get back to them then I'm going to need as much space as possible to bring them back here, that's if I can get anywhere near—"

"When are you going?"

"Look, I need some time, okay? Before I do anything we need to stop and think about how I'm going to—"

"You have to go back. You can't leave them there."

"I don't know what else I can do. It's going to take three or four trips minimum."

"So you make three or four trips."

"Come on, Mike," Donna said softly, taking hold of his arm again and trying to lead him away. "Don't . . ."

He stood his ground, refusing to move.

"Michael," Richard said, looking straight at him, "I'm not going anywhere until morning, if I go back at all. It's too dangerous."

Michael wasn't listening. He stared at the pilot for a few seconds longer before simply turning away and walking away into the darkness. Donna watched him disappear into the night, knowing that there was no point following. There was nothing she could do to help.

41

It felt like days but, in reality, had been little more than a couple of hours. The eleven survivors in the office had remained wedged into the small square bathroom together, hardly able to move, almost too afraid to breathe. In terrified silence they had stood and listened to the world outside for what had seemed an eternity. Nothing out there had been clear enough to be distinct, but they had been surrounded by a constant soundtrack of shuffling bodies and lumbering footsteps. Occasionally there were other noises too—most probably single corpses randomly attacking others nearby.

Their situation was delicately balanced. If they stayed like this then maybe they could make it through to the morning, but what then? Croft could sense that the people around him were struggling. The physical and mental pressure was increasing by the second.

"Need to move," a frightened female voice said, the only

person to have dared speak out loud for hours. Quiet at first, the woman then repeated her words at a louder volume.

"Shut up," Croft hissed angrily at whoever it was who had dared break the precious silence. The cramped confines of the office block bathroom were excruciatingly claustrophobic and uncomfortable, and his reaction was disproportionately strong. What he would have given for a seat. The pain in his leg was agonizing. He didn't know how much longer he'd be able to stay standing.

The woman near to the back of the room was also close to breaking point. "I've got to move, if I don't I'll—"

"Shut up," he snapped at her again, this time managing to keep his voice low. The last light of the dying day had now disappeared and the small room was swathed in a cool, inky blackness. He couldn't see who it was that was speaking. Whoever it was they had to keep quiet. They'd all done well so far. They'd managed to remain almost completely silent and somehow they'd stayed safe. The bodies had temporarily lost interest in the office and its occupants. The doctor knew that it wouldn't take much to bring them back again, and even a lone voice could well prove to be enough. The entire airfield must surely have been overrun by now.

"I can't . . ." the woman moaned. Next to Croft another survivor whimpered pathetically, sensing the fragility of their situation. He could see some movement opposite him now. Was it Jacob Flynn again? Whoever it was they were shuffling backward, perhaps trying to grab hold of the person making the noise and silence them.

"Get off me!" the woman yelped. Croft felt his already aching legs weaken with nerves. Fuck, this was all they needed. Just stay calm and don't panic . . .

"Jesus Christ," he cried out involuntarily. Now it was the doctor's turn to break the silence as another sudden ripple of movement knocked him off his damaged legs and sent him slamming back into the door with a loud smack that rang through the empty building like a gunshot. His weakest leg buckled underneath him and he crumbled to the ground, knocking others off-balance as he fell. He lay on the cold, tiled floor, unable to move for a moment. *This is pointless*, he thought, *absolutely fucking pointless.*

A hand unexpectedly grabbed hold of him and yanked him back up onto his feet.

"Come on, mate," a tired voice whispered in his ear. "You all right?"

The doctor nodded, forgetting that the other man couldn't see, and was about to thank whoever it was that had helped him when he heard it. A single loud bang—the sound of a body slamming a skeletal fist against the outside wall of the building close to where they were hiding. He silently willed the rest of the small group of survivors not to respond but he knew that their reaction was inevitable.

"Oh God," someone moaned. "They know we're here. Bloody things know we're in here . . ."

Before they'd finished speaking there was another bang against the outside wall, this time directly behind where Jacob Flynn was standing. He turned round instinctively and tried to back away but only succeeded in knocking into more people and pushing them into each other.

291

Another bang, then another, then another, then the inevitable sound of countless rotting fists raining down on the outside of the building.

"Let me out," someone next to Croft demanded, trying to force their way past him. He felt his shoulder being grabbed, then he was pushed out of the way. Another hand on his back, square between his shoulder blades, forced him down again and he hit the ground for the second time in as many minutes, the side of his head glancing against the corner of a cold metal radiator. Concussed, he tried to get back up, suddenly aware that people were moving past him and heading out of the bathroom. *Don't go out there*, he thought. *You stupid, bloody idiots. Please don't go out there.*

Cooper, Emma, Juliet, and Steve sat in the middle of the room at the top of the observation tower. Steve stared at his feet, not wanting to look up. Cooper looked out at the clear night sky through the wide window opposite. Emma massaged her temples and Juliet Appleby stared unblinking into the darkness straight ahead. No one had spoken for almost an hour. If time had often felt like it had dragged before, then now it seemed somehow to have slowed down again. Each one of the four survivors had silently made private mental calculations, and each of them had come to the conclusion that if the helicopter was coming back, it would have returned by now. With each minute that passed, the likelihood that Richard Lawrence was ever coming back seemed to reduce.

The sound of shattering glass and cracking, splintering wood disturbed the silence.

"What was that?" Emma asked, quickly getting up from her seat and running over to the window. She leaned forward and peered down. The darkness was disorienting. She was having difficulty making out any distinct movement in the relentless confusion outside.

"What's happening?" Cooper whispered, standing over her shoulder.

"Oh, Christ," Steve moaned from beside another window a little farther down the room.

"What?"

"The office. Fucking things have got inside the office."

From his position he could see a part of the building which was obscured from Cooper and Emma's view. A window had been shattered three-quarters of the way down its longest side. Bodies were already half-climbing, half-falling through the empty window frame. He could see signs that someone was also trying to fight their way out.

"We've got to do something," said Juliet, moving across the room so that she too could see what was happening. "For God's sake, we have to do something."

"There's nothing we can do," Cooper said sadly.

"We have to get the doors open downstairs so that they can get in here."

"We can't," he said. "There'll be a thousand corpses in here before you can take a breath."

"But we can't just leave them," she protested.

"We don't have any choice," Emma said.

"There are people down there . . ."

"There are people up here."

As they watched, a lone survivor pushed his way out through the smashed window, the force of his frantic escape sending several dead bodies flying in different directions.

"Who's that?" asked Steve.

Before any of them had time to answer, it was too late. Whoever it was who had escaped was immediately surrounded and swallowed up by dead flesh. They crowded around the helpless figure, blocking every possible escape route like a pack of starved animals around their doomed prey. Elsewhere, still more of the bodies continued to surge toward the office, drawn there by the sudden movement and noise.

Down below, more survivors forced their way out of the besieged building and were swallowed up by the putrefying hordes. Stunned by the speed of events and their absolute, inexorable helplessness, the people in the control tower above could do nothing more than stand and watch as the office was overcome.

"So will they come for us next?" Juliet asked, her voice wavering with emotion. "Is that what's going to happen to us?"

"They probably don't even know we're up here yet," Cooper answered, "but they will if we give them half a chance."

"It's just a matter of time," Steve muttered to himself.

"You're right," Emma agreed, wiping tears of fear and frustration from her eyes. "They'll realize we're up here at some point and then . . ."

"Then what?" Juliet nervously pressed.

"Just look at them. Their physical condition is deteriorating. They can't communicate or reason. So whatever their motives are, they'll only react in one possible way."

"How?" the now trembling woman asked, her voice barely louder than a whisper.

"They'll try and tear us to fucking pieces," she answered. Her blunt, monotonic delivery belied the mounting terror she felt inside.

In the bathroom of the office block, Phil Croft sat on the floor with his back against the door, determined to keep the fucking things which now filled the building away from him at all costs. But he wasn't stupid. He knew it was only a matter of time.

Reaching into his shirt pocket, he pulled out his last remaining box of cigarettes and opened it up. One and a half smokes left. He lit the first and took a long, beautiful and relaxing drag on it, filling his lungs with nicotine, tar, and smoke. He lit the second, and shoved the glowing stub into a wedge of paper towels which immediately began to smolder and burn. On the other side of the door he could hear thumps, groans, and screams as the ten people he'd been trapped here with were torn apart by the dead. He covered his ears and tried to fill his head with random, pointless thoughts to distract himself from what was happening outside and his own impending death but it was impossible. He'd always been able to block out the horror before, but not tonight. Tonight the terror and hopeless fear was all he had left.

So this is how it ends, he thought sadly as he watched the flames begin to take hold of the paper towels and then begin to scorch and burn the building's wooden wall. He pushed back against the door again—which he could now feel being pushed and shoved from the other side by cadavers—and wedged his feet against the toilet cubicle opposite.

He sat and smoked his last cigarette and waited, wondering whether it would be the flames or the bodies that would get to him first.

From the top of the control tower high above the ground, Cooper watched the building below him burn. Eleven good people lost. How long before either the fire or the dead got to them? He slumped to the ground and covered his face. He didn't want to look outside any longer.

42

Almost first light.

Exhausted, Richard Lawrence had delayed his flight for as long as possible, balancing his physical fatigue with the need to get back quickly to those people they'd been forced to leave behind. Now, seven hours after he'd left them, he flew the helicopter back over the dead land. Beneath him there now seemed to be more movement than ever. Where previously there had only been stillness and an uneasy calm, now the entire dark landscape appeared to be crawling with activity. He could see bodies moving freely, staggering pointlessly from place to place. He wondered whether he was imagining things. Was his nervous mind exaggerating what he could actually see and making things appear worse than they actually were. But how could things get any worse?

This was a dangerous and pointless flight. When he'd left the airfield earlier he had felt beaten and disconsolate. What possible hope could the fifteen or so people left there have against the thousands upon thousands of unstoppable bodies he had last seen heading toward the few isolated buildings in the middle of the airfield? Several times during the journey he had considered turning around and heading back to the island, wondering whether there was anything to be gained from even trying. What good would it do? What would he achieve? The base was overrun: if there were any survivors left there, how was he supposed to pick them up? Would his return do anything more than taunt those left behind and prolong their agony? Would he be able to do more than just fly around the airfield, watching his friends as they waited to die? As bleak and inevitable as the conclusion of his flight appeared to be, he knew that he didn't have any choice. He had to try.

The slowly lifting darkness of the early morning camouflaged the airfield. In his mind Richard still pictured the place as he'd left it hours earlier—a small collection of buildings surrounded by empty space and encircled by the wire fence and the many thousands of bodies beyond. He knew it would look different now, but it was hard to imagine the extent to which the dark scene had changed.

Fear and nerves, confused him. He lost his bearings and flew over the airfield without recognizing it. In the uninterrupted gloom everything looked the same and it wasn't until he was almost over the center of the town of Rowley that he realized his mistake. He turned the helicopter round in a wide, graceful arc and flew back, eventually spotting the airfield—and the fire and smoke to the side of the observation tower—just a mile or so ahead. Like a dark, black scab on the monochromatic landscape, the airfield already looked overrun and lost. Once again he considered turning tail and heading back to Cormansey. There were hundreds of thousands of bodies swarming constantly around the place, filling every square meter of land. Even if Cooper, Croft, and the others were still there and were still alive, could he do anything to help them now?

43

"What are they doing now?" Steve Armitage asked. Too afraid to look for himself, the burly truck driver leaned against the back wall, as far away as he could get from the window without leaving the room. Cooper and Emma remained close to the glass, watching the bodies shuffling below them with mounting unease.

The rear of the nearby office building had been burning for hours now and more than half of the building had been consumed by flame. The fire had attracted the attention of many of the bodies, but many more continued to surround the other buildings. The physical weight of their immense numbers meant they had forced their way into the hangar, waiting room, and other places through windows and doors which had been left open. Those which strayed too close to the burning building had themselves become engulfed by flames. The appearance and bizarre movement of the burning bodies were unsettling and surreal. Ignorant to the heat and flame which quickly consumed them, the corpses continued to stagger around, colliding with other figures and setting them alight too. The fire, although mostly confined to the other side of the remains of the office building, was growing quickly and was eating away at the rest of the structure. Any change in wind direction, thought Cooper, and they might have no choice but to get out of the control tower and take their chances with the baying masses outside.

"They're in at least three buildings now," Emma said.

"Still reckon we'll be safe here?" Steve snapped angrily, looking at Cooper and demanding an answer.

"I never said we'd be safe," he replied defensively, "I just said they don't know we're here yet. Hopefully the fire will keep them occupied and distracted."

"You think so?"

"It might."

"Assuming it doesn't, how long before they manage to get in here?"

"We blocked the door downstairs. They probably haven't got the strength to get past it."

"We didn't think they'd have the strength to pull the bloody fence down but they managed that, didn't they?"

Cooper didn't answer. He knew Steve was right.

"Did you block all the doors and windows downstairs?" Juliet Appleby asked from across the room. She had her face pressed against another smaller window and was trying to look straight down the side of the building. Cooper shook his head.

"No, just the main entrance. That was all we had time to do. Why?"

"Because whether they're going to manage it or not, it looks like they're trying to get in here."

"Where?" Emma asked anxiously.

"I can see a couple of groups of them."

"Doing what?"

"Nothing much at the moment, just pressing up against the door, I think. It's difficult to see much from up here."

"Christ, this is fucking stupid," Steve yelled, increasingly angry and frustrated. "We can't just sit here and wait for them to get in."

"That's just about all we can do, isn't it?" answered Juliet.

"We could make a run for it," he suggested. "Fight our way over to one of the trucks and try and get away."

"Where would we go?" asked Cooper. "You saw what happened to the others." Armitage couldn't answer. The thought of another directionless drive through the decaying countryside was only marginally more appealing than sitting still and doing nothing. It was a last resort, but he knew it might yet turn out to be their only option.

Emma was standing in front of the largest window again, watching what was happening outside. The ground was now completely carpeted in a thick layer of dead flesh and she could no longer see any grass, pavement or runway. The office building was almost completely ablaze and she knew that there could be no one left alive inside. Elsewhere the creatures were tightly packed around the other buildings. Burning bodies still dragged themselves around and a thick, smoglike layer of smoke had settled across the entire scene. The wind was light and directionless and the smoke showed no sign of dispersing.

"What's the roof of this building like?" she asked suddenly.

"What?" Cooper grunted.

"The roof of this building," she repeated. "Is it flat?"

"Not sure. I don't think so. You can't really tell from the ground. Why, what are you thinking?"

"I'm thinking that if we are going to get out of here, then we need to be somewhere obvious so that Richard can see us when he comes back."

"If he comes back," Steve sneered.

"*When* he comes back," Cooper corrected him. "Whether he can do anything for us or not, I'm sure he'll be back. We'd do the same if we were in his shoes. You couldn't just sit there on the island knowing that there still might be people left alive and trapped over here, could you?"

No answer.

"Anyway," Emma continued, "as well as being visible, we need to make sure that we end up somewhere the bodies definitely can't get to."

"Like?"

"Like a flat roof," she replied.

"I think the roof here is sloped," Juliet said, still standing at the window but now looking up instead of down. "And I can't go up there . . ."

Cooper shuffled around so that he had a better view of the rest of the airfield and, more importantly, the few remaining buildings nearby.

"Not sure about this one, but that one over there's a possibility," he said, pointing toward a small utility building nestled in the shadows of the hangar where the plane had previously been housed.

"Just a couple of tiny problems as far as I can see," Steve

grumbled from close behind him. "Getting to it and getting on top of it. Any bright ideas?"

"How desperate are you feeling?" Cooper asked.

"Fucking desperate."

"Me too, so we'll just have to find a way of doing it, won't we? I don't see that we've got any choice."

"How then?"

"Try the usual tricks," he answered, "because they've worked so far. We'll distract the bodies and make a run for it."

"Shouldn't the fire already be distracting them?" Emma asked sensibly. She was right. Many bodies were continuing to crowd around the base of the control tower and were now ignoring the spreading heat and light of the flames.

"She's right. And anyway, that building is at least twenty feet high," Steve sighed. "What are we going to do? Jump up, for Christ's sake? Stand on each other's shoulders?"

"We'll find a way."

"Forget about the buildings," Emma said, her mind suddenly racing. "Using the trucks was a better idea. We could do that, couldn't we? Once they see us on top of one of the buildings we'll have the whole bloody lot of them snapping at our feet. At least with the trucks we'll be able to keep moving."

"But the trucks are even further away," whimpered Juliet. "And how would we drive through a crowd like that?"

"The prison truck's only on the other side of the runway," Cooper said. "Can't see the personnel carrier from here."

"Still don't know how we're supposed to get to it," Steve said.

"Well we'd better think of a way pretty bloody quickly," Emma said suddenly with a new found urgency in her voice.

"Why?"

"Because the helicopter's back."

44

Once he was right over the airfield, Richard Lawrence allowed the helicopter to drift slightly lower, switching on the searchlight and managing to guide it around the area. For a while all he could see were the seething bodies and it took him some time to orient himself and properly identify the dark shapes and outlines of the control tower and other buildings through the smoke. Conscious that the noise and light he had created was again whipping the rancid crowd below into a bloody frenzy, he moved lower still, stopping only when he was level with the top of the tower.

He could see people. The nearby office building had been destroyed and the hangar overrun, but he could definitely see people at the top of the control tower. He had to look twice to be sure it wasn't bodies that had found a way inside. From his high position he could see no obvious signs of any entrance to the building having been compromised. If the dead had forced their way in he would have expected hundreds of them to have pointlessly crammed themselves inside by now, but there didn't seem to be many people inside, and those he could see were moving with purpose and control. They had to be survivors, but how could he get to them?

Cooper's face appeared at the window, confirming beyond doubt to Richard that his return to the mainland had been worthwhile.

"We have to get out there," Emma shouted, suddenly having to raise her voice to make herself heard over the welcome noise of the helicopter.

"But there's no way out," Steve yelled. "Christ, we've just been through this. We're surrounded. They're out the front and they're round the back and—"

"Emma's right," Cooper interrupted. "We have to find a way out and we have to do it now."

"Go for the trucks," Juliet suggested.

"I agree," Emma said quickly, "it's the best option. Richard will see us moving. If we can get to one of the trucks we can drive through the bodies until we reach somewhere where there are fewer of them. Then he can land and pick us up."

"So do we just make a run for it?"

"It's not going to be easy," Emma replied, looking down at the ground immediately around the base of the building. "I think we should try and distract them and get them away from which-ever door or window we decide to use to get out. Then maybe just one of us could try to get across and bring the truck back over here."

Cooper stood behind Emma, thinking carefully. He glanced

up and looked outside. The helicopter was hovering so close that, despite the drifting smoke, the pilot's face could clearly be seen, but the distance was irrelevant. He might as well have been a hundred miles away for all the good it was doing them. Richard looked understandably agitated. Cooper knew he wouldn't wait indefinitely for them to make their move.

"Good God," mumbled Juliet. "Just look at that."

She pointed out of the window down at an area of ground which was almost directly beneath the helicopter.

"What the hell are they doing?" Steve asked, crowding forward to try and get a better view. The four of them peered down to an area of land onto which Richard had angled the searchlight, below the helicopter and slightly to one side. While many bodies continued to react as the survivors had expected them to, others were beginning to behave differently. A large number of them continued to swarm forward and fight with the corpses closest to them, but many others did not. Instead those bodies appeared to be visibly agitated and riled by the noise, light, and wind coming from the helicopter hovering a short distance above their decaying heads. Some of them seemed almost to be cowering. It was hard to believe, but a large section of the bodies were now trying to move away from the disturbance above.

"Fucking hell," said Cooper.

"This is it," Emma announced, "this is our chance. It's like you said earlier, they're changing. They're finally beginning to wake up, aren't they? Bloody hell, those things down there are scared."

"Scared?" Steve said. "Are you out of your fucking mind?"

"The noise the helicopter's making is scaring them. We might not be much of a threat, but that thing is."

308

"Bullshit."

"Might be," she said quickly, "but look at them. Whatever's causing this, it doesn't matter. Point is it might give us a chance to get past some of them."

"How?" asked Juliet.

"We'll use the helicopter as cover. Make as much of a disturbance as we can and try and get Richard's help. Chances are some of them will disappear and keep out of our way."

"Some of them?"

"The rest will probably still go for us, same as they always do."

Much as he hated to admit it, Steve knew that Emma was right. Better to go out there and face five hundred corpses than five thousand.

"We should do it," Juliet announced.

"Do what exactly?" Steve asked nervously.

"Shake them up then go out there and kick their bloody backsides," Emma answered.

"Because if we don't," Cooper reminded them, "then we won't be getting into that helicopter and we'll be stuck here. If we don't go outside and face them now, then we'll be facing them up here when they finally get inside—that's if we haven't burned to death already. Not much of a choice, is it?"

Dividing his concentration among piloting the helicopter, watching the survivors, and watching the bodies below, Richard Lawrence noticed that Cooper and the others had shifted their attention from looking at him to watching what was happening on the ground. He peered down through small observation panels by his feet and watched as the bodies reacted to his presence. He shifted the helicopter slightly and saw that as the searchlight moved, so more shadowy shapes stumbled out of the way. Perhaps if he dropped lower, he thought, more of them would move and he might be able to land and pick up the survivors. He tried briefly, but the number of corpses which stood their ground and still reacted violently was more than enough to convince him that was out of the question. But the presence of the helicopter and the fear—that seemed to be the right word to use—that it seemed to generate among the dead was unquestionably important. It would help. It might give the people on the ground a chance, albeit a slight one. He remembered that the bodies he'd been told about on the island had acted this way. Although quieter and more hesitant than most, they still attacked the survivors when they'd been threatened. The bodies wanted to survive and they would fight when they had no other option.

From his position above the airfield, Richard felt helpless. He had no way of warning the others or telling them what he knew.

Having stood still and watching and waiting for too long, Emma finally decided to take action. All the talking in the world wasn't going to get them away from the airfield and, as Cooper had already pointed out, they had nothing to lose and everything to gain from trying to get away. If they did nothing, their last chance would be gone. The prospect of a relatively safe and secure future with Michael was too great a prize to risk throwing away without a fight. She had to do something.

"Where are you going?" Cooper called after her as she

turned and pushed through the doors and began running down the staircase.

"To Cormansey," she shouted back. "What about you?"

Suddenly feeling pressured into action, Juliet, Steve, and Cooper followed close behind. For all her sudden movement and intent, it was clear that Emma didn't have a plan. They found her at the bottom of the staircase, looking around hopefully for inspiration.

"What now?" Juliet asked.

Through the bitter-tasting, wispy smoke which had drifted into the building, Steve noticed light leaking in from under the front entrance door. A mixture of the natural first light of day and the harsh artificial illumination coming from the helicopter, he edged toward it. Clambering carefully over the tables and chairs which he and Cooper had used earlier to block the entrance, he peered out through a narrow crack between the double doors. There was still a huge number of bodies out there, but their numbers in the light from the helicopter were considerably more diffuse now. He looked up at the aircraft hanging in the air above them. Richard seemed to have worked out what was happening. Steve couldn't be completely sure, but the pilot seemed to deliberately be aiming his light toward the door.

"We should make a run for it," he suggested, his sudden about-face and positive attitude surprising the others. "We should do it now."

"We can't risk just throwing the doors open and going out there," Emma protested. "What if we get split up? What happens when we get over to the truck? Do we just stand there and wait for you to open it up?"

"Worse than that," Juliet added, "if we open the doors and we all go out there, then that leaves this place wide open. We'll have no way back if anything goes wrong."

"We need to get the truck over here," Cooper said. "One of us needs to get over to it, then get it back here to pick the rest of us up."

The sound of the helicopter was deafening, amplified by the long, thin shape of the building itself. Above the mechanical noise they could hear the occasional sound of bodies slamming against the walls, doors, and windows. Although the helicopter seemed to be keeping some of the creatures at bay, its position next to the control tower was also drawing more of them closer.

Steve Armitage could stand it no longer. He was generally a quiet man who was content to sit and wait and watch rather than act, but, occasionally, the pressure of a situation proved too much and forced him into action. It had happened before back in the city when he'd left the safety of the university complex to help collect transport for the group, and it was happening again now.

"I'll do it," he said suddenly.

"What?" asked Cooper, surprised.

"I said I'll do it," he repeated before he could talk himself out of volunteering. "Might as well."

"You sure?"

"No."

Cooper moved forward and looked through the narrow gap in the doors that Steve had been looking through just a few seconds earlier. His view was limited, but he could clearly see the prison truck on the other side of the runway where it had been left. It wasn't going to be easy to reach.

"It's got to be a couple of hundred meters away," he whispered, still looking out through the gap, "and there are still several hundred bodies in your way. Think you can make it?"

"I can do it," Steve answered. "Listen, with enough of those things snapping at my heels, I could run a bloody marathon!"

Cooper nodded and then started moving the tables and chairs which were blocking the doors.

"When you get out there," he said as he worked, looking back over his shoulder at the other man, "you just put your head down and run, understand? Keep moving until you reach the truck. Don't stop for anything."

"I wasn't planning to."

"Ready?" Cooper asked as he dragged the last table away. Steve turned back toward the door.

"Ready," he answered, sounding far from it. He took a deep, nervous breath, then threw the doors open and burst out into the cold morning. The light which poured down from the helicopter and saturated the immediate vicinity was momentarily blinding and the unexpected force of the down draft from the aircraft above threatened to knock him off his feet. The suffocating smell of burning flesh filled his lungs. For a single disorienting second he stood still and stared at the truck on the other side of the runway. His view was relatively clear and, for an instant, the distance he had to cover seemed reassuringly short. But then he glanced to his left and to his right and saw that there were bodies all around him. Though some remained cowering in the shadows, others began to converge on him from various directions. The sound of the door being pulled shut behind him—barely audible over the constant noise from the helicopter above—prompted him to move.

"Shit," he cursed as the nearest body reached out for him. Its hands were bony and hard with much of the putrefied flesh having long since been worn and rotted away. Jogging slowly away from the observation tower, and trying desperately to pick up some much-needed speed, Steve grabbed the skeletal figure by the neck and swung it around, sending it flying into a group of four more ragged cadavers and knocking them down like skittles.

He looked ahead again and tried to regain his focus on the truck. Where before he'd seemed to have a clear passage, now a myriad of shuffling figures crisscrossed ahead of him. More vicious hands lashed out, one catching his cheek and tearing three long cuts from just under his left eye down to his chin. He again forced himself to ignore the bodies all around him and keep moving forward. His mouth was dry and his heart was thumping like it was about to explode but he knew that he had to keep moving. He lowered his shoulder as two more corpses crossed his path. Charging through the pair of them he smashed one away in either direction.

Almost halfway there.

Steve was still a heavy and unfit man, and his right knee was hurting badly as a result of the sudden stress he was putting his body under. He knew that he had no option but to keep running through the pain, but every time his foot hit the ground a piercing, shooting pain ran along the length of his leg from his

314

knee to his backside. The pathways and grass under his feet had now given way to the harder tarmac surface of the runway and he knew that he had almost reached the truck. The ground was littered with the random remains of corpses which had been burned or brought down and torn apart by others and he trod heavily on one which had fallen onto its back. His boot smashed through the rib cage and sent the rotten remains of its innards flying in every direction. As he frantically tried to pull his foot clear he tripped and fell and in seconds bodies had swarmed all over him like flies over food.

"Fuck," Cooper yelled from the control tower as he watched through the crack in the door. More and more bodies piled on top of the helpless truck driver, quickly burying him under a mound of constantly moving, decaying flesh.

"Jesus," Emma wailed, watching through a small window.

Cooper moved to open the door. "I've got to go out there."

"Cooper, don't . . ." Juliet pleaded.

"I can't just leave him."

"Wait," Emma said, pressing her face against the window again. She could see movement from the bottom of the pile of bodies. Steve was still fighting. High above him Richard had moved the helicopter round and dropped lower so that the searchlight was bearing down on him directly. The sudden illumination caused many of the bodies still lurching toward the disturbance to turn and trip away in other directions, looking for cover.

Lying on his back on the cold, hard runway and struggling to breathe through the abhorrent stench, Steve began to kick and punch out at the bodies on top of him. They felt hollow and cold and individually offered little resistance. He felt their decayed flesh dripping and dribbling over him and he could feel himself being soaked through with the vile discharge of their decay. The more they fought, he found, the quicker they deteriorated.

He rolled over onto his front and tried to push himself up off the ground. Still more of them were clinging onto his back. He had no idea how many of the grotesque things were hanging off him and he didn't care. He managed somehow to scramble onto all fours and then pushed hard and stood upright and began to smash the bodies away, swatting them like flies. With five or six of them already thrown to the ground, he found that his torso was suddenly free and the only bodies still holding on were those which clung onto his legs. He began to move forward, his powerful strides dislodging more and more of the pitiful creatures until he was completely clear and he could run again. He battered more of the cadavers out of his path before reaching the side of the truck and slamming into it. With one last groan of effort he reached up to the handle on the passenger door, yanked it open, and hauled himself inside. He pulled it shut, severing a single arm that made a last, misjudged grab for him, and then slid across the cab into the driver's seat.

"He's in!" cried Emma from the control tower window. "Bloody hell, he's done it."

Suddenly sensing that a way out may have just been opened up for them, the three remaining survivors crowded together around the main door and waited for the truck to move. Richard watched events from the relative safety of the helicopter hanging in the air and continued to drench the scene with harsh, artificial light, giving Steve some welcome illumination and a limited degree of protection.

Inside the truck, Steve was struggling. His eyes stinging from the smoke, he slumped forward over the steering wheel. Dripping with rancid blood and gore and soaked through with sweat, he fought to catch his breath and keep his mind focused. He reached out to turn the key and start the engine but then stopped. His chest felt tight. He desperately needed oxygen but the deeper he breathed, the more smoke he inhaled and the worse the pain in his chest became. Beginning as an uncomfortable feeling like a stitch, it quickly became an uncontrollable searing, burning, and ripping pain which started near his heart then spread out across his whole body. His fingers felt numb and were tingling. His feet felt heavy and he struggled to move them onto the pedals.

Steve again tried to breathe slowly and deeply and did his best to ignore the constant distraction of the countless swarms of bodies which thumped angrily into the sides of the truck. Taking his time, he figured that the slower he moved, the more chance he'd have of getting the truck going. His outstretched fingers eventually made contact with the keys and he somehow managed to turn them and start the engine. He pushed himself back into his seat with momentary relief and satisfaction as the truck rumbled into life. Progress was short-lived, however, as another wave of debilitating pain spread quickly across his chest. Groaning with effort he forced himself to concentrate on getting back to the others. He began to move the truck forward and slowly turned the steering wheel to guide the heavy vehicle back toward the control tower.

Still illuminated by the incandescent light from the helicopter, the truck trundled toward the building, mowing down those bodies which foolishly dragged themselves in front of it.

"He's coming," Cooper said, still watching through the gap between the doors. "Ready?"

Juliet and Emma nodded. Emma's throat was dry and her legs felt weak: this was make-or-break and she knew it. Never mind the immediate danger they faced outside, what happened in the next few minutes would undoubtedly decide the direction and duration of the rest of her life.

"What do we do?" Juliet anxiously mumbled.

"When I open the doors," Cooper replied, "you get yourself onto the truck. Doesn't matter if you get in through the front or the back or if you're left hanging onto the side, just get over to that bloody truck and hold onto it, okay?"

She nodded and was about to ask another question when Cooper threw the doors open. The blood-splattered prison truck ground to a sudden, lurching stop just a few meters ahead of them.

"Move!" he yelled. He grabbed hold of both women by the arm and dragged them forward, virtually throwing them out of the building. Bodies began to surge at them from every imaginable direction. Juliet half-ran and half-fell toward the back of the truck, managing somehow to jump up and yank the back door open. She pulled herself inside and then reached out for Emma, who was fighting her way through a dense section of the rabid crowd, struggling to keep moving through the tide of rotting flesh which pushed against her, threatening to swallow her up. It seemed that those bodies which had remained on the sidelines had suddenly sensed an increase in the level of their own physical danger and had chosen to move and attack before the survivors and their machines attacked them. What felt like thousands of vicious hands reached out to grab hold of Emma.

Unexpectedly her speed increased. Running into her at force from behind, Cooper shoved her toward the truck, wedged his hands under her arms, and threw her up into the air. With her flailing hands stretched out in front of her she managed to grab hold of the back of the vehicle where Juliet was waiting. She caught hold of the scruff of the neck of Emma's jacket and roughly dragged her inside. The bodies were no match for Cooper's controlled force. He powered through them and jumped up onto the back of the truck after the others. Hanging half-out of the open door he smashed his hand repeatedly on the vehicle's metal side. The noise was more definite and controlled than the relentless battering coming from the bodies, and Steve knew it was his signal to move again. Doing everything he could to ignore the constant, agonizing pain which still crippled him, he accelerated and turned and drove out toward the gaping hole in the airfield's border fence.

"You okay?" Emma asked Cooper.

"I will be when we get to this bloody island," he replied breathlessly, still standing in the doorway and holding on tightly with each lurch and sway of the prison truck as it moved across the uneven ground. From every direction bodies turned and stumbled toward the powerful vehicle, some being smashed to

319

the side, countless others disappearing beneath its wheels and being crushed. Ignoring the bloody confusion unfolding all around them, Cooper looked up through the drifting smoke and, with relief, tracked the helicopter as it began to follow them away from the buildings.

"What do we do now?" Juliet wondered innocently. Before Cooper could answer the truck began to gradually slow down.

"Steve," he screamed at the top of his voice, "keep moving, man. For Christ's sake, don't stop here."

The truck lurched forward again and accelerated for a few meters farther, and then slowed down. The engine stalled as Steve's foot slipped off the controls, the sudden movement almost throwing Cooper off the back and into the baying crowds. Steve knew that he couldn't drive any farther. The pain was unbearable now. He could hardly move.

"What's he doing?" Emma asked pointlessly. She ran deeper inside and began to bang on the inner walls. "Steve!" she yelled. "Steve! What's wrong . . . ?"

They had stopped just a short distance from the downed section of fence. Even though the crowds were slightly less dense here than they were around the buildings, within seconds of the truck's journey abruptly ending, masses of rotting corpses were already battering against its sides. From his high vantage point, Cooper lashed out at those which were unfortunate enough to stumble and trip close to him, kicking them away.

"We need to get onto the roof," he said as he surveyed the desperate scene. Hundreds of cadavers were now surging toward them like an impenetrable gray mist. The helicopter hovered overhead, its noise and light now attracting easily as many bodies as it repelled. Cooper looked down at the sea of swarming faces in front of him and then glanced up at the helicopter again. "There's no way he's going to be able to pick us up off the ground. We've got to get up."

Turning around he grabbed hold of Juliet and pulled her closer to the door.

"What . . . ?"

"Roof," he snapped. He crouched down and cupped his hands for her to use as a foothold. Groaning with effort and pain he lifted her up. With nothing on the roof for her to hold onto she struggled to get a grip and pull herself up. Cooper dug deep and shoved her a little higher and she managed to dig her elbows down and inch slowly forward. He leaned out of the truck and watched until her feet had disappeared over the top. Seconds later her head reappeared over the edge.

"Okay?"

"Okay," she replied, deliberately looking anywhere but down into the mass of rotting faces which stared up at her.

Emma was next. With the nearest bodies just inches away from grabbing hold of him, Cooper lifted her up and supported her relatively slight weight until Juliet had caught hold of her hands from above and had pulled her up onto the roof. Cooper then turned and scrambled up himself, using the door at the back of the truck to climb up.

The three survivors stood together on top of the truck. Emma looked down at the relentless crowd of decayed creatures below her. Their anger and ferocity seemed to increase as Richard lowered the helicopter down again.

"Get in," Cooper shouted, having to yell to make himself

heard over all the deafening noise. Instinctively crouching down and moving on all fours because of the rotor blades which now seemed perilously close and the wind which threatened to blow them off the roof of the truck, Emma and Juliet crawled toward the aircraft. It hovered just inches away, although the distance between the roof of the truck and the helicopter's nearest landing skid seemed immense. Taking a deep breath Emma stepped across the gap and pulled herself up into the back of the aircraft.

Cooper ran down to the front end of the truck and lay down across the width of the cab. He dragged himself farther forward, leaned down, and banged on the driver's half-open window. He could see the back of Steve's head. He was lying facedown across the steering wheel.

"Come on, Steve," Cooper pleaded. "We've done it. Let's get you up here."

Steve slowly lifted his head, every movement taking incredible effort, and turned to look at Cooper. Then he dropped back down again and closed his eyes.

"Can't," he gasped, his voice dry and hoarse, his breathing shallow and intermittent. "I can't do it."

"Come on," Cooper insisted, although he already knew it was pointless. Steve's face was gray and ashen, his lips blue.

"I can't."

For a second Cooper contemplated jumping down and trying to manhandle the other man up onto the roof of the truck.

"Go," Steve wheezed, trying to lift his head again. The light from the helicopter suddenly shifted slightly, illuminating the inside of the cab and Cooper clearly saw the pain in his face. It was clear that he was beyond help.

"Okay, mate," he said, reaching in through the window and resting his arm on the other man's shoulder. "You're a good man. Thank you." Cooper stood up reluctantly and ran the length of the roof to get to the helicopter. Strangely relieved, Steve closed his eyes again and tried to breathe through the increasing pain until it finally stopped.

"What about Steve?" Emma shouted as Cooper scrambled into the helicopter and pulled the door shut behind him. He shook his head, looked down, and watched the roof of the truck become smaller and smaller as they quickly climbed away.

Below them the airfield was a solid mass of crazed, decaying bodies.

45

More than fifty days since the germ had destroyed almost all of the population of the planet, the final survivors arrived in the air over the island of Cormansey.

Michael had been waiting in the small cottage by the airstrip. Donna and Jack kept him company although no one had spoken for what felt like hours. Finally the oppressive silence was shattered by the constant dull thud of the approaching helicopter. The distant sound increased Michael's uncertainty and nervousness to an almost unbearable level. Almost too afraid to look, he went outside and scanned the skies until he finally spotted the aircraft approaching. He watched every last meter of its painfully long and slow descent to the ground and then sprinted the length of the island's short runway.

Cooper was the first to get out, then Juliet. And then he saw her. Michael ran over to Emma and held her. Ignorant to everything else that was happening around them—the frenzied and excited activity, the tears for missing friends, the cars which approached from various directions, the cheers of relief and cries of sadness—he buried her face in his chest and held her tight.

"I thought I'd lost you," he whispered to her, squeezing her until she could barely breathe.

"No chance," she whispered back, looking up into his face and smiling through her tears.

In a moment of silence Michael stood next to Emma and watched as she looked around her, trying to take in what she could see of the island. He watched her as she tasted the air and soaked up the atmosphere. He watched her as she finally started to relax and he held her as she wept with relief.

Cormansey was a bleak, cold and unforgiving place, but they both knew it was as good as it was going to get.

Epilogue

MICHAEL COLLINS

I spoke to Jack this morning for the first time in weeks. He came by the house earlier, and told me he'd been out walking again. I've often seen him in the distance, marching on his own across the horizon. He told me he's started walking circuits of the island to keep himself occupied.

Very few people visit us here. There aren't many houses more isolated than ours. That was deliberate on our part: we both want to be close to the others, but at the same time we want lives of our own too. Most people have chosen to live in or around Danvers Lye. Some people here want to build a close community; they want to live, sleep, and eat in each other's pockets. They couldn't survive on their own, they need the closeness of others. We don't.

Christ, we could do with having Phil Croft here now. We've really struggled since Emma fell pregnant. People have tried to support her, of course, but it's been difficult and we miss his expertise, his guidance, and his company. It will be hard when the baby's born. At least I'll be able to help more then. At the moment I feel completely useless. The others have been really understanding. They told us about the baby that was born back when they were in the city, and what happened to it, and we know that the same thing could happen to our child. Our medical facilities here are virtually nonexistent, and we didn't have any option but to go through with the pregnancy—not that either of us would have ever done any different. I pray that our baby will be all right. I talked to Donna about its chances. She pointed out that although the mother of the baby in the city had survived, its father had been killed by the germ. She said that maybe the fact that both Emma and I survived will make a difference. I hope that whatever it is that's kept us both alive has been passed down and will protect our child too.

Jack and I had a long conversation about the future today. I've agreed to go back to the mainland with Cooper and some of the others in a few days' time. It'll be the first time we've been back. Providing the weather stays good, the plan is for Richard to fly us over to the nearest port. We'll salvage whatever supplies we can find, but the important thing is to find a suitable boat and sail it back to Cormansey. There's hardly any fuel left in the helicopter now. We'll try to find more, but even so, we need to look for another way of getting to and from the mainland. We're going to have to keep going back there—we'll always need medicines and food and clothing. No doubt we'll become more self-sufficient as time goes by, but at the moment it makes sense to keep scavenging for what we need.

If I'm honest, we're struggling here, and I can't see that things are ever going to get any easier. Some people are talking about trying to get power to the village. They might manage it, but at what cost? It's going to take an enormous amount of effort for questionable gain. How will they maintain the system? Who will keep it working? It's all going to take time, but that's the one thing we seem to have in abundance.

A few days ago I found one of the dead. I'd forgotten how foul they are. I must have walked past this one countless times and not even known it was there. It was slumped in a ditch at the side of the road, massively decayed, and it just lay there and watched me. It tried to move, but it couldn't. It managed to lift its head slightly and the remains of its cold, black eyes followed me until I put a pick through its skull.

For some reason I've been thinking about that body a lot. I find myself thinking about what happened to turn it from a normal, healthy person into that lump of rotten flesh and bone. I wonder sometimes how aware the bodies were of what was happening to them. Did they feel anything? I wonder whether their brains were more alive than we'd originally given them credit for, and whether it was only the deterioration of their flesh that caused them to react and behave the way they did. Did my friends and family suffer? Did they wander around like that, trying desperately to find comfort or familiarity, a release from their pain? I often wonder whether that last body had been looking at me and remembering what it had once been.

It's getting late. Emma is asleep—she has been all afternoon. No doubt she'll wake up soon and then keep me awake all night talking. She still doesn't like to be on her own at night. No one does.

I'm standing in front of the house looking out over the

ocean. It's a bright day, and the water looks deceptively calm and inviting. Everything is quiet, and if I just stand here and listen to the silence then I can almost believe that nothing ever happened. But there's no escaping the fact that our lives have been changed forever, and no matter how safe or comfortable we try and make this place, the rest of our days are going to be hard. We'll have to fight for everything we need, and if our children survive then they'll spend their lives fighting too.

We won a small victory getting here, but it was a pretty hollow one. Our little achievements are insignificant in the overall scheme of things. There might be other people, other survivors, who have been more successful than us, who are more organized and protected than us. Whoever's left alive and however many of us there are, I think our days are numbered. We are remnants of the past. I sometimes feel like an intruder now, like I shouldn't be here. Jack says that whatever the cause, what happened to the world was supposed to happen, and I think I agree with him. We've been brushed aside. I can't help thinking that everything we're doing is going to come to nothing. We're just kidding ourselves if we believe any different. The balance of our world has been changed forever. Mankind is being cleansed from the face of the planet. Purification has begun.

All that Emma and I can do is make the most of the time we have left. That's all that any of us can do.

Outnumbered 1,000,000 to 1, a small band of the living face down the walking dead

Book 2

Book 4

Book 1

Book 3

"A marvelously bleak dystopian future where the world belongs to the dead."
—Jonathan Maberry, *New York Times* bestselling author of *Patient Zero*